HATING MR. PERFECT

SUZANNE BALTSAR

CONTENT NOTE

For all the unlikeable heroines out there. This one's for you.

1

The lighting was terrible, the floor sticky, and the whole place smelled of stale beer and fried food, but they wouldn't have it any other way. All jammed together in an L-shaped corner booth. Between Laney's insistence on being able to walk through "the cutest little town" she'd ever seen, and Bronte's demand for wherever they went to have food, Gem was celebrating her birthday at the dive bar down the street from her apartment in her hometown of Galena, Illinois. They were all together; that was what mattered.

"So, how does it feel to be twenty-five?" Sam asked, tossing her long lavender-hued hair to the side.

Gem was the first one to turn twenty-five out of the foursome, and they'd made a pact long ago to be together as often as possible. Birthdays, special occasions, the good, and the bad, they would be there for one another, always.

"I can rent a car now," Gem said, lifting her glass to the other girls. "But I don't feel any older or wiser after turning a quarter of a century."

Bronte scrunched up her button nose. "Maybe tomorrow."

Laney lifted one perfectly sculpted eyebrow. "Or maybe next year."

The girls all laughed, though Gem forced the sound out. As with any group of friends, each woman had her role to play. Laney was the de facto leader, the most outgoing of them all. Bronte was the sweet one, everyone's conscience. Sam was the brainy one, the problem-solver. And Gem, she was the wild one.

As a joke a few years ago, Bronte had bought Gem fairy wings because she flitted to and fro, had changed majors three times, and still wasn't sure what she wanted to be when she grew up. It didn't help the flighty label that Gem, the shortest of the girls, kept her wavy hair long, halfway down her back, and only wore cruelty-free, organic makeup and clothes. She might as well have been a woodland nymph.

"I, um..." Gem cleared her throat, her eyes on the table. "I opened up a savings account," she finished quietly.

"No shit!" Laney crowed. "You actually read that article I sent you?"

Sam shifted in her seat to see past Bronte to Laney. "What article?"

"It was about money management and retirement. My dad sent it to me...you know him." She rolled her eyes. "But I thought it was helpful, so I sent it to this one," she said, tipping her chin in Gem's direction.

"What did it say?" Bronte asked.

"It explained how much you should be saving every month," Gem said, skipping over the fact that even though she'd opened the account, it didn't actually mean she had any money to save. And she still didn't quite have a hold on the whole compound interest thing yet.

Sam poked Gem's shoulder with her index finger. "Look at you, being all adult-like. Turning over a new leaf, huh?"

"Yeah," Laney added. "I'm glad you don't have your money buried in a jar in your backyard."

Gem gave in to a laugh.

"Tell me—" Bronte started, propping her elbows up on the table, but the uneven legs wobbled, and her still-full gin and tonic spilled over. Sam grabbed a couple napkins to soak it up, while Laney bit her bottom lip, probably trying to rein in her booming laugh before it started.

"You were saying?" Gem said with a snort.

Bronte's clumsiness borderlined on a sitcom gag, but after all these years, they were used to it. "I was saying, what's your goal for this year?"

"My goal?" Gem gathered her hair over her shoulder and started to braid it. "You're funny."

Sam sat back against the booth. "It doesn't have to be a goal. Maybe a wish?"

Bronte shook her head. "A goal," she repeated, digging through her purse. "Let me just get…"

"Please don't." Laney reached her arm over to stop Bronte from pulling out what would assuredly be a pen and paper from her purse to make some kind of list or plan or contract. Bronte was the only one to ever actually stick to New Year's resolutions. "We're celebrating. And I only have twenty-four hours before I need to be back in California, so I'm not wasting them on whatever test you're about to give us."

Bronte tucked a chunk of dark hair behind her ear. "Not a test. I thought we could all come up with something to focus on for this coming year, you know, like a—"

"This is not *Sisterhood of the Traveling Pants*," Laney said, moving to sit up straight. "This is a Friday night with cheap drinks and three of the people I love most in the world." She lifted her vodka and soda. "So, drink up."

Gem raised her glass. "Agreed."

"Here's to one more year older," Sam said.

"And one more year together," Bronte added.

"And life, liberty, and the pursuit of happiness." Laney threw back her drink and then waited, watching as the other three finished theirs.

Sam sputtered a cough, barely finishing the rest of her lite beer as Bronte smacked her lips and Gem swiped her hand across her mouth, shaking her head as the liquor settled in her belly. "Round two?"

"Yeah, but first, for posterity..." Laney stood up and leaned over to the booth next to them where a group of guys sat. They all gazed at her with cartoon heart eyes, nodding at whatever she said, and raised their hands to her, fighting over who would take her cell phone.

Laney handed it off to the one on the end, and he stood, grinning as if she'd knighted him, then waved to the girls. "Come on. Picture."

They scooched out of the booth and rounded to the front of the table. Bronte, Gem, Laney, and Sam all in a row, hands and arms intertwined, smiles on.

"Looking good, ladies," the guy said, stepping back, turning the phone sideways.

"Happy birthday on three," Sam said, from her position at the end. "One."

"It's going to be a good year for you, I know it," Bronte said then kissed Gem's cheek.

"Two."

"It's going to be a good night!" Laney said with a big laugh, dipping her head down toward Gem to reduce the height difference between them.

"Three! Happy birthday, Gemma!"

After a lot of drinks courtesy of the guy Laney had wrapped around her finger, the four staggered, giggled, and danced their way home to Gem's apartment, arm in arm, where they fell asleep huddled together on her floor in a heap of blankets and pillows. The next day, Bronte forced everyone up. She and Sam were both nerds who liked visiting museums, so they had an "education-forward" week-long road trip planned for their summer vacation, and Laney had a flight to catch.

When everyone was gone and Gem was left alone, her phone buzzed next to her. She picked it up, laughing out loud at the picture of them from last night with the caption **THE FOUR HORSEWOMEN OF THE APOCALYPSE** and the red-faced, sweating emoji sent from Laney.

Bronte texted multiple crying laughing faces while Sam replied with a Headless Horseman GIF.

Gem typed out **Miss you clowns already** before holding her head in her hands. She wasn't so much hungover as she was lonely without her girls. As she walked to the kitchen to fill up a pitcher with water, the floorboards creaked under her bare feet. Her pet turtle, Leonardo, crunched on some lettuce. Spot, the goldfish, completed yet another circle in its bowl.

It's going to be a good year for you, I know it. Bronte's words rang in Gem's ears as she watered her plants, their slightly browning leaves silently heckling her.

It's going to be a good year for you.

It wasn't as if last year had been so bad; it just hadn't been great. Here she was at twenty-five, trailing after her best friends, who all seemed to be so far ahead of her in life. She had nothing but a few plants and animals in a one-bedroom apartment, while they had boyfriends and jobs with benefits and *plans*.

For all of Gem's good qualities, the things her friends said made her *her*—passion and energy—she only did things she truly believed in. And the things she believed in left her with a few dollars in savings and a permanent fear of commitment.

Staring down the barrel of a quarter-life crisis, what was a girl to do?

2

The sun set into an orange and purple haze, but the August heat still simmered in the air. Gem rolled her bicycle into a driveway at the end of a large suburban development. Resting her bike on the kickstand, she took off her helmet and tilted her head back to study the home in front of her, which dwarfed the rest of the houses in the cul-de-sac. Between the tall pillars that cast long, dark shadows on the lawn, the carefully carved wood porch, pristine white paint, and high windows surrounded by dark-green shutters, the house looked like something out of a television show that house hunters who walked dogs for a living bought.

But Gem actually had walked dogs for a while, and she could never in a million years afford this place.

A light turned on in a second-story window, shaking her out of the reverie. She combed her fingers through her hair, trying unsuccessfully to tame what the humidity did to it, before digging into her large knit bag to pull out a skirt. With a quick glance around, she stripped off her shorts to pull on the skirt then hoofed it up the long driveway. Sweat dotted her upper lip in the few seconds it took to reach the door, and it opened before she had a chance to knock.

"Gemma Rose Turney, where have you been?" Caroline stood with her hands on her hips, dressed in a yellow cocktail dress and diamond solitaire necklace. With her glossy chestnut hair and wrinkle-free face, no one—sometimes not even Gem—believed she was forty-five years old.

Gem wiped her brow. "Nice to see you too, Mom."

"We've been waiting for you. What were you doing?"

"I was—"

Caroline grabbed her daughter by the wrist and dragged her inside. She inspected Gem, picking at the neon-green tank top with a big peace sign in the middle. "What are you wearing? You could have at least worn a bra."

Gem rolled her eyes. "No one is in for a nip slip, if that's what you're worried about."

Caroline scoffed but gentled her tone as she pressed her hands to her daughter's cheeks. "And put your hair up. Your bangs are always covering your beautiful face."

Gem followed her orders, tying her hair up in a messy bun.

Her mom wrinkled her nose. "And what is that smell?"

Gem smelled herself. "What smell?"

"You smell...like outside."

"Outside? How does someone smell of outside?"

Caroline batted at the air. "It smells like dry air or something."

"That's the smell of nature, Mom."

"Well, I don't like it."

Gem sighed a long-suffering sigh and pawed through her bag again. She found some lip gloss and body spray, and she quickly put on both before turning to her reflection in the mirror next to Caroline. "There. Satisfied?"

She was the spitting image of her mother with brown eyes, high cheekbones, a slender nose, and golden skin. They were even the same height, barely scraping 5'3", but Caroline always wore heels to make up the difference.

"I love you, honey," her mom said, smiling. Her shoulders rose and fell with a deep breath. "I'm so happy you're here."

Gem's eyebrow ticked up suspiciously at the emotion in her mom's voice, but before she could ask about it, Caroline tucked Gem's hand in hers to wind through the house. They stopped at a sitting room with uncomfortable-looking wingback chairs and a grand piano. A dozen people filled the space, laughing and drinking.

"I didn't know this was a party," Gem said, recognizing how underdressed she was now.

"I thought I told you," Caroline said, while waving to Frank, who was making drinks at a small bar in the corner.

Gem shook her head. Her mother hadn't told her. Gem wasn't the only flighty one in their family of two.

"We have an announcement to make," Caroline said as Frank made his way over to the pair and put his arm around Gem's shoulders.

"Gemma, how are you?" he asked with a slight trace of a Puerto Rican accent, offering her a light-colored drink.

"Good." She accepted the glass tumbler before circling her finger in the air. "Nice digs you got here."

He smiled jovially, stepping next to Caroline. Frank, with salt-and-pepper hair and a thick middle, wore his age, unlike her mother's usual choice in men. Gem had taken an immediate liking to him when she met him this past New Year's Day. They had been at a little Thai place and Caroline couldn't decide what she wanted, so he ordered one of almost everything and made sure it wasn't spicy. "Your mother can't handle spice," Frank had told Gem as if she didn't know, and then added with a grin, "Except for me." Gem had laughed and understood why her mom had fallen for him. With his kind brown eyes and a bois-terous laugh, there wasn't much to dislike.

Gem took a swig of her drink, sucking in a quick breath through her teeth. It was fruity and really strong. "What is this?"

"Pitorro, it's like our version of moonshine. I learned to make it from my *abuelo*."

Gem nodded and ventured to take another sip.

"It'll put hair on your chest," he said proudly.

"Great. Exactly what I need."

When Caroline gazed up at Frank with one arm around his waist, he kissed her nose. "Want some, *mi vida*?"

"No, thank you. I learned my lesson the first time."

Gem pointed around the room. "What's this all about, anyway?"

Caroline and Frank smiled at each other, sharing a secret with their eyes, and Gem gasped. "Are you pregnant?"

Frank guffawed as Caroline's mouth dropped to a frown, eyeing her daughter. "Don't be ridiculous."

"Then what is it?"

Frank tugged on Caroline's hand, backing up three steps to the landing. "Excuse me, everybody. Excuse me." The crowd all turned their attention to the pair. "We want to thank everyone for coming tonight. You're all our closest family and friends, and we want you to be the first to know—"

"We're getting married!" Caroline shrieked, showing off her left hand. A sparkling cupcake of a diamond sat on her ring finger, and the party erupted into congratulatory shouts. Everyone rushed forward, hugging and kissing the newly engaged couple.

Gem huffed, soaking up the mild burn of alcohol at the back of her tongue after another sip of her drink. Her mother was a hopeless romantic, and a wedding was nothing new but no less aggravating. Gem loved Frank, which was exactly the reason she wasn't happy about them getting married.

When the crowd finally dispersed, Caroline motioned her daughter over. Gem tossed back the rest of the pitorro in one gulp and choked as it slid down her throat. She wiped her mouth. "Married, Mom? Whatever happened to living in sin?"

Caroline ignored the comment and tucked Gem under her arm, walking a few feet to a man by the piano. Given that his back was to them, Gem could only make out his height and shaggy hair.

"Gemmie, since you'll be my maid of honor, I want you to meet Jason Mitchell. He'll be the best man." Caroline tapped his shoulder to get his attention, and when he turned, she thrust Gem forward like a prized pig. "Jason, this is my daughter, Gemma." Caroline smoothed down some flyaways from Gem's bun. "She's beautiful, isn't she?"

Gem looked up, up, up to the man in front of her to find cool blue eyes assessing her from the top of her head to the feet and back again. The corner of his mouth quirked like he had a secret as he stuck out his hand. "Nice to meet you."

He was much younger than Frank, probably around Gem's age, and she briefly wondered why he would be the best man. But it didn't matter why. She didn't really care. He had that preppy East Coast collegiate look about him, the type of guy she purposefully avoided. Tall and tanned with a jaw that could cut glass.

Gross.

His thick ashy-blond hair, long enough to tickle his earlobes and curl at the ends, was the only thing unkempt about him.

Ugh.

He probably played lacrosse or owned a boat, maybe both, and her skin prickled with bad memories.

Caroline nudged her daughter back into reality, and Gem shook his hand, trying to keep the reflexive disdain from her voice. "Yeah, you too."

Jason's gaze dropped to their clasped hands, his face morphing from arrogance to surprise, but Gem wasn't at all interested in any more conversation and dropped her hand to her side.

Caroline clapped in delight. "Oh, we're going to have so much fun together. Come on, you two, grab your seats for dinner. I put you next to each other at the table."

She all but skipped away as Gem stood in place, frozen between annoyance and disbelief. Her mother was getting married *again*, and she'd apparently have to spend time with a guy who carried the calling card for everything she hated most. "I need another drink."

"I can get it for you," he offered, reaching for her glass, but she snatched her hand away.

"Nope."

He cocked his head, his brow furrowing in a question Gem didn't care to answer.

"I'm good," she said, whirling away from him. She tried to ignore the stare she felt at her back as she uncorked the tall jar of pitorro and took a whiff of the coconut-and-almond scent before pouring two fingers worth of the alcohol into her glass.

After a sip, she pivoted around, catching Jason's attention zip back to the two men in front of him, and she inhaled a calming breath. To get to the dining room, she had to pass the trio currently blocking it, and the closer she got to them, the more details she heard of their conversation.

"What do you say, Jay?" the man with thinning carrot-colored hair asked.

He shrugged. "Yeah, whatever. I don't care."

"Great, I'll call for the stripper." The bald-headed man slapped Jason's back. "I know a girl who..." He dipped his head down, purposely lowering his voice, grinning lasciviously as he finished the rest of the sentence.

Thank the universe Gem didn't hear it, lest she gag. As it was, she groaned at the way the men seemed to drool over the mere idea of a woman like an object. Her instincts about Jason proved correct. "Excuse me."

The bald guy glanced down at Gem next to him. "Well, hello there."

Jason caught her eyes and had the decency to look a little embarrassed. "We were talking about the bachelor party."

Gem shrugged and motioned to the dining room, silently telling the big brute in front of her to move.

Carrot top smiled at her. "Who might you be?"

"The tooth fairy."

Carrot top winked at her, mistaking her sarcasm for flirtation. "Well, you certainly fit the bill, huh? I'm Howie."

The bald one nodded to her next. "Derek."

"Great. Can I get through?"

Derek glanced over his shoulder and shifted as if just now realizing he took up so much room she couldn't get by. She huffed. It was the story of mankind.

Finally seated at the long mahogany table, Gem grabbed her cell phone from her bag to shoot off a quick text to the girls about her mom. She sipped the pitorro with one hand and tapped out the message with the other.

The chair next to her squeaked as Jason leaned down to whisper, "You better slow down."

She angled away from him, the temper she kept under wraps quickly unraveling. "What?"

He tipped his chin to the glass in her hand. "That'll knock you on your ass if you aren't careful."

His unwanted advice grated on the last of her nerves, and she plopped her phone back into her bag with a forceful flick of her wrist. "I'll be fine."

"You probably think—"

That got her attention. She whipped her head toward him so fast, the bun on the top of her head fell lopsided. "You're going to tell me what I think?"

He jerked back, and she felt some satisfaction in the flash of remorse that crossed his features. "What? No." He ran a big hand over his jaw then shook his head. "Why are you so..."

"So what?" Gem raised her eyebrows, waiting for him to fill in the blank, ready to fire back, but Frank stood up, calling everyone's attention to him as flutes of champagne were passed around the table.

"Once again, we want to thank you all for coming here tonight, and we hope you enjoy the feast. But first, I want to thank you, Caroline." He turned to his fiancée. "I didn't think I could love again until you showed up at Angelo's in that red dress, remember?"

Caroline chided him before covering her smile with a manicured hand.

"I thought I had died," he said, painting a picture with his hands as he spoke. "There was an angel standing in front of me. And now, I am going to marry her. I'm the luckiest bastard in the world. To my future wife, Caroline."

Glasses clinked around the table, and Jason held his water up to Gem's. Without saying a word, she tapped her pitorro against it then drained it to spite him as he watched her over the rim of his glass.

She turned away from his icy blues and the column of his throat as he swallowed. Perfection like that was nauseating.

As everyone helped themselves to the prepared catered food, Gem spied her mother at the head of the table, nibbling on dainty bites of the chicken and mushrooms. Their eyes met, and Caroline motioned for her to eat, but instead of picking up a fork, Gem picked up her flute of champagne.

Jason cleared his throat next to her, and she cut her eyes to him over the delicate glass.

"Going in tonight, huh?"

She answered with a smack of her lips that drew his focus briefly to her mouth.

"Might want to hydrate." He gestured to her water with his knife.

"Bold move, telling a complete stranger what to do." By nature, Gem tended to be contrarian, and she wasn't holding back with Jason. Everything about him bugged her, from his tone of voice to the way his knee bumped against hers, driving her to pick at him.

He twisted in his seat, fixing a congenial smile on his face that didn't quite fit. "You better eat. You're going to get sick."

She clucked her tongue. "I don't eat things with a mother."

"Don't tell me you're a vegetarian." He pressed his lips together like he might laugh otherwise.

Gem set down the empty champagne flute with a thunk. "I'm vegan."

"Really?"

"Yes, really."

He shoved a piece of bread into his mouth, saying something under his breath that she didn't catch, but his frown told her it wasn't complimentary. His jaw worked as he chewed, and Gem forced her eyes away from the shadow of stubble on his chin.

One of Caroline's friends leaned forward across the table. "Gemma, your mother told me you'll be the maid of honor."

"Yeah." She nodded, picking up a stalk of asparagus with her fingers to bite it.

The woman pressed on. "Aren't you excited? Weddings are so fun, and with your mother as the bride, I'm sure everything will be beyond elegant."

"I'm sure."

The woman's smile melted at Gem's deadpan response, and she went back to her food.

"You don't sound too excited." Jason leaned down to Gem, elbowing her like they were buddies. They absolutely were not.

She gave him a wry smile. "Fourth time's the charm, right?"

He studied her face, and she refused to shrink under the

weight of his eyes when he said, "Did anyone ever tell you you've got a bad attitude?"

"I'm sorry, I think I misheard you?" She plastered on a fake smile, aiming her asparagus at him. "It sounded like you said I have a bad attitude."

He nodded with a huff, squeezing the crisp white linen napkin he had draped across his lap. "You're being a little rude."

Gem tensed at his casual insult and the way he went back to cutting up his food as if nothing had happened. "I'm being rude?" She shot back in a whisper-shout. "Don't you think calling me rude is a little rude?"

He considered her with one squinted eye before pointing to his plate with his fork. "You should try this. It's so good."

She growled, mad at herself for not being able to squash her short-tempered impulses and irritated with him for continuing to play the stupid game. And for looking so goddamn good while he did it.

With each forkful up to his mouth, the muscles in his arm tightened and released. The veins in his forearm and hand stuck out, strong and masculine. A damn shame.

"I wonder if this chicken had any little eggs in her nest. Or maybe a rooster at home," he mused.

Gem reached for a roll. "Don't antagonize me."

"Is that what you *think* I'm doing?" He flashed her a grin, calling back her unfinished words from a few minutes ago, but this time, she didn't take the bait.

She settled for silence while everyone else discussed the upcoming nuptials and Frank's engineering firm.

3

After the last of the guests had said their goodbyes, Jason was headed to the kitchen to steal some leftover cream puff pastries for the road when a very bad version of "Heart and Soul" drifted throughout the house.

Quietly walking down the hall, he caught sight of Gemma at the piano as her mother sat down next to her on the bench.

"Did you have fun tonight?" Caroline asked her.

Jason stayed close to the wall, eavesdropping. *Fun* wouldn't be the word he used to describe the night, but he did wonder what Gemma's word would be.

"Yeah. Fun." Gemma didn't look away from the keys, swaying, a little tipsy, and even though Gemma and Jason were practically strangers, it was easy to hear the lie in her voice.

"When's the big day?" Gemma asked.

"Next month."

The piano went silent. "Why so fast? You've only been with this guy a couple of months."

Jason hated to admit it, but he thought Frank was moving a little fast too. Although, he couldn't begrudge his godfather happiness.

"Don't say 'this guy' like he's some stranger on the street," Caroline said. "I love Frank very much." She wrapped her arms around Gemma, pressing their cheeks together. "Honey, I know you don't understand, but I truly believe Frank is the one I will spend the rest of my life with. I just can't live—"

"A day without him as your husband," Gemma finished for her mom as if she'd heard that line before.

"Frank's different," Caroline said, so quietly Jason had to lean almost around the corner to hear. He knew he shouldn't be listening in on this private moment, but he couldn't help it. Something about Gemma compelled him to want to know more about her, and it was obvious she wasn't going to give him *any* information about herself freely.

"Frank is a good man. I love him and trust him," Caroline went on. "I hope you do too."

"I…" Gemma left her sentence unfinished, and Jason was oddly disappointed. What was it about Frank or about this marriage that she didn't like? He wanted to know, but Gemma only sighed and rested her head on her mom's shoulder. "Just tell me when and where."

Caroline held her daughter's hand. "September 30th, at the country club."

"Marrying Frank does have its perks, huh?"

"Hey. You, of all people, should know that's not what it's about." Caroline lifted her shoulder so Gemma looked at her, and Jason ducked back into the shadows to remain unseen. "One day, you'll find somebody as wonderful as Frank."

"Don't hold your breath."

Jason had to agree with that one. He didn't know who would be able to put up with Gemma. Maybe an alligator wrestler or bounty hunter.

Caroline stood, calling out, "Jason, can you give Gemmie a ride home?"

He startled, his heart beating fast at almost being caught

snooping on them, and shuffled back a few steps, trying to toss his voice to sound farther away. "Sure."

"Never mind!" Gemma yelled back. "I don't need a ride."

"Yes, you do," Caroline said, as he walked down the hall, all cool and collected, flipping his car keys around his index finger. He offered Gemma a smile, and she turned her back to him.

"It's after eleven," Caroline told Gemma, "and you have a *bicycle*." She said bicycle like it was a whale and Gemma was going to *Free Willy* home.

"I've ridden it at night before." Gemma folded her arms. "I'm good, I don't need a ride."

Though he wasn't really excited about the prospect of spending any more time alone with her, he did not like the idea of Gemma on a bicycle at night. This town wasn't very bike-friendly, so he'd rather see her home safe than hurt. "Ready, Gemmie?"

She threw him a look. "Don't call me that."

"Yes, she is." Caroline answered him as Frank came to stand next to Jason. The men shook hands then Jason kissed Caroline's cheek.

"Take care of my daughter," she said, pressing her hand to his chest.

"Of course." He smiled, and Gemma sulked as she followed him out the door to her bike. Jason pointed to his car, silently telling her where to go.

"What is this? The Batmobile?"

"I wish." He unlocked the doors. "It's a Mercedes-Benz."

He pointed to her bicycle. "What is this?"

"My bike."

"I can see that. I meant, why do you have it?"

"I rode it here."

He only raised one eyebrow.

"My car went to the junkyard a few months ago, and I bought a bike instead. Good enough reason?"

He shook his head. "That's not going in my car."

"What am I supposed to do with it?"

He pretended not to hear the question and got in the driver's seat. She could leave it here for all he cared, but his car didn't have room for it.

"You know what? Thanks, but no thanks. I'll ride home." She sat on the bike a little wobbly and rode a few feet down the driveway then fell over.

He grumbled and stomped over to her. "Get in the car."

"No, I'm fine."

He helped her up with one hand on her elbow. "I told you not to drink so much."

She ignored him, reaching for her bike.

"Look at you. You can't even walk right."

She stuck out her tongue at him. It was like dealing with a toddler.

"Real mature, Gemmie."

"Don't call me that," she snipped.

"Don't act like a child," he barked back.

She started off again, but in a few quick steps, he blocked her, his hands over hers on the handlebars. "Get in the car."

Neither of them moved.

"Gemma," he said slowly, and it was the first time he'd said her name. He hated that he liked saying it. Worse yet, the way her eyes widened slightly, as if she liked it too.

"Jason."

"Get. In. The. Car."

"When. You. Ask. Nicely."

He laughed through his nose. "No."

She tried to get away from him, but with his knees on either side of her front tire, she didn't have any leverage.

"Just get in the goddamn car," he said after a while, shaking the bike a bit so Gemma lost her balance, forcing her off it.

"You're so nice." She hobbled off the bike, and Jason took it in his hands. She sneered at him. "A real prince."

"And you're a real pain in the ass."

They walked to his car, where he somehow finagled the bicycle into the back, then drove to Gemma's place in silence, only speaking for directions. She pointed to an apartment complex. "Right here is fine."

When Jason stopped the car, she hopped out, and he followed, grabbing the bike from the back of the car. She snatched it from him as soon as he lowered it to the ground. "You know your car is ridiculous, right?"

He smiled and crossed his arms. Nothing would make her happy, so he might as well try to have some fun. "Okay."

"No one needs something with so many bells and whistles. It probably has terrible gas mileage."

"Okay."

Obviously annoyed, Gemma worked her jaw back and forth for a moment before she turned, walking her bike up the sidewalk. She had trouble getting it in the door, and he laughed. "Need help?"

"No." For the fifth time, she tried and failed to hold the door open and get her bike inside.

"Okay."

"Stop saying okay, and get over here!"

"Okay."

When he reached the door, he lifted the bike and motioned inside. "After you."

Gemma's second-floor walk-up apartment was a hole. Small, old, and in need of a good cleaning. He set the bike down and stuck his hands in his pockets, afraid to touch anything. "Nice place."

"I'm sure that was sarcastic, but I will say thank you anyway," she said, clicking on a few lamps.

How was there no overhead lighting anywhere? Jason blinked into the sudden brightness then spun in a slow circle. Sketches and watercolor paintings were scattered on the floor, and he admired one black-and-white image of a Joshua tree. She had a drying rack full of clothes sitting off to the side, a well-worn brown couch against the far wall, and an ancient television that had a broken antenna, which sat on top of what appeared to be a table made entirely out of painted soda cans. Homemade picture frames clung to the pea-green walls. He studied one made from popsicle sticks. It held a picture of Gemma surrounded by little kids, who had paint smeared on their faces and hands. She was in the middle of the group with her arms around them, her own face beaming through streaks of orange and blue paint.

A sudden hiss came from the corner, not even a foot away, surprising Jason. A heap of fur lay on top of a bookshelf, and he backed away from it. "What the fu—what is that?"

"George," Gemma answered over her shoulder, opening cat treats. The lump of gray fur leaped down to the floor, and she petted its head.

He grimaced. "*What* is it?"

On cue, the cat spun to look at him, one-eyed and ugly.

Gemma picked him up. "This is Mr. George Clooney. I rescued him. He was attacked by a dog and lost his eye."

"I hate cats." Jason backed farther away, his hands up. "I don't trust them."

George Clooney bounded into another room after what sounded like an offended hiss.

"That's so stupid. What if I said I don't trust..." Gemma coasted her gaze around the apartment as if she could find the end of her sentence on the walls. Then her eyes landed on him, and she thrust her hand. "I don't trust anyone who wears short-sleeved button-downs?"

Jason tried not to laugh. "That's the best you could come up with?"

"I mean...you look like a child. Like you should have a pocket protector."

She was lying. He could tell from the way her attention snagged on his chest, where he knew his snug button-down fit him just right. *He* would be lying if he said he didn't work out for this exact reason. For this exact moment.

"I left it at my math club meeting," he said then pointed at her, continuing the retort. "What about you? I'm surprised you even shave. I thought you nature fanatics didn't do that."

"I'm a vegan and an environmentalist. Whether I choose to shave or not is my choice, not society's. And certainly not because some guy decided it was sexy or not." She aimed her words at him like darts. "Especially you."

"Especially me?" he repeated in a low voice, but she twirled away from him, toward the kitchen.

Jason didn't know what exactly it was about him that pissed Gemma off so much. When Caroline introduced them, Gemma had barely looked at him before she'd judged him. Even as they shook hands, her fingers small and delicate in his, exchanging what felt like static electricity so the hairs on his arm rose, she had still pouted at him, all huffy and harsh-eyed. They exchanged a few words, and it was partially his fault for insti-gating it at some points—he'd give up that much. But he evidently had some new masochistic streak that had him staying firmly planted in her apartment.

He watched as she let her hair down, brown and golden strands blending together to create an almost copper color that couldn't quite decide if it was curly or straight or something in between. She ran her fingers through it—strangely enough, something he wanted to do too—before feeding a goldfish that swam back and forth in a small bowl on the kitchen counter.

Next, she grabbed a banana out of a hanging fruit basket and tossed the peel into a bucket piled up with garbage by the sink.

"What's that?" he asked, standing in the archway of the kitchen.

"A compost pile."

"You're a vegan, and you have a compost heap?"

"Yeah," she said with a glance over her shoulder. Her tank top fluttered with the movement, the outer curve of her breast peeking from the side—of course she wouldn't wear a bra—and he dropped his gaze to the floor so he wouldn't stare. "I have to make up for the huge carbon footprint you're leaving."

"There's nothing wrong with eating meat."

"Except for the fact that those animals are given chemicals from birth to make them grow much bigger than they are supposed to be, kept in cages and pens too small so they become sick and overcrowded, and then, finally, slaughtered in a horrific manner." She broke the banana in half, giving some to a turtle that sat in a terrarium in the space where the microwave should be above the stove. The other half, Gemma ate.

Jason could not believe her. He couldn't believe she was the daughter of the stately Caroline. He couldn't believe she lived like this, that she did and said whatever she wanted, and that she rode a bicycle, for Christ's sake.

He also couldn't believe how attracted he was to her.

"Thanks for dropping me off and everything." Gemma's voice lifted his eyes from where they were soaking in the curve of her ass in her tight skirt, his self-control long gone. "But I have to get up early tomorrow, so if you will..." She pivoted around and ushered him to the door.

"I have one question."

"What?" Gemma opened her door.

He stood in the doorway, facing her. "What's your deal with this wedding?"

She drooped against the doorframe. "What're you talking about?"

"Frank's like a father to me, and I want him to be happy. You, on the other hand, are practically foaming at the mouth over these nuptials."

"You have a real way with words."

He raised a challenging eyebrow. He had to admit he really, *really* enjoyed goading her, immature as it was.

"Not that I should have to explain myself to you," she said, dragging her hair over her shoulder to play with a few ends. "But I'm cynical about my mother's marriages."

"You don't say." When she tossed him a look, he grinned down at her. "I'm sorry," he said, completely insincere. "Go on."

She didn't say anything, and he didn't move from his spot. He only anchored his arms across his chest, waiting for more, and she straightened up, an annoyed curl rounding her lips.

"Husband number one, my father, knocked up my mother when she was nineteen, married her, then ran out on us when I was a year old. Last I heard, he'd found himself a new family in Arizona somewhere. Then there were a few boyfriends who came close to attaining husband number two status, but that glory went to Wayne. He showed up in time for my ninth birthday party with a pet hamster to win me over. He was a good guy, but gone by my twelfth birthday. He left a nice card, though. And this last husband was a young Frenchman, Renard Colbert. She met him at an art gallery I was working in. He was cute, but totally worthless. Did nothing but smoke cigarettes and read poetry all day. He was... *Comment dites-vous* asshole?"

Jason stepped toward her, keeping his voice casual. "So, what you're saying is, you have daddy issues?"

Gemma's skin turned a pretty pink, and she fisted her hands at her sides. A little lightning bolt. "It's a shame."

Jason's mouth turned up into a half smile, and he tipped his head to the side, genuinely curious at what might come out of her mouth next. Everything she did and said was totally unexpected. "What's a shame?"

She put her hand on his bicep and leaned in close, on the balls of her feet. Even though she was a whole foot shorter than he was, she made up for it with sheer boldness. "It's a shame you're so gorgeous and such a dickhead."

He smirked. "You think I'm gorgeous?"

"Fucking douche," she said under her breath, dropping her chin toward her chest.

He took two steps back, running his hand over his mouth and jaw. This one didn't mince words. "You've got quite a mouth on you. I can't believe Caroline lets you get away with it."

"I'm a grown woman. I don't need to 'get away' with anything."

He pushed his hands back into his pockets. No matter how appealing Gemma was, she clearly had a lot of baggage that he wasn't interested in being tied to for this wedding. "You seem to be making some pretty stupid decisions for being so grown up."

Her dark eyes narrowed. "I'm not stupid."

He huffed. "I didn't say you were stupid."

"You insinuated."

He couldn't help but roll his eyes. "You don't think getting drunk at your mother's engagement party is stupid?"

"I wasn't drunk."

She'd drunk so much tonight she couldn't even sit on her bike, but pointing that out would only continue the argument. "Can't you admit when you're wrong?"

"Yes, I can, but I'm not wrong." She folded her arms over her chest.

"Okay, whatever you say."

"Stop saying okay!" When he gave her one of his best smiles in response, she growled. "You're infuriating."

"You aren't exactly a ray of sunshine either." Jason lowered his face to hers so they were eye to eye, their lips were an inch apart. With her breath hot on his cheeks, it was hard to concentrate, but he pushed on. "Let me give you a piece of advice," he said in an almost-whisper, recalling how he'd spotted her quick change at the bottom of the driveway earlier. "If you're going to strip in public, make sure no one is around."

She responded by slamming the door in his face. Then adding through it, "Pretentious bastard!"

4

The next morning, Gem woke up with a headache and a tense neck. George Clooney didn't move from his spot on the comforter, merely opened his lone eye before going back to sleep. She pushed off the bed, the argument she'd had with Jason last night still fresh, and her blood pressure instantly increased.

After brushing her teeth, she stared into the mirror with her slightly bloodshot eyes, only to have her brain ransacked by the image of steely-blue ones, the color of winter. She groaned, her skin warm at the thought of her hand engulfed by his long fingers. He was everything she couldn't stand in a man, and yet here she was swooning over him. George Clooney snuck up behind her, purring, and the daydream was broken as Jason's voice popped into her memory.

"Can't you just admit you're wrong?" She mocked.

In the kitchen, she said good morning to Spot and Leonardo, who poked his head out of his shell. "You like me, right?"

The turtle chomped his mouth open and closed.

"I'll take that as a yes." She patted his shell before swallowing an Advil with a gulp of orange juice then headed off to work.

The humidity was on the rise already, and by the time Gem hopped off her bicycle in front of Bare Necessities, she was a hot, sweaty mess. A bell above her rang when she opened the door to the little corner store that sold all-natural products.

"Finally, Gem! I need your help." Her boss called to her from the back of the store, and she strolled to the storage room, where he jumped down from a small stepladder.

"Morning."

Andrew turned, his platinum hair styled exactly right, while his face was done up all wrong.

Gem raised her eyebrows. "What's on your face?"

"Trying out the new line of vegan cosmetics. Too thick?"

"Way too thick."

Andrew pointed to a shelf. "Grab those boxes for me, please." She did so as Andrew washed his face off at the sink. "I have to do some paperwork this morning. Can you restock?"

"Sure."

After patting his face dry, he walked alongside Gem to the front. "You look tired."

"I am," she answered, setting the boxes on the floor before dropping her arms onto the counter, next to the folders and notebooks Andrew used for accounting.

"What happened?"

Gem pressed her cheek to the cool wood of the counter. "My mom's getting married. Again."

"What number is that?"

"Four."

"Good for her. But why are you so tired?"

She stifled a yawn. "I had a little too much to drink."

He grabbed a bottle from behind the counter and handed it to Gem. "It's ginseng."

"I'm the maid of honor," she said without any pretext.

"Okay." Andrew went to work. "What's the problem with that?"

"The best man is a total tool bag."

"How old is he?"

"I don't know. Maybe twenty-eight or twenty-nine."

"No." He laughed. "I mean the guy your mom is marrying? How old is he?"

"In his fifties, I suppose." Gem opened the ginseng and sank to the floor, ready for a nap even though it wasn't even ten in the morning.

"What's a kid doing hanging out with a fifty-year-old?" Andrew handed an aluminum water bottle to Gem.

"I'm twenty-five." She swallowed the herbs with water. "And I hang out with you."

"I'm not fifty."

Gem smiled devilishly. "Thirty-five...fifty. Close enough."

Andrew feigned anger before taking a seat behind the counter. "So, what's the big deal?"

"The big deal is he's a know-it-all who drives a Mercedes-Benz."

"A Mercedes? Sounds nice."

She snorted. "And he doesn't like cats."

"I don't like cats."

"He wore a short-sleeve button-down. He looked like a Boy Scout."

Andrew fanned himself dramatically. "Always prepared. Who doesn't like Boy Scouts?"

Gem sighed. "The problem is he's too good-looking."

"How dare he!"

From her place on the floor, she raised her fist to the sky in anger. "He should be in magazines. That's the problem. He's arrogant and a bully and incredibly hot."

Andrew mumbled, a sound that told her he was chewing on his pen.

"What?" She moved to peek up at her boss behind the counter. "What are you saying?"

He shrugged, lifting one hand, his fingernails painted dark purple. "Doesn't sound like a problem to me. Sounds more like an opportunity."

"I'm going to take this opportunity to rest my head. Wake me in ten minutes." Gem lay down, closing her eyes, next to the boxes of vegan protein bars she needed to put away.

SANTOS & Mitchell Engineering Group buzzed about the CEO's engagement. Balloons and flowers covered Frank's office. A few men sat around drinking beer and eating hoagies and chicken wings. Jason had his feet propped up on a chair as he watched ESPN on a flat-screen mounted on the wall. Frank seized a chair next to him, offering the young man a beer, but Jason shook his head, biting into a sub.

Frank drank it himself. "I assume you got Gemma home safe and sound last night."

Jason nodded.

"Spitfire, isn't she?"

"That's one way to put it."

Frank's laughter boomed in Jason's ear. "You don't like each other or what?" When Jason didn't answer, Frank slapped his shoulder. "Cat got your tongue?"

"We're not exactly peas in a pod if that's what you were hoping for."

Frank sipped from his beer. "She looks just like her mother, doesn't she? A knockout. She and Caroline could be twins."

Jason continued to eat, his eyes on the TV. He'd spent most of last night bouncing a tennis ball off his bedroom wall, trying to release some tension. And when that didn't work, he closed his eyes and took his dick in his hand, hating himself for coming with Gemma's face in the front of his mind. She was a real knockout who had a mean one-two with words.

"Gemma is nothing like Caroline."

Frank nodded. "That's why I like her so much. You could learn a little something from Gem."

That got Jason's attention. "I could learn from her?"

"Yeah. You need to have a little fun in your life."

"I have fun."

Frank stole a chip from Jason's plate and shoved it into his mouth. "When? With who?"

"My friends."

Frank snuffed out a laugh. "Your friends? You have two friends, Kevin and Luke. I mean girlfriends."

Jason shook his head and wiped a bit of mayo from the corner of his mouth. "You know I don't have any. Nor do I want one right now."

He prayed for a distraction, not wanting to get into this conversation again. He didn't want to commit to just any woman simply because he wanted to please Frank or because he feared being alone. If or when he wanted to settle down, he would. Until then, Jason liked his life fine the way it was.

Thankfully, a buzzer on Frank's office phone rang, followed by a voice. "Mr. Santos, you have a special delivery."

The men in the room whistled as Frank pressed a button on his phone. "Send it in." Then he looked back to Jason. "You need to loosen up, kid." Moments later, his office door opened, and a Marilyn Monroe look-alike sauntered in. "Right on time, Miss Monroe. My friend Jason needs to have some fun."

The woman swirled around to where Frank pointed.

"Anything you say, Mr. Santos," she cooed. Marilyn pursed her lips and winked at Jason before swaying over to him.

Hours later, Jason pulled into his garage, well after his usual time getting home from work. He lazily undid his tie on his path through the back door in the garage and then into the kitchen, which was decked out in state-of-the-art appliances. He grabbed milk out of the refrigerator and drank it straight from the carton. He paused a moment at a picture held up by a magnet on the fridge, the same usual pang of longing burning his chest. It was a young Jason with his parents, huddled together on a blanket outside, a picnic set between them. Jason shared his father's nose and smile but had the same color of eyes and hair as his mother. It was the only picture he displayed of them in the whole house. All the rest of the family photos and mementos were stored in a few boxes, where he didn't have to face them every day.

Upstairs, he pushed open the double doors to his bedroom and sat on his large bed, stripping off his shirt to rub at the lipstick marks on the collar before tossing it in the laundry. He took off his slacks and opened up the doors to the walk-in closet. His work clothes hung neatly on racks, while folded jeans, shorts, and shirts stacked the shelves. Sneakers and shoes were piled underneath. The entire right side of the closet was barren.

He pulled on a T-shirt and mesh shorts and slipped on a pair of sneakers. Closing the closet doors, he considered the bedroom. It was empty. Save for the king-size bed and miscellaneous gray chair and lamp in the corner of the room. He could admit to himself that his bedroom was empty.

His whole house was empty.

And kind of sad.

Frank had been hopeful that Jason had bought the newly constructed townhouse, in the best school district, to fill it with a family, but the pushing and prodding led to no avail.

Jason liked how he lived. He worked hard for the things he wanted and spent his free time doing whatever he pleased. He had a big house, a lot of toys, and a few women to fill up his nights. But still, the fact remained, his bedroom was empty.

He ended up in the driveway, shooting hoops by himself until his cell phone rang. He glanced at the number before answering. "Hey, Bridge."

"Hi, handsome," she said in her typical purr. But for some reason, tonight, he didn't find it as inviting as usual.

"What's up?" he asked, holding the phone with one hand, dribbling the ball with the other.

"It's Friday." Jason ignored the comment, and she continued, in a sweeter voice, "Are we hanging out tonight?"

"Uh, yeah, I guess."

"Let's go out to dinner," she suggested.

"Um..." He took a one-handed shot and missed. "I don't know. I'm pretty tired."

"But we never go out anywhere." He could picture her pursed lips. "Come on, baby."

The pet name grated on him, and the ball got away, rolling into the next-door neighbor's yard. "We went out the other week for ice cream."

"I mean on a real date," she said.

He grabbed the ball and rested it against his hip, remembering Gemma's dark eyes pinning him in place at her apartment, that disaster she called a home. He didn't know why he liked it so much. "How about we watch a movie or something at your house?"

"My pick?"

"Your pick," he agreed, although he was nowhere near as excited as Bridget was. What excited him was the way he felt sparring with Gemma, but there was no way he was going there. "I'll be over around nine."

"I'll make cupcakes."

"Sounds good."

"Chocolate-filled," she said, back to her bedroom voice.

"Sure. Sounds great."

"Can't wait to see you."

Jason hung up and tossed the phone on the grass then took a step back for a shot. He missed.

5

The last week of August flew by in a blur of wedding planning. Caroline dragged Gem along to appointments for invitations, decorations, hairstyling, and now the biggest of them all.

The wedding gown.

Caroline swept open a pink curtain and posed gloriously in the doorframe of the bridal salon dressing room. A long cream dress with a boat neck showed off her thin frame. "So, how do I look?"

Gem put down her magazine and took in the bride-to-be. "Great."

"You think so?" Caroline twisted in front of a mirror, admiring herself from all angles.

"You look beautiful, Mom," Gem said sincerely. Caroline had come from a family of money in Chicago, but when she got pregnant before she was married, they kicked her out. Since then, it had always been Caroline and Gemma.

The sales attendant appeared to explain the bustle to Gem, who only half listened as Caroline continued to fiddle with the dress, inspecting every detail, pointing out any possible snag or stain before the attendant left with a paper full of notes and a tape measure around her neck.

Caroline spun around to Gem. Even in the drab light of the dressing room, she sparkled. "Frank and I want to take you and Jason to brunch tomorrow."

Gem wrinkled her nose. She'd gotten away with not having to interact with him so far, and she hoped to hold off until the actual big day.

"We'll pick you up at eleven." Caroline grinned. "He's cute, isn't he? Frank speaks so highly of—"

Gem opened up the magazine with an irritated flick of the wrist. "All right, all right. You don't have to try so hard. I know you did this to set me up with him."

"Did what? Get engaged?"

"No. The maid of honor, best man thing. I'm not interested."

"First of all," Caroline said, sliding the magazine out from Gem's fingers, "who else would I have as my maid of honor besides my daughter, who is, most of the time, wonderful, caring, and lovely? And second of all, I had nothing to do with Frank's choice of best man." She sat down, wiggling into the few inches between Gem and the arm of the lounger.

Gem shifted over, but there wasn't enough room, so Caroline hoisted her daughter into her lap. "Some things never change," she said with a laugh, then more seriously, "Frank practically raised Jason, so I would assume he would be the only choice to stand next to him on our wedding day. And yes, I thought maybe you two would hit it off, but I'm not going to force you to do anything you don't want to." Caroline took Gem's hand in her own, her eyes drooping like a puppy's. "If you don't want to be my maid of honor, you don't have to."

Gem lowered her gaze to the floor, guilt-ridden. "You're not forcing me to do anything. I'm happy to be your maid of honor."

Her mother's face perked up, and she hugged her daughter

tightly. As if Gem was ever really going to say no to her mom. "And I'll go to brunch tomorrow."

Caroline pulled Gem to stand up next to her, looping their arms together. "This time, Gemmie, I'm going to do it right. With the right man, for the right reasons. I only want you to be happy for me."

"I am happy for you, Mom." Gem smiled at Caroline's reflection in the mirror. "Very happy."

BY THE TIME FRANK, Caroline, and Gem arrived at the café, Jason was already seated at a table outside. He stood up and slid his aviators off before shaking hands with Frank.

"Were you waiting long?" he asked, pulling out a chair for his fiancée.

"About ten minutes," Jason answered, kissing Caroline on the cheek. "How are you?"

She smiled widely, petting his jaw in a motherly fashion. "I'm fine, thank you. I'm sorry we made you wait. Gemma was running behind this morning."

Figured. Jason turned to Gemma, who did not acknowledge him. The sour feelings they'd left each other with after the engagement party clearly hadn't lessened at all, and the irksome awareness that Jason found her deeply attractive was another reason to keep his distance.

The group settled into their seats as a waitress appeared at the table. "My name is Jessica, and I'll be serving you today." She smiled politely, writing down everyone's order until her sights landed on Jason. She smoothed her apron over her hips, color rising in her cheeks as she smiled brightly at him. She was cute, so he played along, sliding his sunglasses back on, pointedly ignoring the daggers Gemma shot at him as he ordered his omelet with bacon on the side.

"You let me know if you need anything," Jessica said to the table, though her attention fixated solely on him.

He replied with a winning grin. "We will. Thank you, Jessica."

Caroline opened her napkin. "Seems like you're quite popular with women, Jason."

He only shrugged. There was one woman, in particular, with whom he was not popular.

Frank wiped his forehead with a handkerchief. "Gem, how do you ride your bike around in this heat?"

Next to Jason, she sipped from her water glass. "It's not bad. You get a nice draft."

Jessica arrived with everyone's drinks, and after passing them out, she placed her hand on the back of Jason's chair. "I love your hair."

He ran his hand through it, the tips curling around his fingers. "Thank you. I grew it myself." She giggled, a bit over the top for his liking, but when Gemma snorted next to him, he kept on going. "What about you? Is that your natural color?" When Jessica nodded, tugging at the black-as-night strands, he smiled. "It's beautiful."

"Could I get more water?" Gemma cut in.

Jessica didn't seem to hear her as she backed away from the table, still only speaking to Jason. "I'll be back with your food in a little while."

"Excuse me," Gemma called after her. "Jessica!"

The waitress didn't glance back.

Frank guzzled down his drink. "So, Gemmie, I know you and your mom went dress shopping yesterday, but she won't tell me anything about it."

"Sorry, Frank. All I can say is that she'll be the most beautiful bride," Gemma said, and Jason watched her from behind his dark shades. The light-green sundress accentuated her shoulders, kissed with a few freckles.

Caroline covered her daughter's hand, smiling, and Jason moved, angling his feet so his left knee almost touched Gemma's right. "Gemma isn't a name you hear very often. Where did it come from, Caroline?"

Gemma's head lolled to the side, evidently bored with him, although her mother sat up tall. "Well, when Gemmie was born, she arrived with that gorgeous tawny hair in a ring around her head like a crown. I wanted to give her a name fit for a princess. But instead of a princess, I got a—"

"A hipster," Jason interjected.

Gemma curled her lip at him. "I'm not a hipster."

"A hipster?" Caroline arched her brow at Frank as if for back-up, but he only fanned himself with his napkin, not paying much attention to the conversation, and she pressed her hand to her chest. "Forgive for being *an old*," she said with a pointed look at Gemma, who grinned in return, clearly exchanging some inside joke. "But my daughter doesn't strike me as a hipster."

Jason opened his mouth to answer, but Gem covered it with her hand. "Exactly. Hipsters wear skinny jeans, listen to jazz music, and read Tolstoy for fun. I'm not a hipster."

Caroline nodded. "Right. If anything, she's a hippie."

Jason smiled under Gemma's palm, her skin soft and sweet-smelling. So sweet he needed a taste and nipped her. She jumped ever so slightly in her seat and yanked her hand away, pressing her thumb against the skin just below her middle finger, and he licked his lips as if he could find her flavor lingering there. It was a travesty that he couldn't.

Behind the shade of his glasses, Jason darted his attention from Gemma's mouth to the curve of her cleavage that rose with each breath. Before he realized it, he moved his hand to her collarbone, brushing locks of her hair behind her shoulder, his fingertips drawing out a blush along her chest. She'd kept her eyes on him the whole time, and it wasn't until she turned away from him that he realized how he missed her stare. She pasted a smile on her face, one he knew was fake because he was doing the same thing, as he dropped his hand. Drumming his fingers on his knee, he relished the fact that he could cause that delicate pink color to invade her cheeks.

Caroline leaned across the table toward her daughter. "Honey, why are you all red? No need to be embarrassed. You know I love that you're basically a reincarnated man who lived and died on some commune from eating poison berries."

That got Gem's attention, and she let out a reluctant laugh at her mother's teasing.

"Yeah, I love that you're into all that environmental stuff," Frank agreed, sinking into his chair. "In fact, we're working on a new housing development that's all green. Right, Jason?"

Jason forced his eyes from Gemma. "Yeah." He cleared his throat. "Yes."

She tied her hair up in a messy knot, displaying miles of creamy skin along her neck, shoulders, and back. "I didn't know you two worked together."

"He is the Mitchell in Santos & Mitchell Engineering Group. Jason's father and I started the company many years ago." Frank unbuttoned the top button of his shirt. "In fact, Jason'll become the CEO when I retire."

"In a hundred years," Jason joked, waving off the future. It was a forgone conclusion, but it wasn't exactly something he bragged about. He especially didn't want to give Gemma any more ammunition to hate him. Although, from the way she avoided any more eye contact with him, maybe she didn't hate him as much as he thought. He certainly didn't hate her either.

Frank pointed to Jason. "I've never known anyone as smart as this kid, except maybe his dad." His face was bright with pride as he spoke to Gemma. "Undergraduate in architectural engineering and an MBA. Jason is transforming us into a green company, and his new development will be the first in the state built with completely renewable energy. Tell her about it, Jay."

He protested, turning his head to her. "No, I'm sure she doesn't want to hear it."

Gemma lifted her gaze from the seam of her dress, surprising him with hurried words. "No, no, I do. Tell me."

Jason shifted forward, one elbow on the table, the other on his knee, and opened his mouth to speak when Jessica showed up with a tray full of plates. She served everyone and, yet again, stuck next to his chair. This time, she boldly placed her hand on his shoulder. "I hope you enjoy your food. I'll be back to check on you in a few minutes."

Gemma held up her empty glass. "Could I have—"

Jessica kept walking.

"Can you stop dazzling her?" Gemma thumped her glass on the table and glared at him. "I'd like some water."

Jason smiled and turned. "Excuse me, Jessica?"

The waitress immediately spun around at his voice. "Yes?"

Gemma let out a huge guffaw.

He pointed to her glass. "We'll need some more water, please, when you get a chance."

"Of course. I'll be right back." Jessica scurried away and was back in a minute with a pitcher of water. She kept her hand on the back of Jason's chair, leaning across him to fill up everyone's glass before leaving the pitcher next to Jason's plate.

Gemma's lips formed silent words that looked to be made of four letters, and he swiped his hand over his mouth to keep from grinning. Frank went back to his talk about renewable energy, and the conversation progressed, although Jason couldn't quite move on from the soft heat Gemma's eyes had shown him earlier.

At the end of the meal, Jessica returned with the check. "I can take this when you're ready." She bent down to Jason's ear. "My phone number is on the card underneath," she whispered. "Call me."

This time, Jason watched her walk away.

"She's cute," Caroline observed.

"A little forward and not very good at her job, but whatever." Gemma bit into a piece of cantaloupe, and at the sight of her dark pink tongue peeking out to lick the corner of her lips, Jason had to forcibly push himself away from the table. He needed more room between them, space for his brain to get back in working order. He shook his head, remembering the combative role he could fill, rather than this dopey character he played now. "Jealous?"

"Of Jessica? No, I'm not jealous of the waitress throwing herself at you." Gemma polished off her water.

Frank reached for the check, but Jason batted his hand away and stuck his credit card in the holder before passing it to another waiter as he walked by. When Jessica returned with it a minute later, she seemed a bit put out, yet he signed the receipt without any further flirtations. "Everybody ready to go?"

Frank helped Caroline up and led the group to the cars, where Jason pressed a button on his key fob. The lights flickered on his truck.

Gemma stopped in her tracks. "You've got to be kidding me."

"What, sweetheart?" Frank asked, opening the passenger side door of his car.

"First, the sports car, and now, a truck?"

Jason stepped next to Gemma, her brusque mood surrounding her like a bubble. It was easy to put her delightful lips out of his mind when they were pulled into a scowl. "What's the issue now?"

"Have you ever thought about the gallons of oil you're burning through every day? The amount of carbon dioxide you're putting into the atmosphere? Almost nine thousand grams of—"

"And there it is," he said, pointing at her with his key. The ever-present nitpicking.

"You really don't—"

Frank cut off whatever argument Gemma had. "Jay, you're coming to the picnic tomorrow, right?"

When Jason nodded, Caroline smacked her forehead. "Gemmie, I forgot to tell you about that. We're having—"

"A picnic. Yeah, I deduced that from what Frank said," she said, still making faces at the truck.

"Deduced." Jason rocked back on his heels next to her. "Good use of vocabulary words."

She sneered at him. "Don't have a master's but—"

Caroline grabbed her daughter, interrupting the rest of her remark. "I'm sorry. I forgot with all the wedding planning and everything. You can come, right?"

"I'm supposed to work at the store tomorrow. Andrew has the day off."

"But tomorrow's Labor Day."

"So?"

Caroline rubbed her daughter's back. "You get that many customers that you need to stay open on Labor Day?"

Gemma shied away from her mother, a miffed breath leaving her, and Jason forced his attention away from her mouth when she said, "Yes, we get enough customers to stay open on Labor Day. Where else would people get their tofu hot dogs?"

Frank choked at that. "Who eats tofu hot dogs?"

Jason laughed at Gemma's frustration, and she looked as if she might murder him. He kissed Caroline's cheek before going to his truck.

Gemma continued, "Besides, I don't want to ride my bike there again."

"That's not a problem. Jason'll take you." Frank tipped his chin to the man in question. "You'll pick Gemma up tomorrow, right?"

He paused with one foot in the open door of his truck. "Uh…"

Frank lowered his voice. "You can pick Gemma up at her work and bring her to the picnic tomorrow."

He started to argue, but Frank straightened his features in his way that made Jason think better of it. "Sure. I can pick her up tomorrow." He faced Gemma. "I'll pick you up at six o'clock."

And with that, he drove off, waving to his adopted father, for all intents and purposes, his future wife, and her surly daughter.

6

Labor Day was unbearable. Swelteringly hot. No one in their right mind left the air conditioning unless they were lucky enough to find a pool. Unfortunately, Gem had neither of those luxuries as she sat behind the counter at Bare Necessities, feet up and fanning herself with an old magazine.

The bell above the door chimed. She knew it was Jason. And he was five minutes early.

He lazily strutted down the aisles, regarding all the merchandise with his aviators still on, picking up random items to study before putting them back down. Like a character in some kind of 80s movie, he stopped in front of the counter, took off his shades to hook them on his shirt, and combed his fingers through his hair. "Nice store you got here."

She eyed him. "Thank you. Nice swimsuit you got there."

Jason glanced down at his green swim trunks dotted with pink whales. "You like?"

She ignored the double meaning behind the question. "You're early."

"I know. Better than being late."

Gem hung her head back, trying to get a little more air. She was *not* going to let him get to her today. The stagnant heat was bad enough without adding his bullshit hot air.

"It's a furnace in here. Why isn't the air conditioning on?"

She dragged her attention up to Jason as he tugged at his shirt, airing himself out. "We don't have any. Saves power."

"No wonder you don't have any customers." Jason shook his head and pursed his lips in that annoying way he had. "You could just invest in eco-friendly HVAC products." He held his hand up, listing them off on his fingers. "Get a programmable thermostat. Reseal the heating and cooling ducts. Get ceiling fans. Do you have radiant heat barriers?"

Of course, he had to know everything about everything when she had no idea what radiant heat barriers were. She stood up with a huff and used a band to tie her now frizzy hair up. A few beads of sweat gathered from her neck and fell in a line down her collarbone, sinking between her breasts. She swiped at it then pushed out her bottom lip, blowing air onto her face, sending her bangs flailing above her head. She tossed the wilted magazine onto the counter and finally faced him, catching him gawking. "What? I know I look awful. It's the humidity."

He shrugged, his eyes openly roaming her body. With her woven cover-up on over her paisley-print bikini, there wasn't a whole lot hiding her body. She pulled her bag over her shoulder, elbowing him on purpose as she passed by.

Outside, Gem had to jump up into the truck. "No Mercedes today?"

"It's for special occasions." He pulled out onto the street. "Seat belt, please."

She buckled in. "Concerned with safety, but not pollution."

"A car can kill you in a second. Global warming will take a few hundred years."

"Well." She huffed. "That's disgustingly selfish. What about the future? The next generations?"

"I'm doing my part." Jason flicked on the radio before she could argue, and emo music blared through the speakers.

"It's too loud," she shouted at him, reaching for the dial. He caught her hand, his fingers big and warm around hers. There was that ever-present heat between them, maybe friction from all their animosity. It had to be that. She couldn't stand to think of the opposite.

Halted at the stop sign, they faced each other. His cool eyes contained a hidden depth, and the more she wondered what his secrets might be, the more she lost herself in the miles and miles of blue. She was slowly sinking into them. Into him.

She had to find a way out.

A car behind them honked, and they both instantly released their hands. He turned the volume down, but neither spoke as they listened to the roaring song.

Jason made a left, quietly singing along to the radio. His voice was low and smooth, and Gem pretended not to notice. "Never placed you as a Paramore fan."

He shrugged and glanced in her direction as she shielded her eyes with her hand. "Forget sunglasses?"

"Lost them."

Without pause, he held out his mirrored aviators, but she hesitated. "Put them on."

She squinted out of the windshield. "No. I'm fine."

He dropped them in her lap. "Put them on. You'll hurt your eyes squinting like that."

"Are you always so bossy?"

"Are you always so difficult?"

After a few moments, she gave in and slid them on. "How do I look?"

He did a double take then a slow, crooked smile unfurled across his lips. "It's a shame."

"What?"

"It's a shame you're so damn gorgeous yet so incredibly annoying."

Gem's mouth dropped at his stolen insult, and she punched him in the arm.

"Hey." He grabbed his shoulder. "That hurt."

"That didn't hurt, you weenie."

He stopped at a red light and tossed her a look. "Weenie? Really?"

Her smile unwittingly transformed into a giggle. Then he grinned, his teeth all gleaming, his eyes shining. Honestly, the audacity of being so good-looking was off the charts.

Arriving at Frank's house, Jason parked on the grass alongside the already crowded driveway. He jumped out and walked around to the passenger side. Gem opened the door to his waiting hand, and her eyebrows shot up in surprise.

"I'm being a gentleman," he said with a relaxed smile, nodding back toward the house. "Come on."

Memories she'd rather keep locked away suddenly flashed in her mind, and she bit her lip, frozen in time, seven years ago.

A newly minted college freshman exploring the social scene. A frat house with a guy, not so unlike the one in front of her now, offering to be a gentleman, to take her hand and get her a drink. Little did she know what would be in that drink. Thank the universe, Bronte, Sam, and Laney had seen it, and they had saved her. They'd gone from near-strangers to best friends in a matter of minutes.

And all because of a pretty boy with a nice smile.

"Gemma, you okay?" Jason asked, stepping closer to drop his hand on the seat next to her knee.

She shook herself out of her years' old nightmare and into the present. "Yeah, fine."

"Are you sure? You look a little pale all of a sudden." He reached for her, but she backed away.

She hated that instinctive reaction, yet sometimes fight-or-flight mode took over. Most of the time, she used her words to fight, but on occasion, her body preferred the flight.

"Sorry," he said quickly, although with a pinched brow. He seemed to apologize out of confusion rather than any real emotion.

"It's fine." She bypassed him and stepped down out of the truck on her own. "I'm fine. Really."

Jason trailed her for a few steps before reaching for her hand, loosely holding on to her wrist. "Is it the party? The wedding?"

Back in fight mode, she rolled her eyes. "No. It's nothing. Don't worry about it."

When she tried to pull away, he stopped her. "You don't have to do this, you know. The party, the wedding, the whole..." He gestured his arm in a circle as if he could encompass her aura. "You don't have to argue with me. We could get along, if you want to."

Standing in front of this man, an actual gentleman who showed no signs of bad behavior—besides the pseudo-cocky thing which Gem hated herself for being into—she thought about the roadblocks she'd put up about certain kinds of guys. If they looked like *him* or had any kind of resemblance, she immediately wrote them off. Even though Jason and his stupidly arrogant grin did have some physical similarities with her real-life nightmare, he was also concerned for her well-being and treated those around him, especially Caroline, like gold.

She didn't want to hold on to her trauma any longer. She had to release it, stop letting it get in her way. So, she did the only logical thing. She poked Jason in his hard chest. "Then let's get along."

He licked his lips and pulled himself up to his full height. She hadn't noticed he'd bent his knees to sink down, closer to her, but now that she did, her heart stumbled over itself as she followed him into the party in Frank's backyard.

The place was brimming with noise. Guests sat at tables with umbrellas, eating hot dogs and potato salad. Jason knew most of them as he waved and said hello. A DJ, set up next to a kidney-bean-shaped pool where a few inflatable dolphins and noodles floated, played classics from the 70s and 80s.

Gem took it all in. "What a tremendous waste of resources."

Jason tipped his chin to the water. "But since it's already wasted, you might as well get some use out of it."

She nudged him with her shoulder. "For the first time, Jason, I think I agree with you."

They made their way to Frank, who manned the grill in an apron with the body of a busty, half-naked lady on it.

"There you are." Frank threw his arm around Gem. "I was waiting for this pretty girl to take a dip in the pool with me."

"You got it, but I'm a little hungry. Got anything on there for me?"

"Go grab a plate from your mother. I have a veggie burger with your name on it."

She walked toward the house, not even out of earshot as Frank said to Jason, "They're disgusting. I don't know how she eats them."

Then Jason laughed. He had a great laugh, the bastard.

7

By the time everyone had finished eating, the sky had turned pink, the heat of the day burned off, and an easy summer breeze took its place. Some guests lounged around playing cards, while others danced to disco music. Gem floated on an inner tube, watching Frank twirl Caroline. A few drops of water hit the side of her face. "Hey, you."

At the sound of the now-familiar voice, Gem paddled around to meet the now-familiar face. He was crouched down toward the pool deck, the right side of his mouth tilted up higher than the left.

"Hey, you," she said, keeping her voice even.

"You're looking a little red," he teased, flicking more water in her direction. "Let me guess, you don't believe in sunscreen either."

"There is a wedding coming up, remember?" Gem held up her arm, studying her skin. She'd put on her normal SPF, but she needed a tan. "I can't look like the abominable snowman walking down the aisle."

Refocusing back on Jason, she noticed he was otherwise occupied, eyes mid-exploration of her body. Not giving herself away, she held still as his gaze coasted down her stomach and legs before moving up to her face, where he promptly blinked away. For the first time ever in front of her, his cheeks turned a ruddy pink.

"You look nothing like the abominable snowman." Then he smiled a smile that made her temperature rise even in the cool water. "You don't have near enough fur."

She couldn't help but laugh. "Okay. You coming in or what? I'm sure you didn't wear those whales to sit around in."

He stood up to strip off his shirt, confirming what Gem already knew—it wasn't just his face that was meant for pictures. His body could have been an ad for some workout equipment or protein shake. The kind of commercial where the camera slowly panned down his flat and defined abs, misted with sweat, with his shorts riding low on his hips.

She shook her head of the idea as he set his cell phone down next to his flip-flops and dove into the pool. He popped his head up next to her, shaking his hair free of water.

"Like a wild animal," Gem said, holding her hands up to block the spray.

He said nothing in response, only gave her a half grin. She felt that little twitch of his mouth everywhere, even down to her toes.

Jason ducked back under the water and appeared at the other end of the pool and propped up a small basketball hoop on the edge. He grabbed an orange ball. "Want a game?"

"Sure." She slipped off the inner tube, holding her hands up for the ball, and when he tossed it to her, she made a big display of catching it. "All right, big guy. Ready to lose?"

He swam toward her, water dripping off his hair and onto his forehead. "I don't know about that, little girl. I should tell you, I'm pretty good at basketball."

She'd heard something from Frank about him playing through high school and even in college. Clearly, she needed a different strategy against this man who could stand in the deep end, while she struggled to keep treading water in one spot. She lowered her voice to a sultry rasp, placing her hand on his shoulder for leverage. "I should tell you, I don't play by the rules."

He glanced down to her hand on him then back at her face. He cocked one brow. "Why doesn't that surprise me?"

Then she splashed him and took off as fast as she could to the net, but he caught her by the ankle and pulled her back before stealing the ball. He sank the shot. "That's one, Gemmie."

She grabbed the ball back, undeterred. "Play to ten?"

When he nodded, she threw the ball as hard as she could toward the net, but it bounced off the backboard and settled a few feet away. They both lunged for it, though Jason's arm outstretched hers, and he easily sank another point.

The game ended almost as fast as it began, and Jason circled Gem like a shark. "Ten-zip. Who's the loser now?"

Never one to give in, she moved over to the side of the pool to catch her breath. "Double or nothing?"

He followed her, his arm lying alongside hers on the concrete edge. "We didn't bet anything."

"Okay," she said, before brushing her wet hair out of her face when a thought struck her. "If I win, you ride a bike for one week."

Something between a chuckle and a groan left his mouth. "I don't own a bike."

She lifted a shoulder, the strap of her top slipping a bit off her shoulder. "I'm sure I can rustle one up for you."

Jason set the thin strap back in its place with only his index finger. She wished for more of his touch, but he didn't notice her begging for it with her eyes, as his attention drifted somewhere behind her shoulder. "All right, and if I win, you have dinner with me," he said then caught her eyes. "Cheeseburgers."

"Ew. No. No way, Jason."

With a teasing gleam in his eye, he tugged on a wet clump of her hair. "I'm kidding. No cheeseburgers, but if you win, you won't have to worry about it."

She didn't know if she believed him or not, and he shrugged.

"Or say you're afraid to lose. It's fine. I won't gloat."

Gem's nostrils flared at the challenge, and he gave her a big grin.

"Look, I'll even give you a free shot." Jason backed off, motioning to the basket, and she swam up to dunk the basketball in.

"Cheap point, Gemmie," he chastised, then dove under the water to grab her legs. She let out a shriek of laughter as he yanked her down. He came up with the ball in hand and scored while she resurfaced, sputtering, wiping her hair out of her eyes. "Tie game."

Fixing her bikini top back in place from Jason's roughhousing, she added a few unnecessary tucks and tugs to draw his attention there. "I didn't think you were the rule-breaking kind, Jason."

Once again, she caught him staring. This time, he didn't blush, only tossed her the ball. She missed the catch and had to swim after it—Jesus, this game was really tiring—and he easily blocked her next shot.

They went back and forth, more grab-handing than shots taken, and in the end, Jason backed her up against the pool wall, holding the ball above his head while Gem clawed at it. "Game point." He tossed her a dark smile then lobbed it over her head and scored before holding his hands around his mouth like a game announcer. "From the three-point line!"

Gem slapped the water. "It's like playing with an octopus. Legs and arms everywhere."

"Come on now, Gemmie. Don't be a sore loser."

"I am not a sore loser." She stared up at him through her wet eyelashes. "Best out of five?"

"I don't know." He looked at an imaginary watch on his wrist. "It's getting pretty late."

She ignored the fact that the floodlights over the pool had turned on to illuminate them, the sky almost navy now, and pushed at his shoulder. "Come on."

"If you insist on continuing to be embarrassed like this—"

"You're so arrogant."

Jason moved close, so close she could see the individual flecks of gray and blue in his irises, and he lowered himself so his chin dipped into the water. He reached for her waist as he whispered, "But you kind of like it, huh?"

Dazed from the nearness of him, she didn't react when he took the ball from her. "One more game, then."

No, she didn't mind his self-satisfied lilt or when he leaned down to breathe out his words next to her ear or even when he slammed into the water so hard, she took on enough water to look like a drowned rat. She did kind of like him. Miracle of miracles.

By the time they finished playing, the moon was high above them and most of the guests had left. Gem got out of the pool and wrung her hair out. A few yards away, Jason snagged towels from a small outdoor shed when his phone rang. "Can you grab that for me?"

She picked it up, taking note of the name *Bridget* on the screen, then exchanged it for a towel. She had no business being curious or even a little jealous. It could be anyone, a coworker, a family member, a nun.

It didn't matter anyway.

He answered with an easy, "Hey, Bridge... No, I'm at a picnic. Not tonight... Okay, I'll call you later."

Gem wrapped herself up in the towel, trying and failing to hold her stupid, stupid tongue. "Bridget?"

Jason only shrugged. She was starting to hate his shrugs.

"So, my dear Gemma, you and I have a date. When'll it be?"

He smirked. She hated his smirks too.

All he did was shrug and smirk. Smirk and shrug.

"No, thanks. I'll pass."

"You can't pass," he said, running his towel over his chest and torso. "That was the bet. You lost three games. I told you it wouldn't include cows."

She pretended to puke.

"It's really not that bad. You couldn't have always been against meat. You must've had it at some point in your life."

Turning her hair upside down to run her fingers through it, she said, "Not since I could think for myself."

He tilted his head so he was also upside down. "When was that? Last year?"

She flipped her hair back and stood tall. Or at least as tall as she could next to him. "For you, maybe. But for me, it was more like kindergarten. I haven't eaten meat in twenty years."

She wrapped the towel around herself.

"Are you cold?"

"Not really." She tried not to shiver, but he noticed and held his hand out, wiggling his fingers, gesturing her toward him.

"Come on, let's get you warmed up." He escorted her inside the house and into the kitchen, where he sat her at the massive kitchen island then proceeded to make coffee, helping himself to the pot, coffee, and all the fixings.

"You know this place well," she said, touching the brass pots and pans hanging above her head.

"I would hope so. I used to live here."

"Yeah?"

He nodded, retrieving two mugs from a shelf above his head.

"Is Frank your long-lost uncle or something?"

"Kind of," he said with his back to her, still only in his whale swim trunks. His back was golden tanned and muscled. Each movement highlighted a new, strong curve, and Gem placed her hands in her lap so she wasn't tempted to reach out to him.

"He and my dad met in college. They were best friends," he went on, pouring the coffee and carefully carrying it over to the island before opening up the refrigerator. "Do you want cream?"

She pointed at her chest. "No animal products, remember?"

He sucked in an audible breath and cringed. "Oh yeah. Sorry." He rummaged inside the fridge. "Uh...there's..." He pulled out a plastic tub. "Can't Believe It's Not Butter?"

She laughed and shook her head. "Sugar is fine."

He handed her the little cup filled with sugar, and she proceeded to dump about a dozen spoonfuls into her cup. Jason watched, shaking his head with a ghost of a smile on his lips.

"What?" she asked, pushing the sugar back his way. "I like it really sweet." She held her steaming mug between her hands, already warming up. "So, why did you live here and not with your parents?"

Keeping his attention on his spoon as he stirred cream to make his coffee a light brown, he answered without emotion. "My parents died when I was thirteen, and I moved in here with Frank."

Gem covered her face with her hands. "Oh my god, Jason. I'm so sorry. I didn't know. I shouldn't have asked."

"It's okay." He tugged on her fingers until she lowered her hands, then sipped his coffee. "Frank's wife had passed away a few months before. We helped each other through it."

She pushed out her bottom lip, really and truly sorry. "I feel so stupid. I didn't know."

"It's okay. Sometimes it feels like a hundred years ago. My life is so different now than it was then." He folded his long body over the counter, resting his forearms on the marble. His face was centimeters away from hers, his voice low and playful. "But," he said pointedly, "maybe if you weren't so judgmental, you'd have taken some time to get to know me."

She brought her hands to her chest, shocked—*shocked*—at his accusation. "Me, judgmental?"

Jason looked around. "Is there someone else in this room who called me pretentious?"

She opened her mouth but couldn't come up with a snappy retort. Not when they were nose-to-nose, breathing in each other's air. Coffee and chlorine enveloped them in an odd but wonderful mixture, and it seeped deep into her lungs. Gem closed her eyes, her heartbeat echoing in her ears.

And after a long minute, Jason was still riveted on her when she opened them again. His eyes were bright and warm, unlike their naturally cool state, and he nodded, answering a question she hadn't asked. *You feel this too?*

"I see you, Gemmie," he whispered, the corner of his lip lifting, threatening to turn into a smile as he stood up tall.

When they finished their coffees, Gem found her cover-up and bag on her way outside. Caroline and Frank were drinking wine on a swing. All the other guests had left, leaving their evidence on the ground.

"Hey, we didn't know you were still here." Caroline lifted her head off Frank's shoulder.

"We're leaving now." Jason tossed his keys in his hand. "But this needs to be cleaned up. I can stay."

"Yeah," Gem agreed, grabbing up a few napkins from a table.

Caroline stood up, taking the trash from her. "No, no, go home. It's past midnight. You need your sleep. Your classes start this week."

"Classes?" Frank asked, scratching his stomach.

Gemma threw two soda cans into the recycling bin. "I run an after-school art program that's a couple days a week."

"Oh, well then, get going. We'll clean up tomorrow. This stuff isn't going anywhere." The older couple chased Jason and Gem out, waving and blowing kisses.

Jason opened the truck's door for Gem. "I didn't know you

were an art teacher."

She imitated him in a funny voice with, "Maybe you should take time to get to know me," then closed the door. She dozed off on the ride home, only to wake up from a tap to her nose. She yawned. "Home already?"

He nodded. "Now, what about that cheeseburger?"

She let out a grumble and rolled her eyes. "Not a funny joke."

He ignored her. "No meat. But you'll still come over for dinner? Sometime this week?"

"Um, okay. I teach yoga Tuesday and Thursday nights."

"That's quite a schedule you got, between the weird tofu shop, art class, yoga, and all the saving the world. Can you even fit me in?"

"I guess I could try," she said through another yawn.

"Said so enthusiastically," Jason quipped. "Where's your phone? I'll give you my number." When she took out a small cell phone from her bag, he practically yelped. "Where did you get this? It's archaic." He flipped it over in his hand. "Is this a first-generation iPhone? I can't believe it. How is it still running? What's the serial number on this? One?"

Refusing to smile, she sleepily stretched forward. "Don't make fun. It's been with me for many years."

He typed in his number and called his phone before she snatched hers back. "I don't like to throw away perfectly good items."

He shook his head at her, his eyes crinkling in amusement. "Should I send you smoke signals instead? That might be easier."

She opened her door and stuck one foot out. "No smoke signals. You'd have to burn down trees for that."

"Okay, no smoke signals. A carrier pigeon?"

Her heart melted at the sight of his lopsided smile, and she jumped to the ground, feeling like she was jumping into a chasm created by Jason Mitchell. Who knew where she'd end up? "As long as it's free-range. You know the address to send it to."

8

Tuesday morning was gray, and storm clouds loomed in the distance as Gem peddled to work. Bronte had texted the group thread earlier about her latest fight with her boyfriend, Hunter. They'd been together since college, and Gem was really starting to lose patience with the guy.

She couldn't help but poke the bear. **You think it might be time to cut the cord? He's hot one day, cold the next. You don't need that**, she texted as she ducked inside the store when the rain began to fall.

Andrew greeted her with a wave of a dustrag. "A good day to get some cleaning done. How was it yesterday? Any customers?"

Gem put her bike and bag in the storage room, bringing a broom back to the front to help. "A few," she responded, sweeping the floor. "How was your day off?"

"Great. And thank you so much for working. We went hiking, had a picnic on the mountain, and had a little too much to drink. You know, the usual. Did you get to do anything fun last night?"

"I, uh…" Her cell phone buzzed in her pocket with a message from Sam, ever the problem-solver.

What do you want to do, B?

"Nothing good, then?" Andrew asked, skirting around Gem and her phone in the middle of the floor.

"No, it was..."

I have to think about it, Bronte texted.

You mean make a list? Gem messaged and added a laughing emoji to soften it.

YES, Bronte responded, and each girl threw up a couple skull and crossbones.

"It was?"

Gem finally lifted her attention to Andrew. "Sorry, what?"

He propped a hand on his hip, his eyes highlighted in a shimmery yellow and white. "Your day, it was...?"

"Remember that guy I told you about?"

He leaned against a shelf and crossed his arms, always ready for tea. "Jason, the Boy Scout. Yes, of course. What happened?"

That was when Gem's phone vibrated with a group Face-Time call. It was the easiest way for all four girls to chat together, and she immediately picked up.

Andrew rolled his eyes. "You know your boss is standing right here."

She stepped next to him and pointed the phone at both of them. Bronte, Sam, and Laney all appeared in their boxes. "Hi!"

Andrew reluctantly gave in with a sigh and took Gem's broom from her to lean on it, grinning into the phone. "Hello, lovely ladies."

The girls all crowed in delight at him, even Laney, who was still in bed, her naturally curly hair spread out on the pillow.

"Am I the only one who ever works?" Gem said, and Andrew snorted behind her. The girls all had similar reactions. Laney was the social media manager for a major league baseball team in San Francisco, Sam was currently working on her doctorate in psychology, and Bronte taught at a middle school.

"I only have five minutes before the bell rings," she said. "This is my free period."

Laney yawned. "And you wanted a team huddle? It's not even seven here yet."

Bronte smiled sadly. "I miss you guys."

Sam frowned. "You all right?"

She only nodded, and Andrew butted in, sticking his head in front of Gem's. "I was just trying to get the gossip from your friend here."

"What?" The three other girls echoed the question, and Gem tugged the broom out from underneath Andrew with a snarl.

Sam's eyes lit up. "Are you keeping secrets from us?"

"No."

Laney got up from her bed. "Okay, let's hear it."

Andrew raised his hand. "She was about to tell me about Jason."

"The guy you said looked like a Boy Scout?" Bronte moved closer to the screen.

"I don't know what's wrong with a Boy Scout," the lone male on the call said. "They're always prepared."

Gem tossed her hand up. "Can't you be like a regular boss and yell at me for not working?"

He scrunched his nose and popped out a hip. "I'm not a regular boss. I'm a cool boss."

Laney caught the *Mean Girls* reference. "You can't sit with us!"

Andrew pointed to his glossy pink shirt, but before he could get another line out, Sam said, "So, what's the deal with Boy Scout?"

When Gem hesitated, Bronte whined, "Come on, quick. I need to hear before all the kids come in."

Resting against the broom, Gem relayed the events from the previous night.

"So, you like him?" Sam asked.

"No. He's impossible."

Laney, now in her bathroom with a toothbrush in her mouth, said, "But you like him."

"We have nothing in common."

"But you like him. Honey, he's hot and single." Andrew waved the dustrag above his head. "What's the problem?"

"Well," Gem started, setting her cell phone down against a jar of honey so she could pretend to sweep. "He might not be single. He got a phone call from someone named Bridget last night."

"Bridget?" Bronte repeated.

"Yep."

"Okay. And?" Laney spat out her toothpaste. "Are you going to ask him about it?"

She avoided the question, diligently sweeping.

"Gemma Rose," Andrew said, and the three girls oohed like she was in trouble.

"You sound like my mom when you say that."

"Good. Your mother's a queen. Are you going to call him?"

"I have a lot of stuff to do today. Yoga tonight."

Sam propped her head in her hands. "It's only a phone call. Are you afraid?"

When Gem didn't answer, Bronte practically cooed. "You are. You really like him. Gemma's in love."

"Hey, whoa. Don't get ahead of yourself."

Andrew picked at Gem's hair like a mother hen, pushing it behind her ears just so. "Yeah, yeah, I know. You don't know how to commit. Daddy issues."

Gem plucked his fingers off where he fussed with her tank top. "That's what Jason said. That I have daddy issues."

"You do," Laney said, wrapping her hair up in a bun on the top of her head.

"I know that." Gem leaned against a shelf. "But I don't want him to know that."

"I think you should call him right now," Laney said, and Andrew agreed.

"I'll even give you a fifteen-minute break to do it."

Gem laughed, waving her arm around as if she wasn't already on a break.

"Yeah, you should definitely call him," Sam said.

Bronte pumped her fist while she chanted, "Call him. Call him. Call him."

The girls and Andrew joined in.

"Fine!" Gem gave in with a growl.

A loud buzzer rang out, and Bronte glanced toward the sound somewhere behind her before smiling back at her screen. "I can't wait to hear how it goes."

"Good luck," Sam said in her singsong voice.

Laney waved at the screen. "Send us a picture. I need to see this Boy Scout in the flesh."

With the FaceTime call ended, Andrew folded his arms, his foot tapping on the linoleum. After a short stare down, Gem pulled up Jason's contact and put her phone to her ear, pacing down the aisle. Andrew tiptoed behind.

Jason picked up on the second ring. "Gemma."

"Jason."

"I'm glad you called."

When she pivoted around, she collided into Andrew's chest, and she nudged him out of the way as he bent down, trying to listen.

On his end, Jason said, "I assume you're calling to make good on our bet."

"You know what happens when you assume," Gem chided as Andrew tripped on her heels, following closely behind. She pushed his shoulder, and he grabbed her wrist, forcing her to hold the phone so he could hear as well. "I could be calling you because I have an engineering emergency."

His laughter rumbled on the other end, and Andrew lifted

his eyebrows. Gem tried to ignore her nosy boss as Jason said, "Okay, then. What's the emergency?"

"There's a huge pothole out front of the store that needs fixing."

"I'm a structural engineer. Call the mayor, she'll fix your potholes," Jason suggested, and Gem could *hear* the smile in his voice. "But first, do you want to come over tonight for dinner?"

Andrew nodded enthusiastically, and Gem palmed his face. "Yeah, I'll come over. My class ends at seven."

"Call me when you're ready. I'll pick you up."

"You don't have to do that. I'll ride my bike as long as it's not raining. I'll call you for directions later."

"Okay. Bring a bib. I'm making ribs."

"Jason."

"Fine. No meat or cheese or anything that tastes good."

She placed the phone back to her ear, much to the chagrin of Andrew. "Hey, don't knock it till you try it."

"Okay. Bye, Gem."

"Bye, Jason," she said, sucking her bottom lip between her teeth to keep from grinning as she ended the call.

"Look at you. You're like..." Andrew circled his hands out in front of her. "Like a blooming flower, all glowing and rosy in the sun."

Gem rolled her eyes at his ridiculous romantic notion.

He tossed her a shoulder wiggle. "Feels good, doesn't it?"

"What?"

"To believe in happy endings." He pinched her arm in a way Gem always thought a big brother might and then handed her the broom. "Now get to work."

BITING BACK A SMILE, Jason pocketed his cell phone, eager to see Gemma again. There was something about her, uninhibited and carefree, so unlike himself, and he couldn't help but want to know more. Be closer to her.

After losing his parents, he coped by walking a tight line. Death and grief were messy, and he needed things to be tidy and neat. Nothing out of place, nothing but perfection to hold him together, to forget what he'd lost.

But Gemma was the opposite. She made him feel things he hadn't felt...maybe ever. From the first moment he laid eyes on her, he'd been instantly attracted to her. Then she'd opened her pretty little mouth and drove him crazy. She made him laugh, made him think. She made him want to follow her zigzag path.

Jason focused on his computer, trying to put Gemma out of his mind, though it wasn't easy with the memory of her in that tiny bikini. She was petite but strong. Lines of muscle contoured her stomach and legs, no doubt from her biking and yoga. He imagined wrapping her arms around his neck and lifting her up to kiss her bowed pink lips, reveling in the feel of her skin against his. Quieting her constant arguing with his mouth.

Gemma was like a summer storm, coming on suddenly, heat and wind threatening to sweep him away. And for once in his life, he was okay with getting caught in the rain.

As the day went on, the seconds slowed, the minutes stretching to long hours once his four o'clock meeting extended from one hour into two. When he finally got home from work, he changed and headed out for a quick run to grind down his nerves that were determined to clog his windpipe and make him sound like a middle schooler whose voice hadn't changed yet, threatening the cool façade he carefully put on every day.

After working up a good sweat, he circled back to his house and slowed to a jog when he had it in his sights. A tall, curvy figure stood at the front door. With a grunt, he caught his breath, his hands on his hips.

Bridget waved. "Hey, babe."

He brushed past her, lifting his T-shirt to wipe his face. "What are you doing here?"

"I wanted to see you." Her dark hair sat in a high ponytail on the top of her head, her navy-blue dress clinging to her curves.

He'd always kept women at arm's length. Bridget was no different, so he ignored her sentiment. "How was your day? You had that big presentation, right?"

"Yeah, it went great. Exactly as planned," she said, leaning against the beveled doorframe. "Aren't you going to invite me in?"

Without saying a word, he opened the door wider and gestured her in. He flipped his sneakers off and tossed his phone and keys on a table next to the door.

"You look good," she mused, dropping her eyes to his drenched shirt, the sleeves cut off so it hung loose around his torso.

He knew that look. "What's up, Bridge?"

"Nothing," she murmured, cozying up next to him, her painted fingernail dragging along his shoulder. He stared down at her hand, tempted to push it away. They weren't strangers but not exactly in a spot where she could show up like this either. "I just..." She drew an invisible little heart on his bicep before meeting his gaze. "I want to know where we're going."

"Where we're going?"

"Yeah, we've been dating for a few months now."

Jason didn't think *dating* was the technical term for what they were doing. Friday night booty calls and occasional midweek hookups did not a relationship make, but he let it slide. She skimmed her finger down to his forearm. "I want to know how you feel about me."

He backed away and shoved his fingers through his wet hair, dropping her hand from his arm. "You're a good friend, Bridget."

"Friends?"

"Yes, friends." He checked the time. It was almost seven, and he needed to get rid of her. "I'm going to take a shower." He moved to the door, but she didn't take the hint.

"Jason, we've been…hanging out for months. We're more than friends," she said, curling her fingertips over the waistband of his shorts. "I want you to admit it." When she leaned in to kiss him, he practically leaped away from her, but his cell rang at the same time, leaving Bridget still by the table with his phone.

"I'll get it." She reached for it, her intent on demonstrating how much they were not *just friends* apparent. Before he could say otherwise, she answered in her syrupy voice. "Jason Mitchell's phone."

The volume was loud enough that he could hear Gem answer on the other end. "Hello?"

"Hi, who's this?" Bridget asked, playing with her ponytail.

"It's Gem." He cringed as her voice wavered. "Is Jason there?"

"Yes, hold on a sec." Bridget passed the phone to him. "It's some girl."

Jason took it, walking away from Bridget. "Gemma, hey, sorry about—"

"I don't think I'll be able to make it tonight," she said like it was all one word.

"Look, I know this—"

"I'm not really feeling well."

"Are you— Gemma, I'm sorry. It's not what—"

On the other end, she huffed. "It's fine, Jason. You don't need to apologize. I'll see you around."

Then she ended the call, leaving him staring at his phone.

Bridget skimmed her hands over his back. "Who was that?"

"The daughter of Frank's fiancée." He didn't owe Bridget more of an explanation, and frustration laced his words. No doubt she was the reason Gem bailed.

Not recognizing the problem she'd inadvertently caused,

Bridget lightly massaged his shoulders. "You said you wanted a shower. Can I join?"

He shrugged away from her hands, but she moved closer, snaking her arms around his neck. When she tried to kiss him, he pressed his hands against her shoulders, gently removing her grip on him, and shook his head. "Go home, Bridget."

9

Determined to make it up to Gemma, Jason headed to Bare Necessities after work on Friday. The small stucco building next to the dry cleaners was drab on the outside, nothing like the colors and smells of the inside. Like before, the bell above his head dinged when he opened the door, and his eyes caught on a sign for vegan brownies and cupcakes. He'd never tried vegan anything, but he had to admit, they looked really good.

"Hi, welcome to Bare Necessities. Can I help you?"

Jason spun around at the voice to find a man with pale skin and wavy bleach-blond hair, styled on top of his head with a sparkly lemon pin. "Hey, I'm looking for Gem."

The man pursed his glossy lips and tilted his head. "And you are?"

"Jason."

His face changed immediately, his hands thrusting up in the air. "Jason! Yes, Jason, so nice to meet you. I'm Andrew, owner and manager of this bountiful vegan oasis. I've heard a lot about you."

"You have?" Jason shoved his hands into his pockets, both surprised and thrilled at that fact. "All good things, I hope."

Andrew looked him up and down with a critical eye before pointing to the bag in his hand. "Come bearing gifts?" When Jason held it up in a silent answer, Andrew patted his arm. "Good man. Gem, darling," he called over his shoulder. "I need your assistance out front."

Jason's breath caught in his chest when she stepped into view, dressed in a flowing white shirt. Her hair caught the sun streaming through the window, and it highlighted the amber hues waving loose down her shoulders. She looked angelic.

Then her dark eyes narrowed on him, her face altering into something a lot less heavenly.

He offered her one of his best smiles.

"Why are you here?" she said, stopping a few feet short of him.

Grabbing the closest thing to him, he held up a bottle of liquid smoke. "Shopping."

She huffed and crossed her arms over her chest.

"I came to apologize about the other night," he said, lifting up the take-out bag from a local burger place. "Since we didn't have dinner together, I thought I could make it up to you."

"I'm not eating meat," she said, and Andrew let out a sound of horror from where he hid two aisles over, not so subtly watching them.

"It's not meat." When Gemma eyed the bag, he offered it to her. "I promise."

She reluctantly took it from his hand and glanced over to her boss, who gestured to the door. "Go ahead."

Gemma smiled blandly at Jason before heading outside, and he followed her to sit on the steps leading up to the store.

"What is it?"

"Open it," he told her, and she pulled out a wrapped-up burger, practically snarling at him.

"I told you I'm not—"

He took the burger from her. "It's black bean and mushroom. Try to do something nice..." he mumbled, unwrapping the edge of the burger. It didn't have the same mouthwatering scent as beef, but it looked okay. He handed it to Gemma. "I got you fries too."

She stared at the burger, suspicion lining all her features.

"I had to try three different places," he said, pointing to it. "Not many restaurants make vegan burgers."

"Really?" She turned to him, her eyes sparkling, and if he'd known that was all it took to make her happy, he'd personally see she had vegan burgers whenever she wanted them.

He nudged her elbow with his. "Yeah. Wasn't that big of a deal."

Only took him an hour.

With a hint of a smile, she bit into it, a slice of tomato falling out of the top. She scooped it up and slurped it between her lips, coating them in juice. Jason tore his gaze away to stare down at the crack in the cement. "How is it?"

"Really good. Here, try." She shoved it at him. "Go ahead."

When he accepted it, she grabbed the bag to dig for a few fries and ate those too.

"Come on," she cajoled. "I want to witness your face when you try your first animal-free cheeseburger and realize how good it is."

"Eh, I don't know about that," he said, lifting it to his mouth. He took a big bite and chewed. It wasn't bad...for cardboard. "It's all right."

"See?" She pointed a fry at his face. "Don't knock it till you try it."

He nodded and handed it back to her. "How's your week been?"

"Busy."

He brushed his hands off. "Mine too."

"Yeah?" She inclined her head, aiming a glare at him, and he readied himself for what he felt coming. "With Bridget?"

He cleared his throat and surveyed the strip mall across the street, while the side of his face boiled at what he could only guess was the same temperature as the surface of the sun. "No, uh, she's..."

Jason and Gemma had met only weeks ago, interacted a handful of times. They were barely friends, more enemies than anything. Although the friction between them threatened to strike up the kindling the two of them seemed to be stumbling around in. She didn't know who Bridget was, and there was no real reason for her to have suddenly acted so funny after she answered the phone. Except if she wanted to fan this spark between them.

Jason had always had a weird obsession with fire. He'd burned lots of holes in rugs as a kid. And he had trouble keeping his hands off the tiny flame next to him now.

He squinted over at Gem. "Bridget's no one. Just a friend."

She clucked her tongue, shoving a couple fries into her mouth in an obvious attempt to stop whatever words were about to come out.

"So, are you coming golfing tomorrow?" he asked to change the subject.

"Golfing?" She crinkled her nose in that cute way she always did and took another bite of the burger.

"Frank and Caroline invited me. I figured you too."

She wiped her mouth with a napkin. "You figured wrong. I'm not much for golf."

"Why not?"

"Swinging a stick around, trying to hit a tiny ball, isn't my kind of thing."

"Bigger balls are more your thing?"

The barest hint of a smile slanted her lips at his terrible innuendo.

He inched closer to her, the toe of his Oxfords nudging her instep. "It's relaxing."

"Yoga is relaxing. Golf is boring."

Trying a different tack, he leaned his elbows back on the step behind him. "How's your art class?"

She polished off the burger and stuffed the garbage into the paper bag. "Good. This week, we learned how to use the supplies and started with the basics. Next week, we'll start drawing."

"How often are the classes?"

"Every Monday and Wednesday."

With his most charming smile, he asked, "And what do the kids call you?"

She perused his lounged position, her eyes trailing down to his leg and back up to his face as if studying a new species of animal. "Why are you so interested?"

He ran his knuckle along his jaw. "I don't know. I thought maybe big kids might be able to come to this class too."

"Big kids like twelve-year-olds, or big kids like you?" She stood up, her denim shorts revealing so much of her legs. Right there. A few inches from his eyes. Instead of wrapping his hand around her calf and burying his face against her skin, he stood up too.

"Big kids like me."

She almost, *almost* smiled. "I don't think you'd fit in the chairs."

Jason tilted his head, learning her face—the arch of her dark eyebrows, her high cheekbones, and of course, her mouth. The perfect Cupid's bow on top, the plump and pink lower lip. He itched to push her long bangs away from her eyes, tuck her hair behind her ears, and kiss her. "What time do you get off? Can I give you a ride home?"

"We close at six. I don't need a ride."

He searched her eyes, finding no hints as to what was going on in her head. He tried again, grazing her elbow with his fingertips. From her slightest jolt, he knew she felt the same electricity that he did when they touched. Though she had a damn good poker face.

"Will you come golfing?"

She shook her head and drew her arm out of his grasp, turning away from him. "I'll pass. See you later, Jason."

He stared after her for a moment, bemused and discouraged. "Call me if you change your mind."

With his keys in hand, he was about to head to his car when he reversed course. He needed to know for sure that the tension between them wasn't only because they were complete opposites, and she needed to know how he felt about her. Jogging back into the store, he caught Gemma by the waist and tugged her to him. He curved his palm against her jaw and softly pressed his lips to hers. At first, she was tentative and still, but when he wrapped both of his arms around her, taking her weight against him, she relaxed into his hold.

She moved her hands into his hair, and she let out a tiny moan as she finally parted her lips. She was his new favorite flavor, and he gently pressed against her neck, angling it to deepen the kiss, tongues and breaths melting together. But as suddenly as she gave in was as suddenly as she backed away with a gasp.

She wiped at her mouth with the back of her hand. "What the hell was that?"

Shocked at her reaction, he held his hands up. "What? I thought—don't you feel anything for me? Because..." He gestured between them with two fingers. "God, Gemma, this is driving me crazy."

"So?" She hissed her words at him. "You can't go around just kissing people. You can't grab someone like that without asking. You can't do whatever you want! I'd like a choice too, Jason."

His breath whooshed out of him. "I don't—" He shook his head. "I'm sorry. I thought you were into it."

Squeezing her fists at her sides, she walked in a tight circle then blew out a long exhale aimed at the floor. "That's not..." She huffed out an angry laugh. "Never mind."

He didn't think he'd ever felt so bad in his life. She was right. He didn't ask if he could kiss her, didn't even cross his mind to. He liked her. He thought she liked him too.

He was so very, *very* wrong.

But the fact that she couldn't meet his eyes told him there was something more going on.

"Gemma, I'm sorry. Are you okay?"

"This isn't the place for this conversation," she said, her gaze skipping around the store, probably looking for Andrew.

He chanced two steps toward her, and when she didn't move away from him, he took another one so he could whisper, "Talk to me. Tell me what's wrong."

She licked her lips, shaking her head almost imperceptibly.

"I'll leave if you want me to, but please, say something."

At that, she shifted her focus to him, her eyes rimmed red and glassy. He waited, completely motionless, more still than he'd ever been in his life, until she spoke.

"I was at a party in college, like, third week of school. It was my first college party." She let out a pitiful laugh and wiped her hand over her face, clearing her eyes. "I went with my room-mate, Bronte, because she'd been flirting with this older guy and wanted to hang out. I don't even really remember much at this point, except for his face."

Jason closed his eyes, a pit forming in his stomach. There weren't many ways this story could end, and he felt like he might throw up. Which made him feel even more like an asshole. If this was how he felt listening to the story, how did she feel living it?

Fuck. He wanted to punch something.

When he opened his eyes, the corner of Gemma's lip was between her teeth, her arms folded like she was cold.

"He was tall and handsome. Wavy blond hair and big arms.

He looked kind of like you."

"Jesus, Gem, tell me he didn't..."

She lifted her head, meeting his gaze. "He didn't."

He didn't know how he was still standing. How could he be when his chest had collapsed?

"He flirted with me, and I thought he was the hottest guy ever, so when he gave me a drink, I took it. Didn't think anything of it. Next thing I knew, I was in the shower, back in the dorm. My friends saved me, they took care of me. Without them..." She lifted a shoulder, not needing to finish that sentence.

"Gemma, I..." Speechless, he held out his arms. He wanted to comfort her, give her some security, but he needed it too. "Can I give you a hug?"

After a long moment, she sank into his arms, though she kept her own clasped together in front of her chest. He didn't mind. He locked his hands together between her shoulder blades. "I don't know what else to say besides it's awful and happens far too often. I'm just so fucking grateful it turned out the way it did, and I'm sorry it happened to you."

She tipped her head up, resting her chin on his chest. "I didn't mean to—"

"No, don't," he said, stepping back from her. "If you're about to apologize or rationalize you being upset with me, don't. I get it, and I get why you might think I'm an asshole. We blond-haired, blue-eyed white guys all kinda look alike."

At that, she put her hand over her mouth, but he could still see the curve of her smile between her fingers. "I don't think you're an asshole for how you look. I think you're an asshole because you're an asshole."

He tossed his head back and laughed. "Okay, whatever you say." Then, because he didn't want to push her anymore, he turned around and walked out of the store. "See you round, Gemma."

AT THE END of the night, Gem closed her apartment door and leaned against it. She sank down to the floor, emotionally and physically wrung out. Exhausted from working all day, from her conversation with Jason, and having to ride her bike home.

Tap. Tap. Tap.

"What?" Gem groaned, forcing herself to stand up after a few moments in which she contemplated ignoring the knocking. She unlocked the door and was greeted by Caroline and Frank.

"That's how you answer the door?" Her mother let herself in. "*What?*"

"Yes, I'm good. How are you? Please, come in." Gem motioned to the couch her mom had already taken a seat on. Frank patted her shoulder on the way in. "So," she said, picking up a few pieces of dirty laundry and a used plate with a bit of peanut butter still on it. "What brings you two over to my neck of the woods?"

"We wanted to talk to you," Caroline said, reaching for her daughter's hand.

"Oh." Gem sat on the coffee table in front of her mom. "'Kay."

"Frank and I were talking. Now, don't get mad."

"I don't have the energy to get mad."

"Good." Caroline stroked the back of Gem's hand then looked to her future husband.

"How long does it take you to get from here to your store?" Frank asked, sitting on the edge of the couch, his elbows on his knees with his hands folded between them.

"About half an hour, why?"

He tugged on his checkered shirt. "And most nights, you're riding your bike home after dark?"

"Yeah."

Caroline chimed in. "You know I worry about you. We both worry about you on that bicycle. And it'll be winter soon."

Frank shifted in his seat to dig into his pocket. "I wanted to buy your mother a wedding present, but she had a better idea." He pulled out a small key fob. "We decided to buy you a car."

Gem's jaw dropped as Caroline bounded up. "It's outside right now. Let's go see."

Out of pure astonishment, Gem followed them outside, where her mom gestured like Vanna White to a small green car.

"It's a Ford Mustang. And electric." Frank pressed the key into Gem's hand. "Go sit in it. If you don't like it, you don't have to keep it."

She did what she was told and sat in the car, gingerly placing her hands on the steering wheel.

"You look good, Gemmie," Caroline gushed, folding her fingers under her chin. "Do you love it?"

Still stunned into silence, Gem couldn't answer, so Frank got in the passenger seat and explained all the controls and how to charge it. "Say something. Do you like it?" When she nodded, his big laugh surrounded them in the small can, and he slapped his knee. "Good. You'll keep it!"

With grateful hugs and kisses, Caroline and Frank left her sitting in the new car and got into their own.

Frank stuck his head out of the driver's side window. "We're golfing tomorrow. Why don't you come? Show off your new wheels."

In a cloud of happiness and gratitude for a man who'd only ever treated her like his own daughter, Gem snapped out of her trance and nodded in agreement. "Yeah, all right. I'll be there."

Caroline might have sprouted wings and flown away if not for her seat belt. "Oh, Gemmie, I'm so happy you're happy."

Frank winked at Gem. "Tee time is ten o'clock. We'll see you there."

10

It was a beautiful Saturday, sunny without a cloud in the sky.
The smell of fresh-cut grass floated on the breeze. A perfect day
for a round of golf, if you liked that sort of thing, and Jason
loved exactly that sort of thing.

What he didn't enjoy was having to feign interest in the
country club gossip Frank and Caroline exchanged with their
friends, but then Gemma strolled up. Much to his chagrin. After
their kiss and the conversation that followed yesterday, he
wasn't sure where they stood: friends, mortal enemies, or otherwise. Although, she didn't seem bothered by anything, her hair
down and completely untamed with waves in every direction,
T-shirt hanging off one shoulder, Aztec print shorts, and red
Converse.

She waved to the group of mostly middle-aged golfers. "Hey.
Where can I get an Arnold Palmer around here?"

Jason sucked his lips between his teeth to hide a growing
smile as Caroline eased away from her friends, towing Gemma
off to the side.

"What're you wearing?" He heard Caroline say to Gemma.
"That is not proper golf attire."

From under the shade of his baseball cap, Jason watched as Gemma shrugged. "I have a bra on."

This time, he covered his laugh with a cough. "Excuse me," he said when Frank paused mid-sentence to glance at him. "Swallowed the wrong way."

"There's a dress code here, Gemma," Caroline said, waving her hand down her daughter's body. "You can't stroll in here like a farmer."

"I doubt a farmer would wear this, Mom."

"You need to get a new outfit." Caroline pressed her hand to her temple, peeking over her shoulder, distress written all over her face as she spotted Jason. She waved him over and thrust her daughter toward him. "Can you *please* help Gemma? She'll need clothes and clubs. Put it on Frank's tab." Before Jason could answer one way or another, she pointed a warning finger at Gemma. "My friends are over there, and I don't want them to see you dressed like that." She motioned her thumb to the pro shop. "Go."

Not wanting to rock the boat any further, Jason followed Gemma inside.

"That happen a lot?" he asked.

She fiddled through some shirts. "What?"

"Arguing over how you dress?"

"Since I was a kid. You'd think she'd be used to it by now, but I guess since she owns her own boutique, she thinks what I wear will reflect on her."

He shoved his hands into his pockets. "She's right, though."

Gemma shot her eyes up to him, a hanger in her hands like a weapon. "Excuse me?"

With the way her gaze narrowed and her tongue darted out to wet her lips, she reminded him of a snake. She could probably taste his fear on her tongue. And, damn it all to hell, it made his dick twitch.

"There is a dress code," he said, earning a quaint little sneer out of her. He lifted a shoulder. Even if there weren't rules about proper attire, he still liked getting a rise out of her.

"Well, Jason, seeing as how you are neither a mother nor a daughter, I think you should be quiet about this particular argument."

Glad to be off shaky ground with her—even if this ground was largely covered in mines—he leaned against a clothing rack, checking out the gloves displayed on the table next to it. "I heard you got a new car." He found a glove he liked and put it on. "I didn't think you knew how to drive."

"I know how to drive. I choose not to." She ripped a skirt and shirt off their hangers and gave him the evil eye on her way to the dressing room as he practiced his swing with an imaginary club.

On his second swing, Jason noticed she'd left the door to the dressing room slightly ajar, lending him an accidental view of her almost-naked body. Her small but round breasts were covered in a blue bra, the subtle curve of her hips and butt in matching panties. She was natural, almost ethereal, a breath of fresh air, and he inhaled as deeply as he could.

Then he sneezed, calling attention to himself. Gem's head shot up from the polo shirt she was pulling over her head, and she frowned at him, slamming the door. "Get enough of the show?"

He slapped his palm over his forehead and dragged it down his cheek with a groan. "Actually, no," he said, loud enough that she would hear. "It was an accident. You were the one who left the door open."

A few mumbled words came from the other side before the door opened again, and she strutted out in her new attire.

"You look nice."

"Shut up."

He waved for her to lead the way toward the counter, where he settled the tab and rented a bag of clubs. He offered to carry it for her, but she insisted she could do it—yet stumbled under the weight when she threw the strap over her shoulder.

Outside, Caroline formally introduced Gemma to her friends and was met with a chorus of how she looked so much like her mom. Caroline wrapped her arm around her daughter, eating up the compliments. In the meantime, Jason tried to push the picture of Gem in her underwear out of his mind. He thought of how much a new pair of cleats would cost, how the trees had started to turn orange. How the wind picked up and would affect his swing, and how Gemma's bangs might settle in front of her eyes with each gust of air and how her nipples might pebble in the cool air.

Goddamn it. He walked away from the group, waiting until the caddies arrived with their golf carts. Frank and Caroline hopped in the first one, leaving Gemma and Jason to the second. When he got behind the wheel, she sat next to him with a sigh. "You're going to be insufferably good at this, aren't you?"

He only grinned as he drove them away.

At the first hole, Caroline started the round off, followed by Frank in his traditional argyle socks and cap. Next, Gem stepped up to the tee, swung, and missed.

Frank coached her from a few feet away. "That's okay, try again. Keep your eye on the ball and follow through with your swing."

She tried again, digging up some earth.

"Don't worry about that." Frank pushed it back in with his toe. "Take another crack at it."

Caroline agreed. "Nobody is keeping score."

"I am," Jason volunteered with a raised hand and cocky smile.

Gem pursed her lips at him before taking a third and fourth swing. Then she hauled off and threw the ball down the fairway. Even then, it didn't get very far.

"That's okay, that's okay," Frank said with a clap. "We'll work on it. Jay, you're up."

Jason set up and swung with a near-perfect follow-through, the ball sailing high into the sky.

"Attaboy," Frank cheered, and everyone piled into the carts to move on, not even stopping for Gem's ball.

When they closed in on the green, Frank tossed another ball down for Gem. The other three easily sank their putts, but she kept missing by a few inches. Five tries later, it finally sank, and Frank patted her on the back. "Don't worry, you'll get the hang of it."

The thought had crossed Jason's mind to offer his help, but he imagined the scowl she'd give him and thought better of it. Instead, he enjoyed watching her swing and miss in her short cream-colored skirt.

The next few holes followed the same pattern, Gem taking a few mulligans and chunking up dirt. After the seventh fairway, she plunked down in the cart with a huff. "Besides doing a one-handed cartwheel on a Slip 'N Slide when I was twelve, this might possibly be the worst decision I've ever made."

"You may want to rethink your criteria for the worst decision ever. Save that honor for something really big like going on a hunger strike to save squirrels," Jason quipped, stepping on the gas, and Gem jammed her Converse up on the dash of the cart to keep from falling forward.

"Can you not do that? And I've already been on a hunger strike. It wasn't that bad."

"You're kidding," he said, eyes wide.

"Of course I'm kidding. People go on hunger strikes when no other forms of protest are available. Come on, read a book every once in a while."

With a shake of his head, he maneuvered them behind Frank and Caroline's cart, idly wondering why her insults kind of turned him on. Was it the way her voice took on that edge of venom? Or was it the way her eyes sharpened, all predator-like? He didn't mind being her prey.

Next to him, Gem hung her head back, allowing him a second to admire her throat as she said, "I can't believe people call this the greatest game ever played. This is the worst game ever played." She lolled her head to the side. "How much longer do we have?"

"It depends."

She rubbed her eyes. "On what."

"There are eleven more holes, and the more strokes that are taken, the longer it goes." He raised his brows at her. "Since you're the worst golfer I've ever played with, I figure another four hours."

"You are quite the charmer."

"I try."

The carts stopped at the next hole, and everyone got out except Gem, who lounged along the bench, her feet on Jason's seat. "I'm going to sit this one out."

"Are you sure?" Frank asked, readjusting his hat.

"Yeah, I need a little break."

Jason assumed she meant she needed to speed up the game a bit. To be honest, he agreed with her, although it didn't keep him from checking in on her. At the ninth hole, she braided her hair, asking him to grab the hair tie she dropped. At the tenth, she gave herself Princess Leia buns and pretended to cut Jason in half with her lightsaber golf club. And on the eleventh, she sprawled out horizontally for a catnap.

After sinking his putt, Jason walked back to the cart and watched her for a moment. Her hair was spread out all over, while his aviators shielded her eyes from the sun. The collar of her shirt gaped open enough to allow a centimeter of blue to be seen, and that was all it took for his mind to race. Those little scraps of blue would star in his fantasies tonight, or rather, in a warm shower. He clenched his jaw, irritated at his own emotions. One minute, he wanted to strangle her, and the next, he wanted to ravish her.

As if she could hear his thoughts—maybe she could, they were screaming in his head—she stirred awake.

"Is it over yet?"

He shook his head and swatted at her leg so she'd move over, allowing him to sit down. "Seven more holes to go."

"Ack."

At the next hole, Frank prodded Gem to try again, and she halfheartedly agreed, pulling a club out of her bag without looking. She wound up and swung. *Whiff.*

"Go help her, Jay," Frank ordered, and Jason was nothing if not a dutiful son.

As Gem lined up to try again, Jason gripped the club in midswing. "First of all, you're using the wrong one. Here," he said, handing her a different club. "That was a wedge. This is a 3-iron."

Her face was blank. "Uh-huh."

"May I?" he asked, alluding to his forthcoming instruction, and she silently nodded. He guided her to the tee, where he engulfed her with his arms, showing her how to properly hold the club.

When her muscles stiffened, he started to back away, but she told him, "It's okay."

Relenting, he stepped closer, his chest flush against her back. "You're too tense. You need to loosen up. Breathe," he told her like it was so easy for him, her hair smelling of vanilla as it tickled his cheek. "That's good. Now, you want to keep your grip relaxed and a slight bend in your knees. Rotate from your hips and keep this elbow straight. Ready?"

He led her movements, lifting their arms up behind them, and in one fell swoop, the club struck the ball high into the air. They faced each other, his lips turning up at the sight of a blush creeping into her cheeks. If he didn't know any better, he might think that tough-girl thing was all an act.

"Good job, Gemmie," Caroline cheered.

"Yeah." Jason readjusted his hat. "Who's next?"

The foursome moved down the fairway, and when it came to Gem's turn again, she lined up behind the ball. This time, Jason didn't have to be told. He wrapped his arms around her, and she glanced back at him.

"Keep your eye on the ball," he told her, and those lovely brown eyes refocused. Together, they hit the ball all the way to the green, and he offered her a congratulatory little shoulder rub.

When they arrived to putt, Gem stepped up to her ball, Jason following. He placed his hand on top of hers and tapped the ball into the hole. "You made par this time."

"That's good?"

"Yeah."

Gem twirled her club like a baton. "Getting pretty good."

He held his hand up for a high five, and when she slapped his palm, he curled his fingers around hers, tugging her closer to him. "With my help. I don't think you could get that ball into the air without me."

She lifted her brow. "We'll see."

At the next tee, she lined up solo and missed.

Jason slow-clapped. "I told you to loosen up." When she shot him a look, he strolled up behind her and put one hand on her hip, the other on her forearm. She connected with the ball and sent it flying. "God, I'm good."

Gem shouldered him playfully, and it took all his self-control not to toss her over his shoulder in retribution. Maybe press her up against one of the trees lining the fairway.

At the next spot, he attempted to help her putt, but she pushed him away, saying, "I can do it. I can do it."

And she did. She sank the putt and danced past him, using

her club like a cane. Obviously feeling her mojo now, she stepped up to the next tee, pointing her club at Jason. "I get this one into the air, I'm driving."

He bowed to her. "You don't, you buy me dinner."

"You're on." Gem stuck her tongue out of the corner of her mouth and wiggled her butt in quite possibly the cutest bout of concentration he'd ever witnessed. She swung, and after the ball rose into the air, she jumped up, whooping. "Get in, loser." She hopped in the driver's seat. "We're going shopping."

"Huh?"

"*Mean Girls*? No? Okay." She shook her head when he sat down next to her. "Never mind."

"Double or nothing?" he asked before she promptly took off, flinging him over a few inches, her laughter ringing in his ears.

GEM WAS woman enough to admit when she was wrong. Golf was fun...or, really, more than bearable. Because of Jason, that gorgeous jerk.

She liked the way he kept his arm up along the back of their bench seat in the cart, and how he coached her gently and without a hint of superiority in his voice. The snug fit of his polo shirt didn't hurt either, or the way his gaze snagged on her mouth from time to time.

Yesterday, Jason was right when he'd said he thought she'd been into kissing him. She very much was, and if it weren't for the way he'd gone about it, who knows what might have happened. Maybe she would've thrown her legs around his waist and pointed him to the back room, where they could have defiled the stock cabinets.

Gemma liked a firm kiss and to be manhandled every once in a while, but she needed a say in the matter, particularly for the first time a man touched her. Not that she ever felt in danger with Jason. He'd always been gentle—his verbal jabs notwithstanding—but she hadn't expected him to kiss her, and it threw her off-balance.

She couldn't help the reaction she'd had, her mind spiraling backward. She was glad she'd told him what she'd experienced in college and that he took it all in stride, openly emotional about it. The fact that he so easily understood her response confirmed he was a good guy and nothing like the one who still lingered at the back of her memories to pop up at the worst times.

After their time together today, Gem could say she truly liked Jason.

When he drove them back to the clubhouse, she dragged her hair over one shoulder, winding it around her fingers. "That's it?"

"We played eighteen holes."

"We did?"

"Well, *we* did. You slept through some." He parked the cart and nodded toward the restaurant deck, where her mother and Frank were finding a table. "Come on."

Then she *really* liked his hand on her lower back. Once seated, he plucked something from her hair.

"I picked this just for you," he drawled, handing her a tiny brown leaf. She twirled it between her fingers, biting back a smile. How could she keep him at arm's length when he could be so cute?

"Oh my god, Jason!" A sweet little voice echoed like a church bell behind her.

Oh, right. That's why.

Without seeing where the squeal came from, Gem could guess who it belonged to.

The statuesque woman strutted right up to their table, placing her hand on Jason's back. "I didn't know you'd be here," she said, massaging his shoulder in a way that showed they were quite familiar with each other. "You never returned my texts from the other day."

With a fleeting look at Gem, he sat forward in his chair so that the woman's hand slipped off him.

"Aren't you going to introduce me?" She smiled at the group, her teeth gleaming white against her honey-brown skin. She wore a pink-and-green sports dress and matching visor. Her straight black hair framed the petite features on her pretty face.

Jason's shoulders rose when he took a deep breath through his nose, and Gem had to hand it to him. He had her fooled.

"Bridget, this is Frank Santos, my friend, and his fiancée, Caroline, and her daughter, Gemma. Everyone, this is Bridget Pozo."

The infamous Bridget. Well, she was beautiful in that blindingly perfect way. If you liked that sort of thing. Jason apparently did.

"It's a pleasure," Bridget said.

"Pozo? As in Nelson Pozo?"

Bridget beamed. "Yes, that's my father."

Frank slapped his knee. "How about that! You tell him I said hello. I owe him a drink one of these days. Caroline, Nelson's the one who hosts once-a-month poker. He's married to Eileen Simpson."

"Oh. Oh!" Gem's mother flicked her manicured hand at Bridget. "Yes, of course! Eileen and I have had a few drinks together. She's so wonderful. And, Bridget, doesn't your smile look just like hers. I wish I had her genes. She could pass for your sister."

Bridget crinkled her nose, lifting a slender shoulder. "I think it's that lifetime's worth of skincare products she won from becoming Miss Illinois way back when."

Caroline clucked in glee. "Well, whatever it is she's using, I'd like some."

Gem rolled her eyes; her mother wasn't even fifty years old

yet and already worried about becoming mummified. She flagged down a waiter. "Something with alcohol, please."

Bridget turned to Jason. "What dumb luck that you're here today, huh?"

"Yeah, dumb luck," Gem mumbled.

"Isn't it perfect weather for golfing?" Bridget asked to the table.

Frank nodded. "Did you play already?"

"No, we're about to. I love it. In fact, I'm in a tournament next week."

Caroline pinched Bridget's watermelon ensemble. "Aren't you the cutest thing? Would you like to have a seat?"

"I'd love to. Thank you."

Not able to take it anymore, Gem stood up. "Here. Take mine."

Caroline frowned at her. "But we didn't even eat yet."

"I'm not really all that hungry."

Her mother moved to stand, but Gem stopped her. "No, don't get up. Sit and eat. I'll talk to you later." She gave a quick wave to the table and sped toward the parking lot.

Jason followed. "Hey, Gemma, wait up a sec."

She didn't slow down, but he and his long legs caught her as she reached the car. "What's wrong?"

"Nothing."

He gently wrapped his fingers around her elbow. "You're upset."

"No, I'm not." Gem was spent. It was too draining to continue this pinball game. The up and down, back and forth, love and hate. It had to stop. He'd claimed Bridget was only a friend when Gemma had asked him about her, but that wasn't the truth.

The facts were that Bridget called him at the Labor Day picnic, she'd picked up his phone when Gem had called, and now, here she was, in the flesh, preening under his attention. Three strikes. Gem was done.

"I'm really sorry about all that," he said.

She put on Jason's sunglasses, having no intention of giving them back. After this fiasco, he deserved to lose something to her. Besides, she looked good in them. "You don't need to apologize. You don't owe me anything."

"I feel like after yesterday—"

"Jason, I don't care." She attempted to open her car door, but he leaned against it, hands in his pockets.

"But—"

"It's fine. Really. Hang out with whoever you want. I'm a big girl, I can handle it."

He pushed his hands through his hair. "I don't think you understand."

Her shoulders caved in, tired of the conversation. "I do understand. I may not be an engineer or have my MBA, but I do understand."

"See," he growled, straightening to his full height. "Right away, you take it to this place it doesn't need to go. You get an idea in that pretty little head of yours and jump off the rails. You need to stop putting words in my mouth."

This situation was unmistakable. Whether he wanted to admit it or not, Jason and Bridget had some kind of relationship, and Gem had no desire to get in the middle of it.

"I jump off the rails?" She pointed at her chest with her car key then at his. "Jason, that girl is in love with you. I'm not going to sit there and have it thrown in my face after you kissed me yesterday."

He threw his hands on his hips. "It's not my fault she randomly showed up here."

"No, but it is your fault for leading me on."

He fisted his hands in his hair then tugged at the hem of his shirt. Once again, she took pleasure in his discomfort because her insides were so knotted up, she didn't know if she'd ever be able to eat again.

"I'm not leading you on!" he finally shouted, his words one big gust of air like he'd been holding it in.

Gem planted her feet wide so as not to be blown away. "Whatever you're doing, you need to figure it out. Because I'm not going to sit around like an idiot, waiting for any crumb of attention from you. Believe it or not, not everyone is impressed by your pretty-boy act. I'm certainly not."

With that, she got into her car and drove away, leaving him in her dust.

11

Jason's cell phone vibrated on his desk, another text from Bridget. Yet another he didn't bother to read. She had been nothing if not persistent over this last week.

After Gem had skipped out on their lunch at the golf course, he definitively ended things with Bridget, earning some tears from her. He'd been surprised she'd felt so deeply about him since his feelings were strictly surface level, but he couldn't keep acting as if what they had was anything close to real. Not when he discovered what real felt like because of Gem.

Her face was in the forefront of his mind, with her hair spilling over her shoulders and his sunglasses covering her eyes. *His* sunglasses. A proud smile crept up to the corners of his mouth, a kind of barbaric emotion rising in his chest, happy that she wore something of his. He had some claim on her, a physical token, and he reasoned that if she thought him as big of a dick as she let on, she wouldn't have kept them. Right?

He tapped his phone on, contemplating calling her to explain his side. He hoped she would listen to him after she'd had the last few days to cool off.

Probably.

Maybe.

But just as Jason put the phone up to his ear, Frank knocked on his office door. "I need your help."

He ended the call before it rang. "What do you need?"

"A tux."

"Oh, uh. Okay."

"Me and you got a date to pick something out after work today," Frank said, plopping down in the chair across from Jason's desk. "Two weeks and I'll be married. Can you believe it?"

Jason played with his pen, spinning it between his index and middle fingers. "Got any nerves?"

"No." He put his hands behind his head, relaxing in his chair, a man on top of the world. "I could never be nervous with Caroline. I wake up every day excited that she's next to me."

"I didn't know you were such a romantic, Frank."

"She makes me that way. I tell you, Jay, being in love is the best."

Jason tossed the pen down. "I'll have to take your word for it."

"That's your own fault," Frank said, not entirely unkindly as he sat forward with his elbows on the desk. "You and me, kid, had some pretty shitty luck. I remember the day Sandy was diagnosed. I never thought I'd be able to go on without her, and then a few months later, she was gone like that." He snapped his fingers. "But, Jason, I wouldn't change it for a second because for every terrible night, there were one hundred really, really wonderful ones. Your parents loved you very much, and I hate that you couldn't have them around longer, but if you keep worrying about losing the people you love, you're going to miss out on something really special."

"I know," Jason said softly. "I know."

"Do you, though? What's going on with you and...what's her name? Pozo's daughter?"

"Bridget."

"Yeah, Bridget. She seems like a nice girl."

"We broke up."

Frank ran a finger under his bottom lip. "Yeah? Thought you said she wasn't your girlfriend."

"You can't remember her name, but you remember I said that?"

Frank winked, his grin open wide, as open and wide as his heart. "What can I say? I only remember what I'm interested in."

Jason grunted and stood up. "Come on, old man, I need a break. Let's go get some coffee."

A few hours later, Frank scratched his head, surrounded by suits of every color. "Oh hell, why are there so many to choose from? When I got married the first time, it was in a suit the color of shit."

"Nice." Jason slid his finger along the brim of the top hat on his head before swinging a cane under his arm. "Are you going for that same look this time around?"

"That's why you're here. I'm not any good at this stuff. You're young. You're hip." Frank pulled him around the room. "What do you think?"

Jason pulled his mouth down, pointing to a big poster that hung on one of the walls, male models all grinning. He assumed they were a groom and his groomsmen. "I think you're supposed to match. Like prom."

"Match?"

Jason nodded resolutely and flipped his cane in the air, catching it deftly as the door at the front of the store swung open. Gem flew in, her attention on her cell phone, a smile gracing her lips as she typed something and then laughed with a little shake of her head.

"What are you doing here?" Frank asked, peering out from behind a mannequin wearing a suede suit.

"Mom sent me to make sure you don't screw it up."

"Oh, thank god. Get over here." He moved to greet her with a hug, and Gemma smiled as she wrapped her arms around him, but she smothered it as soon as she spied Jason over Frank's shoulder.

Taking his top hat in hand, Jason offered her a low bow. She only rolled her eyes and then focused back on her phone as soon as Frank let go of her.

"So, let me get this straight," Jason said, sidling up next to her. "I saw your mom *scold* you for not following the dress code, and yet she sends you to pick out a wedding tuxedo."

She answered with her attention on her cell phone. "I know what's appropriate to wear to places, I just like to wear what I wear. Rules or no rules."

"Of course," he said, nodding, then tried to get a look at what she was doing. "Who are you texting?"

"My best friends," she answered, head still down.

"Must be important."

She lifted her face and angled a brow—he loved that brow—then, without any warning, lifted her phone and snapped a picture. She lowered her attention back to the text thread and messaged the picture, her thumbs racing over the letters in some message he couldn't make out.

"What's that about?"

"My friend Sam is having a stressful day, so we're trying to make her feel better."

"And you thought a picture of me would help?" He didn't know whether to be proud or embarrassed.

She dropped her phone into her purse and smiled at the young man headed their way, speaking out of the corner of her mouth to Jason. "In that getup, yeah."

So, in that case, definitely embarrassed.

"Hi, my name is Remy," the kid said, pointing at his name tag then reaching out to shake Gemma's hand. "What can I help you with today?"

"I'm Gem," she said then motioned to Frank. "And this is my future stepfather, Frank. We need a classic dinner jacket, no satin. Let's stick with one or two buttons."

Remy laced his hands together and nodded. "I like a girl who knows what she wants. You must've done this before."

She snorted, raising an eyebrow. "I've picked out a few tuxedos, yes. My personal marriage, no."

He inched closer to her. "That's good news for all the men out there. We still have a chance."

Jason flung his top hat onto the head of a mannequin and set the cane in its hand, not bothering to tamp down his audible guffaw at the lines this kid was throwing down. He looked barely legal, a few hairs on his chin in a poor attempt at a beard. Jason didn't think Gemma would actually go for Remy, but she smiled sweetly at him as he led her to the back of the store, his hands gesticulating in the air as he spoke to her...about what, Jason didn't know. Maybe the white suit Gemma pointed to, or the fact that Remy could pass for the guy who played Harry Potter in the movies, glasses, bowl haircut, and all.

After a few minutes, Gemma and Remy returned with a tux. Frank nodded in appreciation and took it to the dressing room.

Jason held his hands up, waiting for one as well. "Do I get one too or...?"

Gemma seemed less than pleased to also have to help him, and she tossed her thumb back in his direction as she said to Remy, "Could you find one for him? He's the best man."

Jason expected her to have some sort of direction, like she had with Frank. Buttons and colors and whatever, but she only perched herself on a chair next to the dressing rooms and pulled her cell phone back out of her purse.

Remy wasted no time in picking out a few pieces for Jason to try on and led him back to the dressing room, where Gemma continued to ignore him. Though, she had a pleasant discussion with Remy when he complimented her sweater.

Christ. This guy was like a puppy jumping at her feet for attention. Jason wanted to find a collar to hold him back, tell him to cool it. Go lie down in the corner.

Frank sauntered out of the changing room in his tuxedo and spun around in front of Gemma, who rose to her feet. "You look fantastic, Frank. Really, really handsome."

"Yeah?" He grabbed her hand and twirled her under his arm. "I haven't worn a tux in years, not since…" He pointed to his gut with a laugh. "I feel like James Bond, though, eh? What do you think?" He tugged on the lapels of the jacket.

"I guess you could pass for Sean Connery, if I squint," she said with a laugh.

He chuckled and ruffled her hair. "Sean Connery wishes he was as handsome as me. Okay," he said with a clap of his hands. "You're up, Jay."

When Jason headed into the dressing room, he tried to lock the door but the latch was broken and it crept open a smidge, so he gently closed it again before hanging the suit on the rack. Outside, he could hear Frank, Remy, and Gemma talking about the wedding, and how soon alterations could be done. He stripped down to his black boxer-briefs and socks, and turned, reaching for the white shirt. That was when he noticed the door ajar.

And Gemma staring.

How ironic.

She lifted her eyes from where they were settled somewhere below his hips. Frank's and Remy's voices had faded as if they'd walked away, so he pushed the door all the way open. "Fair is fair, I guess."

He gestured to his nearly naked body, allowing her a better view. She cleared her throat, stood up, and casually scanned him up and down as if she were window-shopping. He smiled gamely. She did not return it. Only walked away.

"It seems like you have everything under control here," Jason heard Gemma say as he stepped into his pants. "I'm going to head out." He rushed to get dressed, but that only made him stumble into the wall when he lost his balance.

"Gemmie, there's no other girl I'd want as my daughter," Frank said to her.

"You aren't so bad yourself."

"Shit." Jason grunted when he pinched a tiny bit of skin of his middle finger in the zipper.

"I'll see you later," Gemma said, and then presumably to Remy, "Thanks for your help."

His chipper response had Jason rolling his eyes as he fumbled with the buttons of the shirt. "It was no problem at all. It was a pleasure meeting you. So...uh..."

Their voices started to fade, and Jason ripped the suit jacket off the hanger, the edge of the hard wood socking him in the eye. He hissed in pain and shoved the heel of his palm against it. "For fuck's sake!"

"What do you think about giving me your number? Maybe I could take you out this weekend?" Remy said, almost inaudibly to Jason's ears.

He hurriedly shoved his arms through the tuxedo jacket, but by the time he got himself together and barreled out of the dressing room, Remy stood at the door, waving at Gemma. She was already on her way out.

12

The following Friday morning, Caroline stopped by Bare Necessities, an unusual occurrence. Gem tossed down her *National Geographic* and sat up behind the counter. "What are you doing here, Mom?"

Caroline placed her designer purse on the counter. "I wanted to tell you we're going to Jason's house tonight."

"Okay."

Her mother inspected the products next to the register, picking up each one. "You should be there around six."

"What? I'm not going."

"Why not?" Caroline pointed to a short, round tub. "What is that?"

"I have a date tonight, and it's lavender body butter. One hundred percent organic and vegan."

"Gemma Rose, why didn't you tell me you had a date?" Caroline lit up in delight while she dug out a dollop of lotion to smell. "With whom?"

"A guy I met when I was helping Frank at the tuxedo place."

"What's his name?"

"Remy."

"Is he cute?"

"Yes."

Caroline rubbed the butter over her hands. "Well, I think you should come to the party first. A lot of Frank's coworkers will be there. Jason finalized the deal today on that development project he's been working on."

Gem perked up. Despite Jason's terrible track record with her, she was interested in his work. "Really?"

"You have to come. This is a big deal for the company." Caroline found a lipstick and drew a small line of it on the back of her hand.

"I wasn't invited."

Her mother waved off the idea. "Of course you were. We're all family now." When Gem chewed her lip in thought, Caroline swatted at her. "Don't bite your lips. It's not—"

"Not ladylike."

Eyeing Gem, Caroline took out her wallet. "Exactly. And you need to come tonight to support Jason, for a little while, at least. He's important to Frank, and Frank's important to me."

"Fine. But only for a few minutes."

"Good, and I'll take the lipstick."

Gem pulled up to Jason's block a little after six. He lived in a townhouse which boasted a two-car garage, basketball hoop, and perfectly groomed landscaping. A few familiar faces greeted her as she entered the front door, and with a quick glimpse around, she noticed the house was bigger than it appeared from the outside, with a huge flat-screen in the living room along with every piece of technology and gaming system imaginable in the entertainment unit. Surround sound music echoed in every room, over the din of all the chatter.

Gem found Caroline sipping red wine in the kitchen. She kissed her cheek.

"Honey, you look so sweet. Where did you find that dress?"

"Thrift store."

"Really? Looks like something you would find at Nordstrom." She touched the straps that crisscrossed over Gem's back. "It gives you a nice shape."

"Thanks." Gem tugged on the blue and gray dress with cutouts at her waist.

Her mom lifted her glass, motioning in a circle. "What do you think of the house?"

Gem surveyed the place. "It's very beige."

"I know," Caroline said in a hushed tone. "He's been here for a few years now, but it's so...blah." She poked her daughter's hand. "Frank is on the deck smoking a cigar, but I don't know where Jason ducked off to. Why don't you see if you can find him?"

When her mother physically pushed her away, Gem begrudgingly moved to locate him, starting with a self-guided tour of the second floor. The first room held an ironing board, a few cardboard boxes, and a desk. The room next to it had only a twin bed, along with a nightstand in the corner. There was a bathroom and laundry room and, at the end of the hallway, double doors. Nosy, she opened them and tiptoed into the master bedroom, like a spy crossing enemy lines. On the right, Jason's clothes filled up less than half the space of the huge walk-in closet. Next, she inspected the attached bathroom, a herringbone-tiled floor with a shower in the corner. The clear glass doors spread from floor to ceiling, and it had more than enough room for two people. Circling back around, she settled her eyes on the king-size bed held up on a plain black bed frame, bookended by night tables on each side. An overstuffed gray chair sat in the corner beside one small chest of drawers.

An unbidden scene unfolded before her, and she closed her eyes to it, hoping to push it away. But her mind had other ideas. Her body coursed with heat, envisioning Jason carrying her through the double doors. She recalled the taste of him when he kissed her, the warmth of his tongue, the pressure of his hands in her hair, tenderly pushing it back from her face.

Her heart tripped over itself as she imagined that same pressure all over her body. His fingers on her hips, stomach, breasts, between her legs. Her spine tingled thinking of them in the shower. She could almost smell the now-familiar scent of his skin and wondered what it might feel like soaped up with bubbles. Soft and hot as water sluiced over his muscles, the planes of his back, the ridges of his abdomen, that length of him that she'd gotten a glimpse of in the tux shop.

Her body ached for it to be real, for some relief. Her nipples pebbled and her thighs clenched together, every part of her aware of how close she was to Jason now. Here, in his bedroom, in his innermost sanctum. If only—

"Hey, you."

Gem jumped, clutching at her chest, and spun around. Jason knocked the breath right out of her, and she couldn't speak as he stood, leaning against the doorjamb, hands in his pockets. "Sorry, didn't mean to scare you. What are you doing up here?"

Sudden cottonmouth made anything more than one syllable impossible. "Hi."

He tilted his head to the side, regarding her with his careful, cool gaze. "Are you okay?"

She nodded, fidgeting with her dress as his eyes roved over her. She wasn't often this dolled up. She'd pulled her hair back in a sleek ponytail and wore dark makeup, but he seemed to appreciate it.

"You look beautiful."

The compliment, though simple, had her heart racing at its honesty. "Thank you."

His lips turned up in an easy smile. "I like that dress on you."

Here he was, totally calm and casual, having absolutely no idea that she'd been fantasizing about how many places they could have sex in his room. She felt the blush creeping up her cheeks and excused herself with a mumbled apology then high-tailed it downstairs as fast as her feet would carry her in the cursed wedge sandals her mother had given her for her birthday.

JASON TRAILED AFTER GEMMA, curious at her strange behavior. He hadn't meant to gawk at her like that, but she was so pretty in her dress. Then when he finally spoke, and she pivoted around, her plum-painted lips opening in a frightened *Oh*, he was torn between wanting to touch her and continuing to stare. He didn't think he'd ever tire of looking at her. Although, she scampered away before he could tell her any of that. He had hoped to fill her in about how he'd broken it off with Bridget and was determined to sit Gem down and finally have it out with her. Tonight.

Back in the kitchen, Caroline, Frank, and Gem were mid-conversation.

Frank offered Gem a drink, but she declined. "I've actually got to leave. I have a date."

"Who has a date?" Jason asked, joining them.

"I do," Gem said, scratching at a cut in the wood of the butcher block island. "With Remy."

"You're kidding. The tuxedo guy?"

She flicked her eyes up to him, her usual intensity back in them. "Yeah."

His shoulders shrank. "The Harry Potter guy? Seriously?"

"Yes." She huffed. "Why? You don't think anyone would want to take me out?"

Irritated that she could never just have a conversation, she always had to turn it into a fight, he dropped his fist down next to her hand. "No. I didn't say that."

She leaned toward him. "That's what it sounds like you're saying."

He met her halfway, frustration at her going on a date invading all his better judgment. "Maybe you need to get your hearing checked."

Beside them, Frank and Caroline watched the argument like a tennis match.

"I don't see Bridget anywhere," Gemma said, her nose all scrunched up.

"She wasn't invited."

"No? That's too bad. Guess it's on to the next one," she snapped.

Jason gritted his teeth. "You are—"

"All right." Caroline stuck her hand out, showing off her platinum watch. "Gemma, don't you have to go? It's almost seven."

Gemma tucked her little black purse into the crook of her elbow, kissed her mother and Frank, and left without another word. This woman.

Utterly exasperating.

He blew out a breath and hung his chin to his chest, rubbing at the back of his neck. He could feel Frank's thoughtful gaze on him, but he didn't have the energy to explain the last few minutes. When Caroline left to mingle, Frank made his move and placed his hand on Jason's back. "Everything all right?"

"Yep, fine." He forced himself to stand up straight to prove it.

"All your hard work is finally paying off."

Jason nodded and rested his hip against the kitchen counter. "Yep."

"Are you worried about the project?"

"Nope." He thrust his hands into his pockets.

"Well, hell, Jay, you don't seem too excited," Frank said with a mixture of dismay and confusion.

"No, I am. I am. It's just that…" Jason paused, trying to get his words and feelings together.

Frank stepped back and snapped his fingers. "Of course. I should have seen this before. My attention has been elsewhere lately."

Jason's brow furrowed. "Huh?"

"You know I consider you my son, right?" Frank said, placing both of his hands on Jason's shoulders to dig his thumbs into the soft spot below his collarbone, like he'd been doing for the last fifteen years, thinking it constituted a massage. In reality, it felt like two blunt dowels being shoved into Jason.

"When I agreed to be your godfather, I never dreamed in a million years that you'd ever actually be placed in my care, but Jason, that was the best thing that ever happened to me. You are the best thing that ever happened to me. I am getting married, but nothing will change the fact that you are my kid."

Frank's eyes teared, and Jason didn't have the heart to tell this man, whom he loved like a father, that he wasn't upset over the impending marriage. Instead, he only smiled and let Frank continue.

"We'll still hang out, play golf. Whatever you want, whenever you want, I'm here for you." He hugged Jason, who couldn't hide it anymore, his shoulders shaking. "It's okay, buddy," Frank said, patting his back. "Let it out."

Jason huffed out a laugh, and Frank froze. "Was that…?" He stepped back, a grumpy smile on his face. "What is wrong with you? I thought you were crying. Here you are laughing at me."

Jason doubled over, his eyes tearing. "I'm crying laughing." He stretched an arm out to Frank, who towed him up to standing. "You're the best. Really. The best."

Frank only shook his head. "And you're an ungrateful little shit."

Jason wiped at his eyes. "I thought I was your child, whom

you so adore." He patted Frank's shoulder. "In all seriousness, you've done a pretty good job being my dad."

The two hugged and clapped each other's backs. When they finally separated, Frank asked, "So, what's the real problem?"

Jason took a deep breath, combed his hand through his hair, and then told the truth. "Gem."

Frank hit his fist on the counter. "I knew it! I knew it."

"You did not."

"Yes, I did." Frank pointed his finger at Jason. "I told you from the beginning. What did I say? I said she was good for you."

Jason bowed dramatically. "Yes. You are the master, the all-knowing."

"Uh-huh." Frank sat back on his heels, placated. "She'll come around. Don't worry."

13

With mere days until the wedding, Gem rode her bike to yoga for some extra relaxation. She needed time to enjoy the quiet of nature before getting ready for class. Her mother had called her no fewer than three times every day for the past three days with any number of emergencies. First with her hair not being dyed the right color, then the wedding singer coming down with a sinus infection, and as of yesterday, a meltdown about a thirty-percent chance of rain. Gem had invited her mom and Frank to come to yoga then immediately turned her cell phone off, hiding it in her closet for good measure. One more frantic phone call and it might have gone down the toilet.

Gem wouldn't be able to help anyone find their center if she was all off-kilter, so she did some breathing exercises on her mat before the class filled up. A few minutes later, Caroline called out, "Hello! Hello!"

Gem got up from her position on the floor. "You actually came."

"You said it would help," her mom said, dropping her bag in the corner of the room. "I tried calling you last night and this morning."

"Sorry," Gem insincerely apologized as she high-fived Frank, who wore sweatpants and a T-shirt a tad too tight around his belly.

He halfheartedly stretched side to side. "Is this going to be hard?"

"You'll be fine," Gem answered, tossing a yoga mat to him.

A few more people filed in, and Gem greeted her regulars before stepping in front of the room, taking her usual spot at the top of her orange mat. That was when she spotted Jason, his tall form ducking in as she began her introduction.

"Good evening and welcome. This is an all-levels Vinyasa flow class." She raised her brow at Jason in question. "I'm surprised to see so many new faces."

He replied silently by pointing to Caroline and quietly removed his sneakers then found an open space in the back with one of the extra mats.

Gem refocused and brought her hands up to her heart, determined not to give him any more attention than necessary. If he wanted to waste an hour trying to impress Caroline, that was his prerogative. "I invite you all to start by planting your feet firmly on the earth, breathing deeply, in through your nose and out through your mouth."

She began the class with some centering breaths then moved through sun salutations. In the front row, Caroline easily transitioned from one pose to the next, while Frank grunted with every exhale. During the more advanced moves, Gem took some time with each student for support or gentle correction, although it took some time to get Frank unstuck from reverse warrior.

"I thought you said this would be easy," he rasped, finally standing upright with her help.

She'd never laugh at any of her students, but she needed to bite her lip to keep a straight face. "I never said easy."

He wiped sweat away from his forehead. "I don't think I'm

going to make it to Saturday. I may have a heart attack before then."

"Don't worry. I am first aid certified," she whispered, patting his back, then continued her instruction on to the next pose. "Nice long inhale, and on your exhale, slowly move into side angle pose."

Everyone followed her except for Frank, who bent to touch his toes, only getting halfway there.

"If you're feeling good today, you can always extend out into half-moon pose."

A few of her students moved onto one leg and hand, and Gem readjusted some before coming to Jason, who attempted the pose, though it was all wrong. "Turn out from your center."

"I have no idea what that means." His usually smooth voice was ragged, but she hesitated to help him. His head hung upside down, his face red and pinched together. "I'm feeling a little light-headed down here."

After everything—the constant arguing, the amazing yet surprising kiss, the whole Bridget situation—she didn't want to be nice to him, but this was her yoga class. She *had* to be nice. "Then pick your head up. Your neck is an extension of your spine. Keep it straight." She placed one hand on his back. "And open up from your hips."

"They are open," he groaned.

She pushed on his hip. "Like this."

His right leg swung higher into the air, and then he came tumbling down, taking Gem with him. His long legs pinned her to the floor as he grinned, hair flopped over his forehead. He leaned up on one elbow. "Like this?"

A laughe escaped before she could stop it, and everyone in the studio paused to see what the kerfuffle was.

"Sorry," Jason said to the class. "My bad." He untangled himself from her and stood up, offering his hand down to help her up off the floor. "You okay?" When she nodded, he pulled his mouth up in playful alarm and held on to her forearm. "Is the drop-in fee extra if I break the instructor?"

"No," she said, tucking loose hair that had fallen out of her ponytail. "I'm fine."

He hit her with his blue gaze full on, silently mouthing *Good*, his pinkie finger brushing her arm as he stepped forward on his mat. The dimmed lights, slightly heated temperature, and soothing chime music were all meant to be comforting, but with that tiny touch, it all whirled together like a hurricane, and Gem and Jason were in the eye of the storm. She'd already been so aware of her body, so connected with the energy flowing in and out of every person, the charge between them was a heavy, pulsating thing. In that moment, everything became sharper.

The sweat dotting his upper lip.

The soft fiber of his T-shirt, clinging to his chest.

The burn of his eyes on her.

She wanted more, wanted to stay in this bubble, but someone coughed, and Jason blinked away from her.

Gem folded her fingers into her palms, bringing awareness back to her body. She was in the middle of teaching class; she couldn't go all gooey-eyed now. She pivoted away from Jason and shook out her arms. "When you're ready," she said, clearing her mind as much as possible, "slowly bring your right foot to meet your left, forward fold."

A few minutes later, the class lay on their backs, but Gem couldn't quite shake the tension away, even as she directed everyone to breathe, reading her daily affirmation in a low voice. She should have been quieting her own thoughts, yet her mind constantly drifted back to Jason and his soft smile and the feel of his fingers on her forearm. When she opened her eyes to check on the class, she found him staring straight at her.

"Thank you for sharing your practice with me, and I look forward to seeing you all next week," Gem said, bowing slightly toward the class before getting up to turn the lights all the way up.

As everyone gathered their belongings, Frank stayed on the floor. "This was torture."

"I thought it was wonderful," Caroline said, wrapping an arm around her daughter. "Frank, sweetheart, come on. While I'm feeling invigorated, I want to go home and go over the seating arrangement one last time."

"Sorry, I can't. I live here now. On this mat. Gemmie, you'll need to bring me some food every once in a while."

Jason shook his head with a chuckle, and the sound tickled Gem's skin. His laugh would haunt her dreams.

"Come on, big guy," he said and hoisted Frank up.

Gem escorted them all outside into the cool night air, a shock to her overheated body, then locked the door to the studio behind her. From the car, Caroline waved out of her window. "Rehearsal is at five o'clock. Don't be late, Gemma. Jason, you're a peach." Frank beeped the horn once, and Caroline blew a few kisses. "See you both tomorrow!"

"I'm not always late," Gem muttered to herself, grabbing her bike from the rack, and Jason stopped in his tracks.

"Where's your car?"

"At home."

He dropped his chin in what looked like exasperation. "Wasn't it bought for you so you don't have to ride that thing?"

"I guess."

"Then why are you still using your bike?"

She glared at him. "Because I like it."

"Get in." He opened the door to his truck.

She only shook her head. "I'm good, thanks."

He tilted his head toward it. "Get in."

"Nope." She threw one leg over the bicycle and settled her feet on the pedals.

"Don't be so stubborn." He stalked over to her, trapping the front wheel between his legs. "We've done this before. You know I win this one." He quirked a smile at her. As if he knew exactly how to persuade her. "Get in my truck, Gemmie."

Following a shorter than normal standoff, she gave up and got into the big red monster.

It was after eight o'clock, and the sky had turned dark navy. Jason pointed at it through the windshield. "It's really not safe for you to be riding a bike when it's so dark."

"I have reflectors." She picked at her long-sleeved bright-white zip-up, evidence that people could see her on the bike.

"But you never know who's on the road. I know you'll be fine, it's the other people I don't trust."

In all of their conversations, Gem had never heard him like this before. Jason's voice was always full of certainty, laced with a little humor. Even when they were fighting with each other, she'd come to expect and sort of look forward to the hint of arrogance.

But this, this voice, was something she had never heard.

It sounded like...like he actually cared for her.

That possibility was a little too suffocating, so instead of pursuing that line of thinking, she changed the subject. "Class was a bit of a struggle for you, huh?"

He kept his eyes on the road, left hand on the steering wheel, his right elbow on the console between them. "The human body isn't supposed to bend like that."

She bit back a smile.

"At least I didn't fall asleep," he said, referring to Frank letting out a rumbling snore during Shavasana.

She couldn't help her grin then and tugged her hair tie out, her hair blowing around her face from the window opened halfway. She ignored Jason's double take from the other side of the truck and gathered it all up over one shoulder to methodically wrap and unwrap it around her index finger.

"How was your date?" he asked after a minute, and she leaned closer to the open window for more air.

"Fine."

"Going on a second?"

When she didn't answer, he hummed inquisitively. "I knew it wouldn't work out. He's what? Fifteen?"

"Twenty-two," she corrected, not sure how she felt about Jason being so positive the date would be a flop.

"Probably majoring in something ridiculous like philosophy."

"He's a political science major."

Jason snorted. "He's a child."

"He is not a child," she said defensively. The date wasn't terrible, but they also had nothing in common. "He's planning on moving to DC after he graduates and is working to put himself through school."

He harrumphed. A literal harrumph. "What could you possibly have talked about? Double-breasted jackets? The subtle differences between white and ivory?"

That growly texture in his tone sounded jealous, and Gem angled her eyebrow in suspicion. "We didn't talk about jackets."

"Colors, then?"

She huffed. "I'm sure I had as much fun with Remy as you have with Bridget."

He stopped at a red light and fixed his eyes on her. "So you didn't have any fun?"

She could lie, but what would be the point? He'd already sniffed out the truth. "I wanted to stab a fork in my ear so I didn't have to listen to him." When he snickered, she jabbed a finger in his direction. "Why are you laughing? Didn't you just admit that you don't have any fun with your girlfriend?"

"Yes," he said without any preamble then drove on when the light turned green.

Gem bobbed her chin, unsure what to say. This night had

been baffling on so many levels. "Well...what... Why are you with her?"

He parked in front of her apartment building and let out a loud exhale, his hand raking through his hair. "I'm not with her."

She didn't know what to believe at this point. Bridget, like a ghost, showed up at the most inopportune times, spoiling any momentum Gem and Jason had gained. "Whatever you say."

He paused mid-step out of the truck and glanced over his shoulder, his face softening from frustration into something that appeared an awful lot like regret. "Gemma, I'm not with her." He shifted closer to her. "She isn't the one I have feelings for."

Gem's breath caught, and she couldn't move, her hand frozen on the door handle at his admission.

"Come on," he said, "let's get you upstairs." He got out of the truck, pulled down her bike, and was halfway to the door before she remembered how to move her legs again.

Once inside, he set the bicycle against the living room wall and glanced around the room, his hand on the back of his neck. "I, uh, guess I'll see you tomorrow." He stepped to the door. "Bye, Gem."

She had felt stifled by him and this *thing* between them all night, but now that his back was to her, she couldn't stand to see him leave. "Wait!"

He whirled back around, eyebrows raised, hair drooping toward his right eye.

"Do you—" She bit her lip, pointing to the kitchen. "Do you want a snack or something? I'm kind of hungry."

His eyes roved over her, and she picked at the hem of her jacket, her bare feet rubbing against each other after she'd kicked off her shoes. As if he really liked her chipped toenail polish, he grinned. "Yeah, me too."

He was a ridiculous man.

She pulled out hummus and chips, while he sat down on one

of her mismatched chairs, scooting it away from Mr. Clooney, who lounged on his back on top of the table. His silver eye followed Jason's movements.

"Your cat is freaking me out."

"George, off the table." Gem snapped her fingers, and he vaulted from the table to a cabinet by the doorway to the couch in the living room.

"That's pretty impressive to do with one eyeball."

"He's missing an eye, not a leg," she said, pouring them drinks into mason jars.

"What is that?" he asked, his lip curling up slightly at the sight of the whitish liquid.

"Coconut water."

He lifted one of the glasses. "If it's water, why isn't it clear?"

She sipped some from her own glass. "Because it comes from a coconut." When he only held it aloft, examining it from side to side as if he'd find a bug or something in it, she jostled his shoulder. "It's full of nutrients and replenishes electrolytes after a workout. Try it, it's good."

"I highly doubt that," he said with a skeptical eyebrow raise.

"You liked the vegan burger." She pushed the glass toward his mouth with one finger on the bottom. "Don't be such a baby."

He growled something unintelligible then took a big gulp.

"So?"

He wagged his tongue. "Ugh, gross. Tastes like a mix of feet and cereal milk that was left out overnight."

"How many toes have you been sucking on that you know what feet taste like?"

"Hey, don't kink shame," he said with a laugh through his cringe. "And I'm assuming that's what feet taste like." He wiped at his mouth. "It's offensive to call that water. How do you drink that?"

"I have to change. Help yourself to whatever." She poured

him a glass of regular old tap water then ambled down the hall, smiling to herself. At least he tried it. Most people didn't even taste her vegan offerings. She shucked off her jacket and lifted her oversized T-shirt over her head before she discovered it.

The monster in the corner.

Her phobia took control of her body, her lungs releasing a screech before she could stop it. "Jason!"

"What? What's wrong?" He bounded down the hall instantly, running into her as she sprinted from her bedroom. They collided with an *oof*, and he grabbed her shoulders, a half-eaten chip still in his hand, as his eyes scanned her body in panic. "Are you hurt?"

She shook her head. "Spider."

"What?"

"In my room." She shivered. "There's a gigantic spider in my room. You have to kill it."

"You're kidding."

When she shook her head, he shoved the rest of his chip into his mouth and pressed his lips together, suppressing his stupid smile, and she bounced on her toes, covering her eyes. "Please, Jason, don't laugh at me. Please."

He skimmed his fingers back and forth over her shoulders. "All right. Okay. It's okay. I'll take care of it."

He walked down the hall to her bedroom, with Gem following close behind, slowly rotating his head side to side, probably taking in the hand-drawn pictures everywhere, the clothes piled up on her unmade bed.

"Where is it?"

"There." She pointed over his shoulder.

"Where?"

"Right there." She grimaced. How could he miss it? It was enormous. "By the bed, on the wall."

"Oh, that little thing?"

"Little?" she nearly shouted. "It's huge! Like a half-dollar!"

He grabbed a tissue and promptly killed it. "A half-dollar? I don't think I've ever seen that coin in real life, and this thing was, like, a dime at most."

"Is it dead?"

He held the tissue open to her, with black legs mangled in every direction. She threw her arms up, squirming and sputtering.

"Coming from the girl who doesn't eat things with mothers," he mocked her, throwing the arachnid corpse away in the trash before turning back to her. His cocky grin dropped, and he paused in the middle of whatever he was about to say. His attention leisurely tracked down her body, in contradiction to how he'd studied her mere moments ago.

This time, his eyes blazed, pupils widening, and Gem suddenly realized—two seconds after Jason did—that she only had her pants and sports bra on. Her skin dotted with goose bumps, and she crossed her arms over her chest, hiding her hard nipples.

"Are you cold?" he asked, stepping closer.

"No, spiders make my skin crawl."

But it was too late. He knew the truth, the sound rough when he let out a low, "Mm-hmm."

Slowly, he reached up and skimmed his thumb and index finger down a wave of her hair. "You amaze me sometimes."

"In a good or bad way?" Between his concentrated stare and gentle touch, she could do nothing but move closer, dragged in by his gravitational force. She released her arms from around herself to hold on to his forearm.

"In a very good way." He dropped his head a fraction of an inch, so close yet so far away. "You need a ride tomorrow?"

"In the red Transformer out there?" she quipped, leaning toward him.

He squinted one eye thoughtfully in an attempt at being cute. It worked. "I was thinking the Mercedes."

Gem huffed and pressed up onto her toes, weaving away from him slightly so he had to catch her with a hand on her waist. "That's worse than the truck. How about I pick you up in my new electric car?"

"Am I even allowed in it with red meat and gasoline in my veins?" His focus shifted back and forth between her own eyes as if he were memorizing the exact color of them.

"I'll permit it this one time," she whispered so close she could smell the hint of salt on his breath from the chips.

As he moved closer, her heart fluttered. With every passing second, she grew eager for his mouth on hers, but he held back. Waiting for permission.

What a ridiculously perfect man.

"Kiss me, Jason."

And that was it. His mouth met hers in an explosion of *finally*.

Finally, she gave up the battle she'd fought against him.

Finally, she felt the plushness of his lips and the scrape of his teeth.

Finally, she could let go of the anxieties holding her back.

She wrapped her arms around his neck, bringing her body flush with his, and he pressed one hand against the small of her back, thrusting the other into her hair, adjusting the angle of his lips to coax her tongue out to meet his. When a quiet moan escaped the back of her throat, he trailed his hand over her neck to wrap his fingers around her shoulders, tenderly pulling away.

He swallowed thickly, his throat working hard. Gem wanted to lick it.

"I should go," he murmured and released his hands from her completely.

Gem shook her head. "You don't have to. We didn't even get to eat anything."

His laugh was breathy. "I'm not hungry right now." He

swiped his palm up over his face and into his hair. "At least not for food."

"But—"

He kissed her forehead. "Gem, let me be a gentleman tonight, huh? We gotta big couple of days coming up."

She couldn't argue with that, but also…he could stay a little bit longer.

He plucked at her pouty bottom lip with his thumb and grinned her favorite crooked smile. She was no match for that smile. All his smiles, really, but especially that one. Her body drooped against his, her head on his chest so she could hear the rumble under her ear when he said, "I promise I won't be so gentlemanly next time."

Then he tipped her chin up to him and ran his fingertips down her cheek, blazing a trail of fire. "Have a good night."

Before she could snap herself out of her daze, he'd walked out of her bedroom and down the hall, calling back to her, "Pick me up at four thirty."

Then he was gone with a quiet snick of her front door. Gem flung herself onto her bed, one arm over her feverish forehead. She was in trouble.

14

When Gem pulled up to Jason's, he was already standing outside. Coming to a stop, she rolled down her window, and he ducked his head to see her. "You know what time it is?"

She pursed her lips, glancing at the clock on her dash. "Uh... 4:37. Why?"

He pressed his hand against the door and heaved out a sigh. "Do you genuinely not realize you're late, or do you not care?"

"Oh." She let out a carefree little laugh.

"Oh?" He opened the passenger side door and dropped into the seat, adjusting it so his legs had more room. "That's all?"

"What? I'm seven minutes late, big deal."

"Gemma." He tugged at his hair.

Her teeth sawed into her lower lip, doing nothing to contain her amusement. "Jason."

He pointed out the windshield, his stress about being late ratcheting up. "It takes, like, twenty minutes to get to the country club from here on a good day."

"Yeah." She nodded and pulled away from his driveway. "We'll get there just in time."

He wiped both of his hands down his face, and when she giggled, he groaned out a low, "I can't with you right now."

"Relax. We'll be there in plenty of time."

"I can't relax when traffic will add at least ten minutes to the drive time." If there was one thing she had to know about him, it was that he was always on time. "I'm buying you a watch."

"A watch? Who wears watches anymore?"

He stuck out his left arm, his wrist right under her nose. "I do."

Briefly taking her eyes off the road, she held on to his hand, twisting the brown leather strap back and forth. "Yes, you do."

She sounded all squeaky and very un-Gem-like. "What's the voice for?"

"You have nice hands, is all." She dropped his hand, letting it settle in her lap, and he lightly gripped her cotton-covered thigh. She wore some kind of adult onesie pants thing. He didn't understand it, but she looked damn good in it.

"You have nice everything," he said in possibly the least smooth compliment he'd ever given. She glanced his way, her dark eyes sparkling with mirth, and he couldn't stop himself. "You're gorgeous, but I hate that you're so tardy all the time."

"Tardy," she repeated, laughing again, and the fact that he could put that look on her face, tease that unabashed sound from her, made him feel ten feet tall. "Sorry, Principal Mitchell," she said seriously, "it won't happen again."

"Already on to role-playing, huh?" He tightened his grip on her thigh a bit. "I could get down with that."

She flicked at the collar of the white button-down he wore under a camel-colored sweater. "You look very academic."

He leaned toward her. "You like it?"

She lifted one shoulder, a few strands of hair falling out of her loose braid, and she tucked them behind her ear. "I'm not feeling super well-behaved, if that's what you're asking."

"Are you ever?" he mumbled and shifted in his seat, forcing his hand off Gem's leg. His mind reeled with possibilities of what he could do to this misbehaving girl, starting with stripping her of that black one-piece suit and bending her over the nearest hard surface.

"I don't like being told what to do," she said as if he didn't know.

"Yeah, I got that."

"And you can't help but follow directions."

He nodded. They were polar opposites, two hemispheres with completely different seasons, and he didn't know if they could ever meet in the middle, but he was damn sure interested. He'd always wanted to visit the equator. Being with Gem felt like that, blistering heat. Burning sensations everywhere. Hell, that kiss yesterday was enough to consume him late into the night. The early birds had begun to chirp before he'd finally gotten the taste of her lips out of his mind.

And he was desperate for it again.

She made him feel out of himself, a little out of control, and he liked it.

But he didn't like arriving ten minutes after five. Caroline frowned up at Jason as if it'd been his fault, and he pointed at Gemma with one hand, holding the other up in innocence.

"Snitch," she hissed, batting at his stomach.

He very much enjoyed Gemma feeling free to touch him however and whenever she wanted, whether it was a short grasp of his wrist or a light whack to his torso. As long as she was comfortable doing it, he welcomed it all.

"Let's get this rehearsal started, then," Caroline said, gesturing to a woman in a light-pink pantsuit, although rehearsal was a loose term.

The real ceremony was slated to last only thirty minutes or so, but they spent over an hour staging the entire ceremony, poring over every word, line for line, and each tiny movement, before practicing the kiss a few times to make sure it wasn't "too showy." As Caroline and Frank spoke with the officiant, the maid of honor and best man were banished to the corner to fold programs.

Jason creased the corners at exact angles while Gem gave up after one minute and found a pen to play tic-tac-toe, poking him every few seconds to make his X mark.

"These look great," Caroline said, finally finished up. "Thank you both."

"No problem." Gem smiled up at her mother, and Jason tugged on her hair. She fluttered her eyelashes at him.

She thought she was cute.

"Oh, but look at this," Caroline said, motioning to the table settings that had already been put up for the following day. "These napkins are all wrong."

Frank stepped in, struggling to release the taupe cloth napkin from Caroline's death grip. "I know you want every-thing to be perfect, but you have to let the people here do their job. I don't want you stressed out."

"These ugly folded napkins are stressing me out. They're supposed to look like a rosebud, not a cone."

"I think they look okay," Gem said, causing her mother to fight Frank again for the napkin.

"Honey, honey," he said, giving one last hard tug on the cloth then tossing it to Jason behind Caroline's back. "We'll be late for dinner." He kissed her temple. "I love you and I respect your wishes for a napkin to be folded like a rose, but if you want a groom with both of his arms, you better leave now because I am ready to chew one off."

"Oh, you." She rolled her eyes in a rare display of impatience, but one Jason had seen Gem wear on multiple occasions. "Let's go. Where did you make the reservations?"

Frank clucked his tongue. "Somewhere real nice. Very

lively."

The foursome found themselves in front of a massive stone building with a neon orange-and-blue sign.

Caroline scrunched up her face. "Who are Dave and Buster? I thought we were going to hibachi."

Gem slapped a hand over her mouth and tucked her face into Jason's shoulder, hiding her snort-laugh. Jason only dragged a knuckle over his top lip, much smoother about it.

"I think we could all use some old-fashioned amusement, especially you, *mi vida*," Frank said, opening the door. "Let's eat some greasy food."

Caroline stepped cautiously inside. "I don't know about the grease. Oil and satin gowns do not go well together."

The group was shown to their table, where the bride-to-be decided on a liquid diet. One-and-a-half fruity drinks later, she joined an air hockey game with a middle school kid. She tugged up her skirt, trying and failing to bend far enough over the table, balancing on one foot, her other shoe somewhere under the game table.

When she scored, she whirled around, waving. "Gemmie! Gemmie, look, I made it!"

Jason elbowed Gemma. "She looks like you."

"Like me?"

"Messy hair, shoes off, tipsy. That's you."

She feigned anger, pointing a piece of edamame—one of the few vegan options—at him. "Are you accusing me of being a bad influence?"

He plucked the bean from her. "You were the one who convinced her to order the second drink."

"And," she started, motioning to her mother, "she no longer cares about rosebud napkins. Ergo, we don't have to care about rosebud napkins. You're welcome." Then she flicked another bean at him and got up from the table to meet Caroline.

Jason squeezed the beans out with his teeth and tossed the

empty pod down into the basket, watching as Gemma slung her arm around her mom's shoulders. He'd noticed that even though they argued a lot, the bond they had was strong. There were never any real hard feelings between them, and they tended to forgive each other as fast as they got angry. He admired that about the duo.

Across from him, Frank took a big bite of his burger. "Things are going good."

"Is that a question?"

Frank shook his head, chewing, and motioned toward Gemma with a ketchup-covered thumb.

Jason smiled, watching as she bent down, trying to put her mom's heel back on. "Yeah, things are good."

Swallowing, Frank wiped off his hands. "I like her for you."

Jason turned away from the mother and daughter pair, now laughing about something. "You trying to make us into some kind of Brady Bunch?"

"No, I'm serious."

And that was exactly what scared Jason. This man had often pestered him about his personal life, had mentioned how Jason was wasting his time with meaningless hookups, but *this* was different.

Only a few weeks ago, Frank had spouted off about Gemma being fun and that Jason needed more fun in his life, but it wasn't that simple. In less than twenty-four hours, Frank would marry Caroline. Jason wasn't related to Frank biologically, but they were family, nevertheless, meaning Caroline would also become family. Jason couldn't take this blossoming thing between Gemma and him lightly. The repercussions of it going wrong would ripple, not only for the two of them, but also for Frank and Caroline.

If Jason was going to do this, he had to go all in. Or not at all.

Gemma reappeared next to him, her eyes bright with joy,

Caroline's hand in hers. "I think the clock has struck midnight for this Cinderella."

Caroline's smile drooped to the side. "Gemmie told me about a potato remedy for dark circles. Do we have potatoes at home?"

Frank stood up, tossing his balled-up napkin down onto his plate. "I think so. If not, I'll stop at the store."

"You're too good to me," she said, having trouble with her cardigan, and Gemma reached around, holding one sleeve out to help. Once she was put back to rights, Caroline leaned down and kissed Jason's cheek. "You take care of my girl for me, okay?"

"Yes," he said instantly and wholeheartedly. It was an easy question to answer. Took no thinking at all.

Then Caroline towed Gemma in and rubbed their noses together. "Don't stay up too late. I don't want you to have dark circles either." She patted her daughter's cheek. "Potatoes, who would've thought?"

Frank led Caroline out of the restaurant, and Jason held up the gaming card to Gemma. "You feel like seeing what Ms. Pac-Man is up to?"

She shot him two finger guns. "Winner with the most tickets gets to pick out the prizes?"

"What?" He huffed out a laugh. "You going to force a stuffed animal on me?"

She spun away from him, her braid swishing with the movement. "We'll see."

If he won, his prize would have nothing to do with light-up toys and everything to do with wrapping her hair around his hand and feeling those pliable lips on his again. He caught up to her, leaning down to her ear, almost missing her tiny shiver when he said, "We will see."

They played some classic arcade games, a few rounds of Skee-Ball, and one intense motorcycle race. There was some name-calling, a couple arguments, and a lot of not-quite-accidental touches to her shoulders and back.

"I do believe it has come time to pay up," he said, leading the way to the prize corner, plastic baubles and knickknacks in neat rows.

Gem grabbed a small Styrofoam football and tossed it in the air as Jason held up a shot glass.

"No, no shot glasses."

"That's not the game, Gemmie. I won, I get to pick out your stupid prize."

She put the football back and picked up a slap bracelet. "Well, contrary to what you think about me, I don't do shots."

"What I think about you?" He frowned. "What do *I* think about you?"

She flicked her wrist, curling the bracelet around her other arm with a crack. "That I'm completely irresponsible."

"Gem, I don't think that at all." He set the shot glasses down and walked back to her, unfurling the neon-colored bracelet from her arm and slapping it on his own wrist above his watch. "You have multiple jobs, two of which are teaching—that's the height of responsibility."

"They're not full time, though. No benefits, no insurance." She held up his arm, examining the two adornments on his wrist. One simple and brown and worth a lot more than the plastic bracelet covered in swirls of pink and green and purple glitter, although at the moment, he wasn't sure which one he liked better.

"So? That doesn't matter," he said. "That has nothing to do with the type of person you are."

She looked up at him, her eyes boring into his. "What type of person do you think I am?"

"I think you're caring, in a real, tangible way. You care about people and the consequences of the choices we all make. You care about the environment and..." He circled his hand not currently in Gemma's grasp behind her, as if he could encompass everything. "You care about what happens in the world, and you care very much for your mom. You might annoy the hell out of me, Gemma, but I think you're smart and funny and exactly what this planet needs more of."

Her attention fell back to his wrist, and she skimmed her index finger over the face of his watch and the slap bracelet. "You thought I was rude when we first met, and I was. I made a snap judgment about you, and I shouldn't have. I'm sorry."

He gulped back his words to placate her because he knew—he somehow felt it—that she needed to get whatever this was off her chest.

She turned his palm flat against hers. "I think you're attentive and considerate and so damn perfect with your dumb shiny loafers and ironed shirts." She moved her fingers in line with his, her skin warm and slightly clammy as if she was nervous. He wanted to tell her there was no reason to be nervous, but she continued, "I've always been confident in who I was. I didn't care that people thought I was a slacker or—"

"You're not a slacker."

She tossed him a reprimanding look for interrupting. "I've always gone where the wind's taken me, and that's how I like it. But lately, it's felt... It feels like I've been falling further and further away from the pack. My friends are all gorgeous gazelles, leaping and running, and I'm the one with the broken leg about to be eaten by a lion."

This time, he couldn't help it; he needed to understand why she felt like she was living in the wild as opposed to standing in this crazy-loud Dave & Buster's. "Gemma, just because you don't have a full-time job doesn't mean you're going to be eaten."

Lacing her fingers with his, she nibbled on the corner of her mouth, and he would lose his patience if she didn't spit it out soon.

"It feels like you're the lion."

Jason worked his jaw, momentarily stunned into silence by her confession, but when she offered him a small, tight smile, the knot in his chest unwound a little.

"I think part of the reason I've been so defensive with you is because I always felt some kind of, I don't know, pull or something. I didn't want to believe it." Her little smile widened to show her teeth. "I didn't want to believe I could like someone so…" She waved her hand down his body.

"Flawless?" he guessed with a grin.

"Exactly," she said, shaking her head in mock scorn. "I don't know if you've noticed, but you and I are completely opposite. I'm not exactly the sweater-set Barbie type, and my credit score is horrible."

He sniffed, tugging her close with their joined hands, guiding her toward the counter with her prize in hand. "I don't care that you don't have a 401(k) or whatever it is you think you're missing or self-conscious about. And you don't care that I am, much like Mary Poppins, practically perfect in every way."

"I'd like to stuff you in Mary Poppins's bag if I could."

"That's my girl," he said and handed over the gaming card to the guy behind the counter before slapping his prize, a temporary tattoo, down. "Where do you want it?"

"I'm not putting that on."

"Yes—" he drew her arm toward him, turning the inside of her forearm up "—you are. Them's the rules."

She began to argue, but he laid the sticker on the soft skin above the inside of her wrist and bent over it, lowering his mouth. He heard her suck in a quick breath when his tongue glided over the thin paper, and he took extra care to massage the wet sticker onto her flesh. Their gazes met, and she licked her lips, leaving them wet and so damn tempting.

If she thought she'd be eaten, she was right. His baser instincts were slowly surfacing, and the more she opened up to him, the closer he got, the more he wanted. Like an insatiable animal.

He peeled back the paper to reveal a two-inch, black, fire-breathing dragon, and his fingertips skimmed over her skin. "That, Gemma, is art."

"My mother's going to kill me. I hope you're satisfied when you're sitting in the police station, being questioned about my whereabouts."

"It's not that bad."

"You have met my mother, haven't you? You think she'll be fine with this on my arm at her wedding?"

He sucked air in through his teeth; he hadn't thought of that. His mind was only on her skin. Seeing, feeling, touching, licking *more* skin.

"Sorry," he said.

"No, you're not."

He laughed and tossed a hand out in thanks to the guy behind the counter, his new slap bracelet shining under the fluorescent lights above. "You're right, I'm not."

Back at Jason's house, Gem parked her car and twisted in her seat. "So, what do you think of my little battery-powered car?"

"Not bad. It's faster than my Hot Wheels."

She pinned him with one of her you're-about-to-be-lectured stares. "Electric cars emit fifty-percent less carbon dioxide in their lifetimes than those that run on gas."

"Yeah, but electric cars still run on lithium batteries, which account for something like thirty percent of emissions when they're made."

She tossed her hand in the air. "It still comes out in the negative column if you think about how much less carbon would be produced if every automaker switched over."

"It's negligible."

"You're an engineer," she said accusatorily. "Come up with a new way of powering my car!"

He hated to state the obvious, but... "Even if I did, that still won't change the handful of companies that are responsible for the majority of emissions."

"It's little changes, but if everyone made these little changes, we could come together to push for bigger ones." When she swiped her palm over her forehead, he caught sight of her tattoo. "You can't be so nihilistic. Why are you smiling?"

He lightly took hold of her arm and smoothed his thumb over the dragon. "This."

"I hate you for it."

"I know," he said, leaning over the console between them to glide his fingers up her cheek and into her hair. She closed her eyes and nuzzled into his palm, breathing evenly through open, inviting lips. "So pretty," he said, then kissed her.

Like the night before, he didn't feel any hesitation from her. She grabbed at his sweater, her fingers groping for purchase at his shoulders, and when he teased her with nibbles of her exquisite lower lip, she chased his mouth. She craved this as much as he did, her tongue searching for his, and when he finally gave it to her, she moaned and he wanted to gobble up all her little noises.

First kisses were usually about finding a rhythm and learning what each other liked, but with Gem, each kiss was as if they'd done it hundreds of times before. Like his whole life was only practice for this moment, for these kisses with this woman.

Curling his palm around the bottom of her throat, he kissed down her chin and across her jaw, her mouth close to his ear so he could hear her panting breaths. He smiled against her cheek then backed away. "I have to go to this big wedding tomorrow, and I don't have a date. You wouldn't know anyone who might be interested, would you?"

A slow smile etched across her face. "Maybe."

His gaze narrowed on her mouth. "Maybe I'll see you tomorrow?"

"I won't be the one in white," she said coyly, and Jason kissed her one more time before exiting the car. He moved his thumb over his mouth, savoring the feel of her lips on his.

Yes, he was in. He was all in.

15

It was unseasonably warm for being the last day of September. The sun had not yet set but was low enough to provide shade over the lawn. The surrounding trees of green, brown, and yellow formed an enclave for the wedding ceremony.

Stationed under a canopy of cream linen next to the officiant, Frank swiped at his forehead with a handkerchief then fidgeted with his calla lily boutonnière. Next to him, Jason casually tucked his hands in his pockets, gazing out at the one hundred guests sitting in front of them, while a trio of violinists played a soft waltz.

"How are you feeling?" Jason whispered from the corner of his mouth to Frank, who played with his tie, cleared his throat, and tugged on his sleeves. "Anxious?"

"I didn't think I would be."

"I'm sure once you see her, you'll feel better," Jason said, hoping to calm the older man down.

Frank gave Jason's neck a squeeze. "You're a good kid. I love you, Jay."

"I love you too." He patted Frank's shoulder as the music changed, and everyone swiveled their heads to the back.

Gemma slowly floated down the aisle, awash in a dark gold dress. A ghost of a smile graced her red-painted lips, and her dark eyes sparkled at Jason from under long eyelashes. When she reached the front of the aisle, she mouthed *Hi* at him then took her place opposite him. He got a flash of her bare back, bare from the low cut of her dress—the straps meeting at a point just above her tailbone—and he blew out a breath.

God, she was magnificent.

The guests stood when the violinists began the wedding march. Caroline appeared, a glowing vision. Her eyes welled with tears when she saw Frank, who couldn't control his broad smile.

"You look beautiful," Frank said softly, reaching for his bride's hand under the canopy, and Jason glanced over her at Gemma, catching her eyes.

Hi, he mouthed back.

The officiant began the service by welcoming everyone and read a few passages before introducing Gem. She stepped forward, unraveling a small piece of paper.

"This poem is titled *Maybe*, but the author is anonymous." She glanced over to Caroline and Frank, who were staring into each other's eyes, and then to Jason. He smiled at her, and when she seemed to drift somewhere else mentally, he motioned to the paper. With a blink, she got back to the task at hand, holding the paper, though she barely looked at it as she recited,

"Maybe we are supposed to meet the wrong people before meeting the right one so that, when we finally meet the right person, we will know how to be grateful for that gift.

Maybe it is true that we don't know what we have got until we lose it, but it is also true that we don't know what we have been missing until it arrives.

Maybe the happiest of people don't necessarily have the best of everything; they just make the most of everything that comes along their way.

Maybe the best kind of love is the kind you can sit on a sofa together and never say a word, and then walk away feeling like it was the best conversation you've ever had.

Maybe you shouldn't go for looks; they can deceive. Don't go for wealth; even that fades away. Go for someone who makes you smile, because it takes only a smile to make a dark day seem bright.

Maybe you should hope for enough happiness to make you sweet, enough trials to make you strong, enough sorrow to keep you human, and enough hope to make you happy.

Maybe love is not about finding the perfect person, it's about learning to see an imperfect person perfectly."

She finished the poem and balled the paper back up into her hand, and Jason had trouble keeping his attention on the bride and groom while they recited their vows. Gemma blotted at the corner of her eye with her knuckle, and he instinctually checked his pockets for a tissue to give her but came up empty. She ended up hiding her tears behind her bouquet of white roses, and he bit into his lip to control his stupid grin.

We don't know what we have been missing until it arrives.

With rings exchanged and a candle lit, the officiant introduced everyone to the new Mr. and Mrs. Santos. Frank picked up Caroline, swinging her in a circle, entirely disregarding the kiss protocol, and the guests went wild as they made their way back down the aisle.

Jason stuck out his arm to escort Gemma. "Hey, you."

"Hey, you," she echoed, wrapping her hand around his bicep.

He slanted his chin down to her distinctly naked forearm. "How long was it before she noticed the dragon?"

"A few hours, longer than I thought it would take."

"She was probably preoccupied," Jason said, waving at a few friendly faces, "being her wedding day and all."

"Though she had enough time to supervise the alcohol scrubbing."

"The next one will have to be permanent, I guess," he replied, moving his arm so he could hold her hand.

Her fingers laced with his, and she tipped her head back, her pinned-up, curly hair scraping his shoulder. "I would have to lose an awfully big bet for that."

He arched an eyebrow. "I'll see what I can do."

THERE WAS a short photo session with the bridal party on the carved white staircase, and Gem molded herself to Jason's side, smiling at the camera. A few weeks ago, she never would have guessed she'd be attending another one of her mother's weddings. Especially next to this blond and blue-eyed rascal of a man, yet in this moment, tucked up against him with his fingertips drawing circles against her spine, there was nowhere else she wanted to be.

Inside the reception, Mr. and Mrs. Santos had an intricately choreographed number for their first dance to "This Will Be" by Natalie Cole, and Jason bowed his head down to Gem's ear, whispering, "He's surprisingly light on his feet."

"It must be all the flexibility he gained in yoga class."

"If that's true, call me Fred Astaire."

Gem only nudged his side. When the dance ended, everyone took their seats except for Jason, who picked up his water glass as the MC passed him the microphone. "Many of you know me, but a few of you may not. I'm Jason, the best man, and I'm grateful you could all be here to celebrate this special day with Frank and Caroline. I have put up with this..." Jason motioned toward Frank, who smiled in delight.

"Put up with that son of a bitch!" someone shouted from the back, and the guests all laughed at the suggestion, but Jason continued with a shake of his head.

"No. I've put up with this guy for over fifteen years now,

talking about the great love of his life." He took a few seconds to scan the room, dazzling the guests with his smile. Gem included. "Sandy was Frank's first wife, as most of you know, and sadly passed away too early. But fortunately for me, I was taken into his care a few months later and became the great love of his life." The guests broke up in cheers.

He went on, glancing down at Gem. "Gemma read a poem about hoping for enough trials to make you strong and sorrow to make you human. Frank, you have had enough of both."

Jason's voice broke as he gestured to his friend and adopted father, and Gem reached out, hanging on to his suit jacket. It wasn't enough comfort, but it was some, at least.

"I'm so grateful for everything you've given me. You deserve to have all the happiness in the world, and I'm so glad you have found the woman who knows how perfectly imperfect life can be. I hope that one day I will be as in love as you two are." Jason lifted his glass. "To Mr. and Mrs. Santos."

Frank walked over to him, throwing his big arms around Jason's neck, saying something only they could hear. Jason nodded a few times and swiped at his eyes with his index fingers before sitting back down at the table. Gem wiped uselessly at her cheeks, and he unfolded a napkin to dry her tears.

"I never thought you'd be the type to cry at weddings," he said, and she laughed through a sniffle.

"I never thought *you'd* be the type to cry at weddings. Your speech was really good."

"I said what I felt." His winter-snow eyes pierced her, stealing her breath. "You and that poem inspired me."

She stared down at the napkin, finding a few mascara marks on it, and she huffed. "Do I look a mess?"

"Absolutely not. In fact—" he grabbed her hands and steered her to the dance floor "—I think you look—" he spun her under his arm before placing his left hand on her back "—like an sun goddess."

Gem laughed as he led her into a simple two-step. "Where'd you learn to dance so well, Fred?"

He released her with one hand and circled her back to his chest. "I'm not usually. Must be my partner."

He dipped her backward, and she lifted her leg like in an old movie musical. "Call me Ginger."

By the time they took their seats, the first course had been served, and a woman with salt-and-pepper hair patted Gem's hand. "You two make a sweet couple."

"Thank you, but we're not—" She peeked over her shoulder at Jason. They hadn't had any explicit conversations about what was unfolding between them, but if she were honest with herself and this random woman in front of her, she wanted a relationship with Jason. Much to her own astonishment.

The man in question smiled at her, crooked and mind-shattering, his arm draped over the back of her chair. He traced a finger down her shoulder. "Do you want a drink?"

For the seventy-eighth time today, she blinked out of his stunning orbit. Then blinked again. And he grinned as if he knew exactly what he was doing to her.

He brought the back of her hand up to his mouth for a kiss that lingered a little longer than socially acceptable. "Gemma. Drink?"

She nodded, marionette-style. "Wine."

"Preference?"

"White," she said, even though the gerbil, straining to get the wheel of her brain back on track, reminded her that white wine would give her a headache tomorrow.

"I'll be right back."

"You're not what?" the woman said, dragging Gem's attention back to her when she tapped the table.

"I'm sorry?" Gem raised her brow in confusion.

"You and Jason." The woman moved forward in her seat. "You're not a couple? You could have fooled me with the way you two look at each other." She introduced herself. "I'm Joann, Frank's administrative assistant."

Gem shook her hand. "Oh, hi. Nice to meet you. I'm Caroline's daughter, Gemma."

Joann smiled, poking at her salad. "I could tell. You look just like her." She speared a cherry tomato. "I never thought I'd see this day. Frank married again. Jason smiling and happy with a girl."

Gem paused with her water glass midair. "What do you mean?"

Joann held the tomato aloft. "Well, after Sandy passed, Frank was crushed."

"I mean about Jason. What do you mean, happy?" Jason had never struck Gem as being *unhappy*. Was he unhappy?

"Jason is… He was always so broody," Joann said, munching on the tomato. "Even as a teenager, he was always so serious. And girls would fawn all over him."

"Brooding? Really?" Gem scoffed. From the moment they met, Jason had been constantly laughing. At her. And then, of course, there was that ever-present arrogant smile.

"Speak of the devil." Joann pointed to Jason's chair.

He arrived with three drinks held between his hands. "Chardonnay for Gem, Kahlúa and cream for Joann, and ginger ale for me."

"You know me so well." Joann winked at Jason, accepting her drink. "Gemma and I were just talking about you," she said casually, sipping her cocktail, as if she hadn't broken rule number eight of girl code.

"You were?" Jason crossed his right ankle over his left knee. "Anything interesting?"

Gem flicked her hand in the air. "Oh, you know, only how she knew you when you were awkward and geeky."

He bent his head to her. "Those two words are not in my repertoire. Try super masculine and cool."

"Yes, the bow tie is very cool and masculine," she teased.

He patted it down. "I think it's fetching."

Gem did too, but she wasn't about to tell him that. His head was big enough as it was. She inched closer to him but spoke to Joann. "Do you have any good stories? Maybe an unfortunate haircut or prom incident? Did Mr. Perfect here flip out like Carrie?"

"No, no pig's blood." Joann leaned her temple on her index finger. "But he was homecoming king, if I remember correctly."

"Of course he was." Gem rolled her eyes when Jason jutted his chin out, extra peacocky.

"You're sitting next to royalty, Gemmie."

16

After the cake had been cut and the china cleared away, the dance party commenced. Caroline, usually never one to do more than a slight hip shake on the floor, let loose with the twist. She bounded over to Gem, reaching for her hands, spinning them both in a circle.

Gem hadn't ever seen her mother so full of joy. "You're glowing."

Caroline grinned, her cheeks pink, eyes slightly wet. "Gemma, I know you and I don't always see eye to eye, and you haven't always understood the decisions I've made, but I did everything with you in mind."

With all the guests dancing and singing around them, Caroline pulled Gem closer. "I always thought you deserved better than me."

Gem jerked away from Caroline's hold. "What? Mom, no, I—"

Caroline only smiled. "I was so young when I had you, and after your dad left, I didn't think I could do it on my own. I never felt good enough."

"Mom—"

Caroline shushed her with a fingertip to her own lips. "This is important. I know I didn't set a good example for you in that way. I settled for men who weren't good for me—and certainly not good enough for you—and I'm sorry. It took me a long time to realize I was strong enough on my own and that I didn't have to force a man into our lives just because I was afraid of failing you as a parent. I was afraid of being alone."

Gem's eyes burned with tears. Sure, she'd argued with her mother a lot, but she'd never blamed her for the choices the men in their lives had made. "You are strong, Mom. I always thought you were. And you did raise me on your own. Those other men..." Gem waved her hand off. "You thought you weren't a good enough mom or wife, but they weren't good enough for *you*."

Her mother smiled through her tears and hugged Gem. "I love you. Have I told you that lately?"

Gem smoothed back a chunk of hair that'd come down from her mom's French twist. "Not today."

"You're the most amazing girl." She kissed Gem's cheek. "You're everything I'm not and everything I wished you would be. Smart, independent, and so damn stubborn."

Even in the middle of the crowd, Gem's chest swelled with pride from her mother's compliments. They might as well have been the only two there. "You like that I'm stubborn?"

Caroline held her daughter's face between her hands, saying seriously, "It's one of my favorite things about you."

"I love you, Mom."

"But I need one more favor," Caroline added with a sheepish smile.

Gem snorted a laugh. "What?"

"Could you house-sit while we go away?"

The music changed and slowed down to something mid-tempo, and the women swayed back and forth. Gem nodded her answer. "Sure. Did Frank tell you where you're honeymooning yet?"

"Still a surprise. I hope it's somewhere—"

"May I cut in, Mrs. Santos?"

The two turned to a guy with his hand out to Gem, and Caroline delighted at the thirtysomething man sporting a trim goatee. "Oh, hello."

"Hi." He smiled at Caroline then at Gem. "I'm Martin. I work with Frank."

In Gem's three-second hesitation, Caroline took over and propelled her daughter toward him. "I'm going to find my husband. You two have fun!"

Gem smiled politely and took Martin's hand as he smoothly tugged her closer, guiding her in a slow circle. "I must say, you've stolen quite a bit of attention away from your mother tonight."

"I have?"

"I think most of the men in the room would agree."

Gem tried to force some imitation of a smile, but she wasn't interested in him or his one-liners. When he asked to get her a drink from the bar, she declined and found Frank for a spin around the floor. He danced his jacket and tie off, pulling at his suspenders, jumping in circles during "Shout," and by the time Gem finally got away, laughing and panting, the DJ called all the single ladies to the middle of the floor.

It was time for the bouquet toss.

Gem stalled until a family friend yanked her out to the front of the giggling group of women, and Caroline threw it over her head right to Gem, who sidestepped it. A little old lady picked it up and held it over her head like a trophy.

Next up was the garter. Frank, sweaty and sans suspenders, disappeared under Caroline's dress to reemerge with blue lace in hand. He twirled it around his finger as a large group of men formed, hooting and hollering. He threw it like a baseball into the center of the rowdy crew, where Jason's long arm reached up to catch it, and Gem shook her head in amusement as she sipped on a glass of champagne.

The band played some cheesy burlesque music, and someone brought a chair out to the center of the dance floor so Jason could push the garter up the old woman's leg. He made a production out of it, pretending to peek up her dress and then pass out. The woman, loving every second of the attention, laid a big kiss on him at the end of it.

When Jason strolled up to Gem a few minutes later, she wiped lipstick from his mouth. "Do you need a minute to yourself?"

"Got me hot under the collar." He undid his tie, leaving it hanging around his neck, and the look really started to make Gem hot under the collar. The man was lethal in a tux.

The music slowed down, the bandleader humming the first few notes of a Jason Mraz tune, and Jason held his hand up by his chest. "I think I've lost my date. 'Bout yay high, eyes that can murder a man. Sharp tongue but soft lips. Have you seen her?"

Even as his gaze narrowed to her mouth, his eyes twinkled with humor, and Gem wondered how this Prince Charming could have ever been the brooding type. She took his hand and let him lead her into a slow dance, enjoying the feel of his arms around her waist, her fingers toying with the ends of his hair at the nape of his neck. "I must admit, I'm a little jealous."

He splayed his hands wide against her spine, warming her from the inside out. "You should be. Cousin Mimi has been pinching my ass for years."

"She's your cousin?"

"Frank's eighty-four-year-old cousin, who was left a ton of money by her multimillionaire husband. She spends most of her time in Florida, but I get ten dollars in my birthday card every year."

She rested her temple on his shoulder. "I wish I'd have known that earlier. You know I like a big bank account."

She felt his chuckle rumble in his chest then his breath on her as he kissed the top of her head. When he moved one of her hands from around his neck to place her palm against his heart, she tipped her head up. With his steady heartbeat under her fingers and his heavy gaze on her, she thought he might open up his chest and allow her a peek around.

"You asked how I learned to dance. It was from my parents. They danced around the house all the time."

The grief was evident in the hunch of Jason's shoulders, as if he didn't want anyone else to hear his words, and Gem held on to him a little tighter. She'd never lost anyone she was close to but recognized how he struggled—still—with the reverberations of it. She pictured Jason as a young boy with his parents. She wondered if his father was the first one to teach him how to play basketball, if his mother sang to him at night. Then she imagined what it might feel like to have all that gone in an instant. How easy it might have been for a young teenage boy to cling to the things he could control and create a perfect image of himself to hide the raw, broken bits inside.

Everybody protected themselves in different ways. Gem did it by pushing people away before they could get too close. Jason did it by showing the world how *fine* he was.

So, she offered him the only thing she could in that moment —herself.

"It sounds like your parents had a lovely relationship. I'd like to hear more about them one day, if you're willing."

His throat bobbed on a swallow, and he nodded, wrapping his hand along her jaw, his thumbs skating along her cheekbones. He slowly lowered his lips, his breath smelling sweet like cake icing, and she stretched up to meet him halfway.

"Jason, hi!"

GEM AND JASON spun around at the sound of the voice. *That* voice.

It was Bridget.

And she was coming toward them.

"You've got to be kidding me," Gem murmured, stepping away from Jason, although he loathed to let go of her.

"What are you doing here?" he said to Bridget, sure she was not on the guest list.

"I was having dinner with my parents on the patio, and we wanted to congratulate the happy couple." She held out her hand to Gem. "Hi, I'm Bridget."

"I know. We've met."

"Oh." Bridget smiled ruefully. "Sorry. Um, Jason, could I talk to you?"

Gem's head toggled between Bridget and Jason, and he wanted to show her there was nothing between them anymore. He shoved his hands into his pockets. "Yeah. Sure."

Bridget's normally bright eyes dimmed, her hands uncharacteristically restless by her waist. "In private. Please, Jase?"

It was unlike her to ask for anything. Bridget was a go-getter —in work, in romance, she took. She didn't ask. He got a weird feeling about it, and he looked to Gem to gauge her reaction.

She huffed, tossing her hand out to him. "Whatever, *Jase*. I'll be at the bar."

He watched her walk away, the silky material of her dress clinging to her hips and ass, and he ran a rough hand over his face.

"Did I interrupt something?" Bridget asked, raising her shoulder.

He sighed and pointed to a couple of empty chairs at a table. "Yeah. What's up?"

She smiled, although it didn't reach her eyes. "That tuxedo fits you really well."

"Bridget, what do you want?"

"To say hi."

His attention fell to the bar, where a dark-haired guy had crept up next to Gem. He worked at the firm...Matt or Mark or something. Jason started to stand, needing to go to Gem. "Come on, Bridge, this isn't—"

She stopped him with her hand on his wrist. "Where are you going?"

"I have a date."

"Don't go." She added her other hand, towing him back down to his chair. "I need you."

"I told you. I can't be with you," he said, watching as Matt or Mark touched Gem's elbow, sliding a drink of something dark in front of her. Jason ground his molars at the audacity of this guy, although Gem pushed it away and accepted a new drink from the bartender.

"Please, Jason," Bridget said, her voice rising in what sounded like alarm. "My mom's sick. That's why we're out to dinner tonight. My dad thought it might take her mind off it. She got the results back a few days ago, ovarian cancer."

Jason sank back down into his chair, briefly forgetting about Gem and Matt/Mark.

"Bridge, I'm so sorry." He gathered her up in his arms as her eyes turned glassy, and he handed her a napkin from the table. Letting her cry on his shoulder for a few minutes, Jason found his focus floating back to Gem every once in a while, her actions becoming looser, her laugh a little louder with every sip of her drink. She'd told him she didn't do shots, but from the lime she sucked on, it looked like she was downing tequila.

"She's starting treatment next week," Bridget said, stealing Jason's attention.

"That's good. How's she feeling? How are you feeling?"

They'd broken up, and even though he would rather be with Gem at the moment, he also didn't want to leave this woman who needed support at the moment.

"She's trying to be strong, she's putting up a good front, but I'm so scared. They only found it because my mom had been having pain for a while. She tried to ignore it, thinking it would go away, but..." She held the napkin against her eyes, and it darkened with a mix of tears and makeup. "I'm sorry to dump this on you, but I saw you here and you look so handsome, and I felt, I don't know..." She lifted her face to him, her pretty features marred with streaks of mascara. "I miss you, and I needed to tell you."

"Bridget, if you need someone to talk to, I'll be there for you. But only as a friend, okay?"

She nodded, a wave of fresh tears springing to her eyes, and lunged forward, hugging him.

Back at the bar, Mark slid his hand up Gem's shoulder, and she shifted as if to nudge him off. That was when Jason's eyes met hers, and he exhaled harshly. He needed to go to her. "Bridge, I hate to—"

She cut him off with a kiss on the mouth, and Jason startled, immediately taking his hands off her, lurching his head back. "Bridget, no."

He pushed away from his chair, panic flooding his chest at the way Gem's face turned stony. She'd seen it, and she tossed back her drink in one gulp then gestured for another. *Fuck.*

Bridget stared up at him, crestfallen, and he tried to let her down as easy and fast as possible. "You're going through a really hard time right now, I get it. You need someone to be there for you, but I'm not that guy, Bridget. I'm sorry. You deserve someone who will give you his full attention. I meant it when I said I'll be there if you want to talk, but that's it."

She nodded and covered her face with the napkin again, and he gave her one more apology before heading straight to the bar, where Gem teetered on the edge of her stool, laughing with Matt/Mark, who didn't seem at all concerned.

Jason grabbed at Gem's wrist, righting her. "Come on, I think you've had enough to drink."

Matt/Mark lifted his glass in Gemma's direction. "She's all right."

"Yeah, I'm all right."

Jason motioned to the door, tugging on her hand again. "Gemma, let's go."

"No," she snapped and pulled away from him. "I'm having a good time with..."

"Martin," the other guy supplied. "Don't worry, I got her. I'll take her home."

Jason hated him. Hated everything about him. His goatee, his stupid drunk laugh, and his complete disregard for Gem's safety.

"Seriously, Gem. It's not funny anymore. Let's go."

Martin put a hand on Jason's shoulder. "Buddy, don't worry—"

Jason glowered at his hand then back at his dopey face. "Listen, Mark."

"Martin."

"I've seen you around, so I know you work for Santos and Mitchell. That means you know I'm Jason Mitchell, head of the development department." He shoved Martin's hand from his shoulder. "I don't give a shit what your name is."

Martin's face dropped, his ears tinged pink, a kid caught with his hand in the cookie jar.

"You know damn well Gemma is not fine, so you can put your dick away because she's sure as shit not going home with you." Jason stepped up, literally, toe to toe with Martin, lowering his voice to drive the point home. "And if you continue to disrespect the CEO's new stepdaughter, I will make sure somebody else has your job. I'm positive there is a college intern somewhere who could do it."

Martin stuttered a response as Jason hauled Gem off the stool to the closest exit. Rage took over. Rage at that motherfucker, at Bridget's bad fucking timing, and at Gem's own senselessness. After everything she'd experienced, she was going to let it go down like that?

Yet she dug her feet into the floor, twisting her arms. "Let go of me."

He managed to get her out of the reception area and into a hallway, where he crowded her against the wall. He meant to shield her, but when she glared at him, he backed away two inches.

"You were making a fool of yourself in there," he said, his anger picking the worst words he could have chosen. But he couldn't do anything now. They were out there.

"Fuck you and your high horse," she said, jutting her chin out.

Feeling out of control, he yanked at his hair. "Gemma, how could you do that?" He waved his hand back toward the reception hall. "You're drunk, and that guy was all over you. Why would you—"

"Why would I drink and flirt with a man paying me attention? Oh, I don't know, Jason, because it feels good. Because I like it. Because I can and I want to. Don't think I'm some damsel in distress because I told you something from my past, and now, you're a white knight saving me from any random guy. I don't need that from anyone, including you."

He didn't think she needed saving all the time, but that guy didn't strike him as the most upstanding citizen. Besides, she'd come as his date. But as usual, it was two steps forward and one step back. Here they were, fighting. Again.

He jammed the heels of his palms against his eyes then shot

his arms out to the sides. He was crawling out of his skin. She only stood there, arms crossed, face completely rigid.

"You can't go around doing whatever you want," he said, grasping at straws.

"All right," she said casually. "So, you can go around kissing any woman you want, but I can't have a drink with someone?"

"That's why you got drunk and hung all over him? Because you're mad at me?" He wanted to punch something—preferably Martin—but more than anything, he wanted to go one goddamn day without having words with Gemma. He curled his fist against the wall, barricading her in. "I'm tired of this tit for tat game, Gemma."

She needled her index finger into his chest. "Don't blame this on me. You kissed her. Right there, in front of everyone."

"I didn't kiss her. She kissed me."

"Semantics." She ducked under his arm.

"Her mom is sick and—"

Scooping up the side of her dress, she bent down and kicked off her heels, dropping down two or three inches, but she set her shoulders back, her gaze unrelenting. She aimed straight for his heart. "I didn't make a fool of myself, Jason. *You* made a fool of me."

Direct hit.

Then she grabbed her shoes and walked away.

17

Gem woke up, still in her dress, with one leg hanging off the bed and George Clooney asleep next to her head. Groaning, she rolled to the floor, the long silk gathering around her knees. The pounding in her temples recalled the bottle of white and that musty Uber ride home. Not exactly how she'd expected the night to go.

An old-school clock on her nightstand flipped numbers, 10:23, and she wiped her eyes, rubbing makeup off onto the back of her hand. Her mother and Frank were leaving on their honeymoon this afternoon, and she needed to get up and shower. But at the moment, everything was a tad blurry.

She grabbed her cell phone from the floor, her home screen flooded with well-wishes and questions about the wedding from the girls, begging for photos. She hadn't plugged it in to charge last night and the battery life was at four percent, enough to text her friends a selfie with the message **long story**.

She let out a pitiful laugh. Her hopes for a future with Jason went down the drain, along with her dignity. What a waste of a perfectly beautiful dress.

It was the exact reason why she never planned more than a

week in advance. She was a fly-by-night kind of girl, remaining unattached and uninjured. Yet here she was, on the floor of her apartment. Disappointment settled in her bones like cement, keeping her there, as a physical ache bloomed in her chest.

She and Jason were on the cusp of something amazing, so to have it wither in her hands like the brown leaves of a plant that never really had a chance to grow made her want to throw the whole thing in the compost bin. Forget it ever happened.

Fortunately, now that the wedding was over, she could.

The pads of her feet throbbed as she toddled to the shower, where she turned on the cold water. Each drop pricked her skin like a needle, erasing the feeling of Jason's searing touch. If only she could somehow bleach her brain of the memories. Of the emotion weaving over his features as he gave his toast and then talked about his parents while they danced. Of him pressing her hand against his heart, of the small glimpse she had of his insides.

Then his reaction of her drinking with...Mark? And, of course, Bridget.

She wanted—needed—to forget it all.

When Gem pulled up into the Santos's driveway, her mom and Frank were in the midst of loading matching suitcases into a limo. She took out her sunglasses and, goddamn it, they were the ones Jason had given her—she couldn't escape him—but put them on anyway to cover the dark circles, before stepping out of her car.

"You're just in time." Frank beamed, bear-hugging his new stepdaughter. "Did you have a good time last night? I did." He kissed both of her cheeks. "Looks like somebody had a little too much fun."

With rosy cheeks and her hair unusually loose around her shoulders, Caroline grabbed Gem's hands. "We're going to Thailand! Can you believe it?"

"Thailand. Nice," Gem croaked.

"What should we bring you home?" Caroline asked as she double-checked her purse, presumably for her passport.

Frank raised his index finger. "How about a monkey? I hear they hang out anywhere, in houses and restaurants."

Gem had to clear her throat before answering. It cracked anyway. "No thanks, Frank. No wild animals."

"All right, then." He clapped. "Asia awaits, Mrs. Santos. Let's get going." He held the door open.

Caroline kissed Gem's cheek. "Make sure you turn the alarm on before you go to bed."

"Okay."

"And water the plants in the foyer."

"I will. Have a good time."

"I left some cash in front of the coffeepot."

"Honey, she can handle it," Frank said, laughing as he drew his wife into the limo and shut the door. Caroline blew kisses from the window when they drove off, and as soon as they were out of sight, Gem made her way into the house.

She headed to Frank's den, decorated with leather recliners and a sectional. Long shelves were stacked with hundreds of movies, and a projector screen hung down from the ceiling. She took a running leap onto the couch, pulled a knit blanket around her, and drifted off to sleep for a long winter's nap.

WEDNESDAY AFTERNOON, Jason drummed his fingers on his desk. A cold cup of coffee sat untouched next to the phone as he read the report in front of him for the hundredth time. He cursed and sank down in his chair as his mind wandered to Gemma. Also for the hundredth time.

He'd texted her once every day since the wedding, and even though he understood why she was upset, he still half expected her to respond. The scent of vanilla followed him everywhere;

he couldn't get it out of his head. He dreamed of her pink lips, her fingers in his hair, and her naked back under his palm. Even those minor physical remembrances of her had him waking up every morning painfully hard.

He had to see her, convince her of the truth. He felt nothing for Bridget because Gemma had stolen his heart from the moment they met, no matter how hard they both fought against it. He'd briefly toyed with the idea of going to her apartment, but he knew she'd hate that—find it wholly presumptuous—and probably not let him in anyway. So, there wasn't much left for him to do. Maybe tomorrow he would go to her yoga studio. It was public, and she couldn't very well throw him out of the class.

Or could she? He wouldn't put it past her.

Setting aside that particular debate, he laser focused back on the report, and by the time he checked the clock again, it was after eight o'clock. The floor had emptied except for the maintenance workers. He still needed to send out a contract Frank had signed, but after scouring his desk and Joann's office, the papers were nowhere to be found. The only other place he knew to look was Frank's home office.

Everything was dark when he opened Frank's front door. He turned off the alarm, flipped on a few light switches, then went upstairs, where he rustled through desk drawers and a filing cabinet before finally locating the folder he needed. Sudden movement caught his eye, and he reared back. Gemma was there, a flip-flop raised over her head as if she were about to pummel him with it.

"Oh my god, Jason." She heaved out a breath and slumped backward. "What are you doing here?"

"What am I doing here? What are *you* doing here? And did you really think you could do actual damage with a flip-flop?"

"It's the only weapon I had." When she tossed the shoe at him, he batted it away. "And I asked you first."

"I need to send this contract out." He held up the papers as evidence and watched the fear drain from her eyes, replaced by fire, apparently remembering herself.

"How'd you get in?"

"I know the alarm code and have keys." He held up said keys. "I did live here. What's your excuse?"

"House-sitting." She brushed her hair back from her face, the movement calling focus to her body. He'd been too preoccupied before to notice she wore only underwear and a thin white shirt. He could see right through it.

He forced his eyes up from her nipples, and for fuck's sake, he deserved an award for that. "Did you get my text messages?"

"Yeah." She threw a hand on her hip, an annoyed scowl slanting her lips, her fingers lifting her shirt enough to display a two-inch-wide strip of skin above her purple boy shorts. They were his new favorite thing, and he shut his eyes to them, losing his train of thought. "You don't, uh, wear clothes anymore?"

"I was in bed. Sorry I don't meet your pajama standards. I'm sure you sleep fully dressed."

The mental picture of her in bed had him shooting his eyes back open, and he felt the papers fold under his tightening grip before throwing them down. "You always do this. You blame me for this high-and-mighty bullshit. I'm not like that."

Gemma muttered an argument under her breath, and between the stress at work and the direction this conversation was headed, Jason's temper exploded. His arms flew out at his sides. "I don't have standards. In fact, if I had my way, I'd prefer you completely naked. All the time."

She huffed, her lip curling in anger. "Do you think I'm dumb? You must."

"What?"

"You think I'm going to fall for that? You come in here and toss around a few ridiculous lines about getting naked and think I'll come crawling back?" She took two steps closer to him, hissing, "You get to do whatever you want, thinking you can pick me up and put me down at your leisure? You're wrong. I'm not going to wait around for you. I am not anyone's second choice!" She had risen up on her toes, shouting the last word at him.

Jason held his hand up to quiet her. "Believe it or not, Gemma, but you don't exactly give off that weepy kind of woe-is-me vibe, and, quite frankly, I wouldn't be here, in this never-ending cage match with you, if you did. You don't have to tell me how fucking tough you are. I already know. So, can you, for once, shut up and give me a chance to explain?"

"There's nothing to explain. You left me at the reception to go play nice with another woman."

"I know, and I was wrong," he said, but his irritation got the best of him. "Something else to add to the list. Along with the car I drive, what I eat, what I wear, everything I say. It's all wrong."

"Because you are wrong. You can't talk to me the way you do. You can't—"

"You think this is all my fault? Everything we've ever said or done to each other since we've met? It's all my fault?" Jason stood right in front of her, his breath ragged as if he'd run a marathon—being with Gemma sometimes felt like that—as he stared down at her. With their bodies mere centimeters from each other, Gemma's indignation started to wilt, and something close to tears took its place.

"You can't look at me the way you do and then choose some other girl," she said in a barely audible voice, and if he could have ripped his heart out of his chest to show it to her, he would have.

"I can't help it. I can't help looking at you." He dared to touch her, his fingertips tracing over her jaw. "I can't stop this. What do you want me to say?"

"I want you to tell me the truth," she said hoarsely.

He ventured lower, curving his hands around her neck. "The

truth is I've never felt like this before. I know you don't believe me, but I don't fight with people, Gemma. I don't like rocking the boat, and I normally don't like people I argue with every day like I do with you. But that's why it's different. I want to be here with you. For some godforsaken reason, I would rather fight with you than be with anyone else."

"You're right. I don't believe you." Gem's voice was small, and her eyes, usually so bright and full of spirit, dulled.

And it was Jason's fault.

His body coursed with a need to show her how it could be between them. All he wanted was to quiet her dissension with his mouth, but he needed her to come to him. He had to prove he wasn't the guy she thought he was. He clasped her arms, his fingers holding her biceps. "Believe me. I'm here, Gemma, and I'm not letting you go."

When her forehead pressed to his sternum, she mumbled words into his chest, and he lifted her chin. "What?"

"You make me feel stupid," she said.

He bent his knees, getting closer to her eye level. "Why?"

"For wanting to be with you."

His heart galloped away, and he couldn't help his smile. He molded his hand to her jaw. "That's not stupid."

"It is when you grow up with a mother who only ever concerned herself with jumping into relationships. I never thought I would be like that, but that's what it feels like with you. Like I'm jumping without looking."

He breathed out a sigh, drawing the tip of his nose along hers. "But you're not jumping alone. I am too."

She swallowed, taking a moment to digest his words, and he held steady, although his eyebrows rose slightly in question. "Gem?"

Stretching up on her toes, she tangled her fingers in his hair to pull him close so she could touch her lips to his, and in that instant, he forgot about everything else. Gemma and her perfect, smart mouth and her fearless yet sensitive spirit had ruined him. Past Jason no longer existed. Future Jason had yet to be shaped. As long as it was by her hands, he didn't care what it looked like.

He moved his hands under her T-shirt, sinking his fingertips into her waist, and he parted her lips with his tongue as he pressed her up against the doorframe. Lifting her slightly, he dragged her leg to his hip and left openmouthed kisses across her throat, nipping at her ear. She arched against him, sweet and soft and *his*, and he couldn't get enough of her, couldn't touch or kiss or breathe in enough.

Gem roamed her hands over his body, down his shoulders, chest, and stomach before unbuttoning his fly and slipping her fingers between his pants and underwear. He bit into the soft skin at the curve of her shoulder to keep from howling in pleasure as she familiarized herself with the feel of him. It wasn't until she slid her thumb under the elastic, scraping against the root of his cock, that he froze. "Stop."

She paused, her fingers wrapped around him. "What?"

He hung his head, exhaling roughly. "I don't have any condoms."

"I do."

He slowly raised his head, his defeat rallying to anticipation. "You do?"

She tossed him the sexiest smile he'd ever seen over her shoulder and towed him down the hall to the guest bedroom. She rummaged through her knit bag and held up what appeared to be a tiny tin can.

"What's that?"

"A condom."

When she tossed it to him, he caught it in one hand and flipped the packet in his palm.

"It's vegan." She pointed to it. "With recyclable packaging." Then she pointed to him. "Now, take your clothes off."

He laughed, grabbed her hips and tossed her on the bed, before peeling his shirt off. Gem propped herself up on her elbows, shamelessly gaping at him, and he stripped down to black boxer-briefs, allowing her to look her fill. He'd never lacked confidence, but under her wanton gaze, he felt enough strength to scoop her up and fly her out into the universe.

As it was, though, he had better things to do and crawled onto the bed next to her. "Your turn."

She raised her arms so he could lift the shirt over her head, then it was his turn to stare. He'd seen her before, at the pool in her bikini. He'd had a hint of what her lithe form felt like under his palm, but with her laid out before him like a feast, he didn't know where to start. He trailed kisses from her chin to her belly button and back, leaving goose bumps in his wake. He smoothed his hands over one of her breasts and then the other, sucked at the pink tips until she writhed beneath him, her hips rising off the mattress. Still, he took his time, kissing the small birthmark on one of her upper ribs, then stroked down her sides, tugging at those hip-hugging panties of hers.

She grabbed at his neck, trying to drag his mouth back to hers, but he only lowered himself down her body, tucking his nose into the apex of her thighs. She smelled like heaven, and he kissed her there, over the cotton.

"Please, Jason, please, please," she panted, tugging at his head, her heels digging into the bed on either side of him.

"Don't worry. I'm here, and I'm not letting you go," he said, reminding her of his promise, dragging her underwear down and off her legs. He sat back, admiring her. "You are beautiful."

She let out a rough breath and sat up, reaching for him. She wrapped her hand around his hard length. "I'm already naked. You don't have to sweet-talk me."

It took every ounce of restraint in him, but he gently removed her hand and kissed her palm before pressing the back of it into the bed, holding her still as he moved back down between her legs. His first taste of her had him groaning, her flavor and heat filling his mouth. He lapped it up, her noises and jagged exhales filling his ears, and he could feel her tension growing, her legs straining around his shoulders.

"Right there, right there, right there," she said, and he slid one finger inside her while he sucked and nibbled and tongued her. She tried to buck away from him, incoherent words tumbling from her mouth, but he only pressed more firmly against her, using both his hands to angle her hips up.

He kept his eyes focused on her as she fisted the comforter in her hands and growled out her pleasure in complete abandon, her climax rippling over his tongue. His hips thrust against the mattress of their own accord, his need bubbling up until it was almost impossible to think of anything but being inside her now.

Now.

Now.

"You look fucking incredible when you're wild like that," he said, grabbing the tin and struggling to open it in his haste. She laughed and stole it from his grasp, flicking her dark eyes up at him from under heavy lids. She removed the condom and carefully slid it down his shaft, giving him a playful tug before pushing him down on the bed.

"I want to see it again," he said and yanked her leg over him, holding her steady as he lined himself up at her entrance and she lowered onto him inch by delicious inch. "Fuck," he ground out, closing his eyes. He knew it would be good, but this, this was *so good*. He feared if he dared to look at her, he might spontaneously combust.

But then she made the choice for him, dragging his hands up her body to place them over her breasts. "Touch me," she ordered, and he snapped his eyes open, her fingers demonstrating how she wanted to be pinched and pulled. "Make me wild."

He did as she asked and played with her nipples, rocking his hips up against hers, and she licked her lips, staring down at where their bodies met. Her skin was flushed and dotted with sweat, and there was never a more gorgeous sight.

"Yes, like that," she whispered, tilting her weight forward, finding the angle she needed. "Jason."

He loved the sound of his name on her lips. Loved how she moaned it. Loved how he could feel her pulse quickening around him.

"You're close, I can feel it," he said and pulled her body down toward him so he could suck one of her nipples into his mouth, holding on to her hips to piston up into her harder, faster. He gritted his teeth, the familiar burn building deep within him, his spine stiffening, his skin going hot all over. "You look so good riding me like this, Gemma. I want to feel you come on my cock."

She tossed her head back and forth, lost in her pleasure.

"One more. Come on, Gem. Give it to me." With his pluck at her other nipple, she was coming again, and he gave in too, stuttering his thrusts, his mouth finding any part of her to suck and hold on to as he left this earthly plane.

"Hey," she wheezed out, pushing off him with her hands against his chest to settle against his side. "You'll leave a mark."

He laughed and wrapped one arm around her, the other flopping over his forehead. "Sorry, not sorry."

They were both slightly clammy but cuddled together for a few moments before she walked to the bathroom. He needed a few minutes to himself anyway to get his scrambled brain back into functioning order.

Once she finished, he took her place, cleaning himself up, planning on having some more naked time, but when he reopened the door to the bedroom, she was poking her head and arms through her T-shirt. "Hey, whoa, what are you doing?"

She raised an eyebrow at him as she covered up all her good bits.

"I set one rule, and already, you're breaking it," he said, settling back on the bed. "I said if I had my way, I'd want you naked all the time."

"When do I ever let you have your way without a fight?"

"Never." He grinned, looping a finger around the collar of her shirt to tug her in for a kiss. "But I'm okay wrestling it off you."

"Don't stretch it out!" she whined, bobbing away from his hold. "This is one of my favorite shirts. Perfectly worn-in."

"Yes," he agreed. "My favorite too. But, really..." He tipped his head off to the side, in the same direction all their other clothes lay on the floor. "Off, please."

After a few seconds, when he really wasn't sure if she'd comply or not, she stripped it off. "Only because you said please."

He immediately pressed a kiss to her breastbone then her throat and curled her into his side. He buried his nose in her hair, inhaling the intoxicating vanilla scent.

"I like you," he said in the understatement of the century, and she snuggled in closer to his chest.

"I like you too."

Not too long later, with this wild woman firmly held in his arms and his breaths matching hers, he drifted off to sleep. His body satisfied, his mind at ease.

18

Gem rolled over onto her stomach, her arms and legs starfishing to the corners of the bed. Her eyelids fluttered open to find a note on the pillow next to her, scribbled in permanent marker.

I had to go in to work early. You're too cute to wake up when you sleep. —*J*

A nervous energy started in her toes, spread up through her fingers, and before she could stop herself, she texted the girls. **Guess where I am right now??**

When they didn't immediately message back, she took a picture of Jason's note and sent it. Still, no response.

Don't make me squee on my ooooooown

A few seconds later, Sam got back to her. **Tell me that is the Boy Scout's handwriting?! That means you forgave him?**

Gem had, of course, kept her girls up-to-date on every high and low between her and Jason for the last month and a half. Bronte, ever the optimist, thought it would all turn out fine. Laney had told Gem to follow her gut. Sam, though, was warier. She'd been through the wringer with her parents' relationships and didn't fully trust Jason after so many run-ins with Bridget.

We have to talk more about that situation, but I know and trust that he was never stringing me along.

If you say so. Sam sent a Michael Scott GIF, displaying her mocking suspicion.

I like him, Gem said simply.

Then I'm happy for you. I'll save my judgment for when I meet him. We are going to meet him, right?

Gem sent a couple upside-down smiley faces. **You know I'm not a long-term planner.**

Sam's only response was a side-eye.

After throwing on some clothes, Gemma headed to work, avoiding Andrew's eagle eye for what he said was "morning-after face," and set up shop in the back room, sorting through new merchandise.

During Bronte's lunch break, she FaceTimed Gem. She pointed at Gem with a carrot stick. "You look different today."

"I would hope so. I saw God last night."

Bronte tossed her head back in laughter. "It's good?"

Gem widened her eyes and nodded once sluggishly.

"Ugh. Okay." Bronte waved her hand, swatting at an imaginary fly. "Don't brag," she said with a smile, although Gem didn't need to know Bronte and Hunter's history to see the longing in the slight downturn of her mouth. "So, now what?"

Gem stacked a few face toners on the floor then flattened the box they'd arrived in. "I don't know."

"Are you guys together or...?"

"I don't know. It only happened last night. We didn't do too much talking."

Bronte set her chin on her fist, dipping a small piece of broccoli in what looked like ranch dressing. "I figured, but did you think about it at all?"

"Think about what?" Gem ripped open another box.

"The future," Bronte said, as if she were telling Gemma it was Thursday.

Thinking about the future. Easy for Bronte, the ultimate planner, to say. Sam had her next few years mapped out with her schoolwork. And Laney, she didn't need a plan with all her luck; good things simply fell into her lap.

Gem was the odd one out. A lifetime of men disappointing her didn't exactly bode well for making future plans. She'd rather stay loose, focus on today instead of worrying about tomorrow. Making plans led to expectations, and unmet expectations led to worlds of hurt. She'd rather avoid that, if possible.

After hanging up with Bronte, Gem finished her work, eager to head to the yoga studio. It was a welcome change from Andrew's relentless questions all day.

What does Jason do for a living?

How much does he make?

Does he own a house?

Is his hair really as soft as it looks?

Yoga was exactly what she needed, and she began the class with her eyes closed, as usual. "Clear your mind." She inhaled through her nose. "Relax your mouth." And exhaled through her lips. "Let the tension from today roll away with every breath." Another inhale. "Arms up." And exhale. "Swan dive to forward bend."

The class followed as she folded in half, taking more deep breaths. "Back up to mountain pose."

Gem rose back up, opening her eyes, and there was Jason in the back of the room, hands pressed together in front of his chest. The butterflies woke back up, fluttering in her stomach, her heart beating at the speed of their flapping wings. Heat flushed her cheeks, and she bit her lip, covering the idiotic smile she knew she'd been sporting all day.

Continuing the class, she felt his eyes on her the whole time. Attempting to keep her back to him as she helped students adjust their movements, she made her way past him, but he stretched out his long arm and flicked her thigh.

She whipped her head around to find a grin plastered across his face.

She hated that she loved that face so much. She'd forgive a lot for that stupid grin.

At the end of the hour, everyone left except for Jason, who stayed seated on his mat as Gem went about the room, picking up her supplies.

"I was thinking we could have pizza tonight," he said, and she piled up a few blocks in the corner of the room, tossing him a look.

"It's weird I have to keep reminding you I'm vegan, when the night we met, that's, like, all you talked about."

"Patently false," he said, towing her down to his lap as she approached him, and positioned her legs on either side of him. "I did my research. I grabbed a few frozen vegan pizzas from the store after work."

"Really?" She played with his hair—because, yes, it was incredibly soft—feeling her cheeks stretch wide. She didn't think she'd ever smiled so much as she had in the last twenty-four hours.

He nodded, moving his hands to her thighs, where he plucked at the material covering them. "I love these pants on you."

"Does that mean you're coming over to my parents' house tonight?"

"Well, when you put it like that..." He laughed, and she grimaced.

"This is weirdly incestuous, isn't it? We're basically stepsiblings."

"It's fine. We're not related," he said with a sideways smile, kissing away her horror. "Nothing untoward." He kissed her chin. "Back to the issue at hand. Is it okay with you if I come over tonight?"

When she made a show of thinking about it, he slipped his

hands to her waist, underneath her shirt. "I'm coming over. With pizza. The cardboard kind for you, the real kind for me."

She smacked his wandering hands away and stood up, lugging Jason up with her. He walked her out after she locked up, and he opened her car door for her, leaning inside to kiss her cheek. "I'll be over in an hour."

After stopping at her apartment to feed all her animals and give George Clooney a scratch behind his ears, she was off again to Frank and Caroline's house. By the time she'd showered and changed, she heard Jason thumping around in the kitchen.

His back was to her as he grabbed plates from the cabinet, the muscles in his back visible beneath his tight gray T-shirt.

"Smells good," she said, and he turned, his eyes alight as he took her in.

"Those pants look familiar."

She pinched the long flannel pajama pants that she'd rolled up around her hips. "You said I never wear real clothes."

"So, you stole mine?" He pulled out a stool for her at the kitchen island. "Where'd you find them?"

"I went on a little tour of your room when I got home." She sat down and propped her chin in her hand, watching him slide on a mitt to remove the pizzas from the oven, placing them on hot pads on the counter. He was so domesticated.

"These pants were hiding a few *Playboys* in one of your drawers." She held up her right hand. "But I won't tell. I didn't even know they still printed physical copies anymore."

"Hey, when you're thirteen and your friend's older brother offers you pictures of naked ladies, you don't turn it down, no matter the format." He offered her a plate with a slice of her pizza on it. "Your cardboard, madam."

When she bit into it, he paused with his slice halfway to his mouth, a piece of pepperoni sliding off with a glob of cheese.

"What?" she asked mid-chew, and he shook his head, bemused.

There was something about his enigmatic smile, the same one he'd worn the first night they met when he'd insinuated he had caught her changing from her shorts to her skirt in Frank's driveway, that told her he had another secret.

"Nothing." He bit into his own animal-product junk. "How was your day?"

Maybe it was the comfortable way he spoke about Bare Necessities and laughed about Andrew, but the effortlessness of their conversation scared her. An everyday, home from work, kiss on the cheek kind of conversation. It was scary because it was so easy. Ease that slipped minutes into hours, days into weeks, years into decades, and suddenly—as Jason waxed poetic about the science behind the eco-friendly renovations to the Empire State Building, and how he was trying to use those same principles on new developments—she could see it all.

Dinners after work.

Quick kisses over coffee in the morning.

Texts about items they needed from the grocery store.

The future.

"You okay?" Jason asked after a while, wiping off his fingers on a napkin, almost his entire pizza devoured. Gem had only gotten down two pieces before she gave up, a slightly woozy feeling in her belly like she'd drunk too much.

"Yeah, yeah. I'm fine. I was...wondering if you brought dessert with you too."

To answer, he hopped over to the gym bag he'd packed and pulled out a box of condoms.

She put her hands on her hips. "First of all, those are made with casein, and second of all, it's really presumptuous of you to think I'd let you stay over."

"Is it, though?" He closed the gap between them. "Technically, this is my home too." He linked his arms around her middle, inching his mouth closer to hers. "And in that case, I don't need your permission. You're only babysitting this little sardine can, after all."

She murmured her assent. "Good point."

Speaking against her lips, he said, "I don't know what casein is."

"Those condoms aren't vegan. Casein is a milk protein that the latex is—"

He shushed her with a kiss, his tongue teasing into her mouth. "We don't have to use them if you don't want to. I have a lot of ideas about what else we can do."

Her body practically hummed in anticipation, and he backed away two inches, raising a challenging eyebrow. "First one upstairs gets the first orgasm."

Gem pushed off his chest and bounded out of the kitchen. Jason's laughter reverberated off the walls as he chased after her. She had lots of ideas too.

THE NEXT FEW days were a blur of sex, Gem's homemade blueberry-and-banana pancakes, Jason's favorite superhero movies, and more sex. They woke up Sunday morning in his old bedroom. A few posters still clung to the gray-painted walls, along with one framed photo of Jason in a cap and gown next to Frank.

Jason yawned and rolled onto his back, blinking awake in Gem's direction. She stretched like a cat, languid and soft, and he ran his hand along her stomach, saying, "Morning."

Refusing to open her eyes, she draped one arm over his torso. "I couldn't sleep last night. You were squirming all over the place."

"Really? Sorry. Must've been my dreams." He ran a hand over his face. "Have you been awake long?"

"No." This time, she crooked her neck back to look at him,

her bangs falling in front of her eyes. He opened his mouth to let her know how pretty she was in the morning, but she cut him off, asking, "What were you dreaming about?"

"My parents."

"Do you dream about them a lot?"

He shrugged. "Sometimes."

"Do you want to talk about it?" She stacked her hands on top of each other on his chest, elevating her chin on them, and he was once again struck by how simple it was to tell her the truth. He'd always been private, particularly when it came to his family, but he wanted to tell Gemma what happened. He wanted to tell her everything.

Mistaking his pause for something else, she backtracked. "You don't have to tell me if you don't want to."

He offered her a little smile and wound a lock of her hair around his finger as he spoke in a soft tone. "When I dream about them, they're alive. They're talking and laughing and dancing, sometimes with me. It's like I'm ten again or something. My friend is really into psychics and stuff, and he said that when I have those dreams, it's them trying to communicate with me." He huffed out an incredulous laugh. "I don't know about that."

Gem put a hand over his heart, drawing lazy figure eights. "What were they like?"

Memories inundated his mind, and he sighed in contentment. It had taken him almost a decade to be able to think of his parents without getting choked up. "My mom's name was Jane, and she was the quintessential mom, cooking and baking. She was the mom who brought the orange slices to basketball games. You know that kind of mom?"

"I've heard of her," Gem said, giving him a half smile. "What about your dad?"

"Everybody called him Bill, except for her. She called him Billy. That's what I remember most about him. The way he perked up when he heard her say his name. I was just a kid, but I knew they loved each other a lot."

"What happened?"

Even though Gem could ask any and all questions she wanted, that one was still tough to answer. He wasn't there that night, and when he was younger, his imagination used to spiral out of control, inventing terrible images of what it might have looked like. Anchoring himself to the present and Gem's deep brown eyes, he told her, "They went out to dinner, and my dad was driving them home when a drunk driver hit them from behind."

Gem's eyes closed tight, wincing at the information.

"Their car spun out of control and flipped. My parents weren't wearing their seat belts. They were dead before the ambulance arrived."

Jason had been through enough therapy to be able to relay that information with some detachment. As a thirteen-year-old kid, he didn't know how to process his grief, though as he got older, it had been to have every detail in his life in order. No surprises, good or bad. It was better for him to take the straight and narrow; he could see exactly what was coming and where he was going.

As if Gem could read his thoughts, she leaned up on her elbows. "That's why you're so straitlaced."

"Hmm?" He tipped his chin down, brushing her hair off her shoulder. "Why I'm what?"

She counted off with her fingers. "You're super smart, good at everything you do, your house is spotless. I mean, you even make your bed. What single guy does that? You like everything perfect."

He rolled onto his side, supporting his head with his hand, thinking back to those middle school years. "I wasn't always like that. I went through a rebellious period. I was having trouble dealing with everything, and I got into trouble. I was drinking, smoking a lot of pot, staying out late."

She wrinkled her nose. "I can't picture it."

"The last straw was this party the summer before I started high school. Frank found me at this kid's house at one in the morning or something, and right there, he laid into me. Verbally kicked my ass into the next county, screamed at me about how acting that way wasn't going to change anything." He shook his head; a shadow of guilt still followed him around, even all these years later. "You know, he had his own stuff to deal with too, and it made me understand what an extra burden I was to him by acting the way I was. He needed me as much as I needed him, but I was too high to notice. It took him finding me at that party, yelling and crying at me in the front yard, for me to finally see it."

"And look at you now," Gemma said, sitting up with a playful tilt of her lips, "you're as uptight as they come."

He guffawed and scooped her up, wrestling her back down to the mattress. "I'll show you uptight."

She shrieked with laughter, trying uselessly to push him away as he blew raspberries down her stomach. He wiggled her legs apart with his own and laced their fingers together as his tickling turned into kisses. "Every day with you, I feel like I'm being unraveled."

"Yeah?" Gem writhed under him. "What are you doing?"

He lifted a brow. "You said it yourself. I like to be good at everything I do, and practice makes perfect."

He moved his lips to the inside of her thighs and came to hover over the soft pink skin between her legs, prepared to stay down there for hours and then, "Gemmie! We're home!"

Jason froze with his mouth barely touching her, and Gem let out a pitiful moan, "Unbelievable."

The honeymooners were home three days early. She rolled

away from Jason and grabbed the first articles of clothing she could get her hands on. "You owe me one orgasm."

He held his hand out for a high five. "As many as you want, Gemmie."

"Ugh. God, don't call me that *now*." She gestured to him, naked and half hard, sprawled out in bed, then let out one more groan before heading downstairs. He tossed on jeans and a long-sleeved thermal T-shirt, interrupting Caroline, dressed in a gold sarong dress and looking tanned and refreshed, mid-conversation with Gem. Frank, on the other hand, hunched over a chair, his face drawn and pale.

"Oh, Jason, I didn't know you were here," Caroline said, stepping up to give his cheek a kiss and his hand a squeeze. "It's so nice you were here to keep Gemmie company."

Gem's eyes snagged on him, and he pressed his lips together to keep from grinning. "So nice."

She rolled her eyes.

"Frank got food poisoning, so we decided to cut the trip short," Caroline said.

"Oh, man." Jason pulled his mouth to the side. "How was it besides that?"

Frank grunted while Caroline rubbed his back. "It was wonderful. The resort was so peaceful, and the spa was out of this world. I had the best hot stone massage of my life. Frank even tried acupuncture. Everything was great up until..." She frowned, motioning her thumb to Frank then inspected her daughter. "What are you wearing?"

Gem held out her arms as if only realizing now what she'd put on. Jason's red boxer-briefs and white undershirt sagged off her body. "I, uh, must have gotten the laundry mixed up."

Jason held his hand up. "Anyone want coffee?"

Caroline helped Frank up. "Actually, hon, I'm going to put him to bed, but help yourself."

They trudged upstairs, leaving Jason and Gem alone, and he smiled down at her. "So, breakfast?"

"How are you so casual about this?" she said, following him into the kitchen.

The past few days, they'd been eating at the island, but he pointed to the table in the sun-room next to the kitchen. "People have gotten food poisoning before. No big deal."

"I mean..." She clenched her jaw tight, her words muffled through her teeth. "My mother and Frank."

He kissed her jaw and scrunched up his underwear on her. "You're killing me in this."

"Don't change the subject."

He opened the refrigerator for orange juice and the mixture of berries and gross vegan yogurt Gem had stored in there then set it all on the table. "You worried about being caught?"

"Like we're fourteen-year-old kids, yes, it's a little awkward."

He laughed and grabbed a pan to cook himself some eggs. "What's so awkward about it?"

"I don't even—we don't..." She gestured between them and sank down in a chair. "What are we supposed to say to them when we haven't even talked about it ourselves?"

"Then let's talk about it," he said, cracking two eggs in the pan.

Gem picked up a spoon and dished out her yogurt and berries into a bowl. "Okay."

"Okay."

Then they stared at each other for a minute.

"You first," Jason said, attention on his scrambled eggs as he scraped the pan with a spatula.

"Okay, well." Gem dragged that word out into three syllables. "I don't want to sound like an annoying girlfriend or anything, but..."

Jason looked up from his food to find Gem staring intently down at hers.

"What was the situation with you and Bridget?"

He grabbed a plate from the cabinet. "She wanted a boyfriend. I wanted to be friends."

"With benefits," she corrected, and he felt his cheeks heating with embarrassment over the whole situation. "How long were you—" she bent her fingers up in quotation marks "—friends?"

"A couple of months." He spooned out his eggs and sat down at the table with her, silence descending between them. He poured himself orange juice and played with the glass, rolling it back and forth between his palms. "Since you asked that question, does that make you my annoying girlfriend?"

"Annoying?" she repeated, pausing with a berry halfway to her mouth.

"You're the one who said it first."

She pointed her spoon at him. "But you don't have to agree."

"But I do." Jason grinned, quickly snapping his mouth around her bite of breakfast then sticking out his tongue. "Nope, still gross."

Gem threw a balled-up napkin at him.

"You never answered my question," he pointed out, lifting his juice to take a gulp.

She dipped her spoon back into her yogurt mixture, swirling it around. "I liked playing house with you for a couple of days. What do you think?"

"I think," he started, swallowing the last bite of his eggs. "I kind of like the idea of you being my annoying girlfriend."

Gem scraped her bowl with the spoon, the noise like nails on a chalkboard.

"You don't like that idea?" he asked, his voice sounding squeaky in his ears.

Setting her spoon down, she sat up, breathing deeply. "You aren't the only one afraid of commitment."

"I am not afraid of commitment. I'm afraid of losing..." He trailed off as his gaze drifted to the window, his words suddenly dust in his mouth as his terrible imagination got the best of him.

But there was Gem, wrapping her fingers around his hand, her lips curling up into a promising smile. "I'm not letting you go."

19

Monday afternoon, Jason peered into a classroom window where Gem held up a cutout of a pumpkin with a three-dimensional face made of different types of material. With her back turned, he used the opportunity to sneak into the room. He sat down at a table, his long legs barely fitting under it.

A boy raised his head to him, scrunching up his nose. "Who are you?"

"Jason."

The kid examined him up and down. "Did you fail a grade or something?"

Jason whispered, "Do I look like I failed a grade?"

Gem stopped in her tracks. "I am trying to explain the directions for your project, Cole, so why are you talking?" She pivoted around and raised a brow. "Ah, we have two troublemakers today."

"He started it." Jason pointed to the kid next to him. Cole shook his head in denial.

Gem tsked, her glorious lips trying and failing to hide her laugh, as she handed out the rest of the supplies to the class, including Jason. Once the kids started the project, she bent over his shoulder. "What are you doing here?"

"Art." He sorted through scraps of newspaper, felt, and cardboard before finding a piece of green tissue paper and tugging on her ponytail. "You smell good."

"Thank you. You know you're in a class of ten-year-olds, right?"

"Yep."

"Okay then, have fun," she said and proceeded with her class, which Jason fully participated in, to all the kids' amusement.

At the end of class, Cole gave his new friend a dap and ran out of the classroom. "Bye, Jason!"

Jason waved. "See ya, buddy."

Gem crossed her arms.

"What?"

"You and Cole are best buddies now. Going for pizza and beer later?"

He stalked over to her, hands in his pockets. "Apple juice and peanut butter sandwiches."

She yanked on his tie, lowering his face to hers, and kissed him, nipping playfully at his bottom lip. "You finished work for today?"

He nodded, giving her a little pat on the ass, then she started to clean up, wandering from table to table and back to the closet in the corner. "Want to give me a ride home?"

"That's why I'm here," he replied, putting scissors away before escorting her out of the classroom and the building. He carried her bicycle to his truck, trying to mask his annoyance. "Isn't it getting a little cold out to still be riding this?"

"It's not snowing yet." He grumbled at her carelessness but decided not to pick that particular battle. When he turned out of the parking lot, Gem held up his art project to assess it. "You did a pretty good job."

"Pretty good job? That's an awesome mixed-media pumpkin," he said, proud of himself for remembering the terminology Gem had gone over during class.

She slid on his aviators. She looked so good in them. "Maybe we could sell it at the auction."

He leaned his elbow on the console. "What auction?"

She removed the elastic from her ponytail and combed her fingers through her hair, letting it settle over her shoulder. He resisted burying his face in it, missing her smell even though they'd kissed goodnight less than twenty-four hours ago.

"Every year, the museum has a fundraiser for Artist Point, which is the program that employs me. They auction off stuff by local artists—paintings, sculptures, even some of the projects from the kids. We actually raise quite a bit of money. And since you're..." she paused as if she were afraid to say it out loud, "... my boyfriend, that makes you obligated to go, right?"

"I suppose I could pencil it in. Anything for the kids."

"Truly magnanimous of you." She poked his side before taking a look out of the window. "Where're you going?"

"Home."

"This isn't the way to my apartment."

"I know. I'm kidnapping you."

"Damn it." She banged her fist on her door. "I didn't pack my weapons in my purse tonight."

"Eh, I don't know that you need much more than your mouth. Cut somebody to the quick with that." She ran her tongue over her teeth, and he brought her hand to his mouth, kissing her palm. "Don't tease."

Inside Jason's kitchen, Gem stuck the pumpkin on the refrigerator with a magnet then studied the picture of Jason with his parents. He stood behind her, crisscrossing his arms over her chest to her shoulders, and she angled her head to ask him, "How old were you there?"

"I don't know. Maybe five or six." He was so young and happy in that moment with his parents, even though he had no memory of getting the photo taken. He only knew what it had been like, their little family of three. He didn't need Gem to say anything to let him know she would allow him time and space to be open with her about it, because he felt it in the way she turned in his arms, clinging to his neck. She pressed one hand to his heart and kissed his neck, silently repeating the promise they had made to each other.

She wasn't letting him go.

He rested his forehead against hers, his voice barely audible. "Thank you."

"For what?" she breathed.

"Being you." He lifted his head and then slowly quirked his mouth to the side. He had been so patient during her art class and on the ride home, he didn't want to wait any longer. "Let's go."

In one swift motion, he threw her over his shoulder and carried her upstairs to his room. She yelped in laughter when he tossed her on the bed. "I had fantasies about being carried through those double doors," she said breathlessly, fixing the hair that had fallen over her face. "But not like that."

"I couldn't wait any longer. I owe you from yesterday." Wasting no time, he tugged off her pants and made himself at home between her legs, nibbling on the tender skin of her upper thigh before moving to her pubic bone. When she growled out his name in impatience, he let out a laugh against her before dragging the flat of his tongue up her slit.

Gem gasped his name, digging her fingers into his hair, and he held her hips down so she couldn't wiggle away under the onslaught of his sucking and pulling at her clit. From the way her breath sped up and her belly clenched, he could tell she was on the brink, and he moved away, wanting to draw this out longer. Torture her just a little.

He rained sloppy kisses up and down her legs as she tried to drag him back to her center, whining, "Jason, come on."

Instead of giving in to her, he took his time, bringing her to the edge, then backing off before she could find relief. Finally, she screamed in frustration, her fingers digging into his scalp. "Jason! Please! I'm dying!"

"But I like playing with this pretty pussy. I want to drive you crazy, like you drive me crazy."

"I hate you," she said, throwing her forearm over her eyes.

"No, you don't." He smiled against her skin and slid two fingers into her exquisite wet core, finding the spot deep inside her to bring her to climax. She cried out, and he lifted his head, swiping a palm over his mouth. Providing Gem pleasure might've been the sole purpose he was put on this earth, to be the reason this glorious creature glowed from the inside out. It was his favorite thing.

He tweaked her big toe. "So, dinner in, like, half an hour?"

GEM PANTED ON THE BED, her fingers balled up in the sheets, holding on with a death grip. From the door, Jason gave her one more sizzling look. He raked his eyes over her body and licked his lips as if he had just finished dessert, before letting out an appreciative sigh and leaving the room.

Lured by the sound of pots banging around the kitchen, she eventually stood up to collect her brain and underwear. She hadn't known Jason very long, and they'd only solidified their relationship status yesterday, but accepting her invitation to the auction and now him making her dinner, it all hit her at once.

This was real.

This was setting dates and sharing calendars and attending potlucks or whatever it was couples did.

Gem and Jason. Coupled up. She was going to try to make a real go of this.

Wild.

The scent of tomato sauce and garlic bread brought her back to the present, and she was about to leave the bedroom when a picture on his dresser caught her eye. It was framed in popsicle sticks and looked like one that hung on the wall in her living room. She picked it up to inspect it. The photo, from last year when she had volunteered at a summer camp, showed her and the kids covered in rainbows from finger painting day. She turned it over. A messy note was scrawled on the back, *For Miss Gem, Love, Peyton.*

She brought it to the kitchen, where Jason stirred spaghetti. "Jason?"

He set down the spoon, leaning his hip into the counter. "Hmm?"

She remained silent, holding up the picture.

"Oh. About that." He smiled impishly. "I may or may not have stolen that."

"What? When?"

"The night I dropped you off."

"After yoga? The night you killed the spider?"

He laid his palms against her throat as he massaged the nape of her neck, but she wasn't going to be thrown off the scent. She was a dog with a bone. "When?"

He didn't answer, but his eyes told the truth, and she gaped. "The night we met? You drove me home. We fought the whole time, and then you took this?"

He nodded and twisted back to the stove, his face redder than she'd ever seen. Behind his back, Gem stared at the frame in her hands. "I thought you couldn't stand me."

He ignored her, setting the table, but she stopped him with her hand on his wrist. "Hey. Make me understand."

He suddenly circled around, trapping her in his arms,

burying his face in her hair. "I wanted you the moment I saw you. But you were—are—so frustrating. I needed a piece of you."

"So, you stole a picture of me? Like some creep."

"Yeah. I'm an awful creep. Forgive me for stealing it?"

She lifted a shoulder. "I didn't even realize it was gone until now."

He chuckled, heating her neck with his breath, then picked her up in a bear hug, tilting his head back for a kiss. "Hungry?"

"Starving."

Setting her down, he kissed her, gently holding her against the counter. It was cool against her back, a contrast to the skin of her stomach growing warm when his hands moved underneath her shirt. She moaned when he traced the shell of her ear with his tongue, and she found his belt loops with her fingertips, inching his hips closer to her own. Which was exactly when the pot of water boiled over with a loud hiss. Steam swamped them.

Gem brushed her bangs back from her damp forehead, the heat from dinner nothing compared to this near-constant fever. No matter how many times he kissed her, how often he had his hands on her, it was never enough.

She was full of want and need and wasn't ready for the fever to break yet. She hoped it never would.

Jason opened up a window, waving away the last of the steam. He still hadn't changed out of his work clothes, making the show of him finishing dinner all that much more enticing. He wore dark, fitted pants that showcased his long legs and tapered waist. His white shirt flaunted the muscles in his broad shoulders, and when he emptied the pot into a colander in the sink, his forearms flexed from under sleeves that were rolled up to his elbow.

"It's ready," he told her, dipping his head toward her chair.

She loved that move, the tiny head nod directing her where he wanted, always right next to him.

Gem didn't have a whole lot of experience with boyfriends, but this one seemed to be pretty perfect.

After dinner, she stood to take the dishes to the sink, but he snatched hold of her waist. "Leave 'em. Let's go upstairs."

"I can't. I need to go home." When he attempted to sit her on his lap, she dug her heels in and he put on a pained face. She drew her finger across his narrowed eyebrows. "I'm opening the store tomorrow. What do you want me to do? I don't have any clothes here." He didn't move, so she yanked him up out of his chair. "Give me a ride home?"

He looked none too pleased but grabbed his keys from the counter to drive her home. He carried her bicycle upstairs to her apartment and jumped when George Clooney lunged at him from behind the sofa. "Jesus!"

"What are you, six-three, six-four, and you're afraid of a cat?" He ignored her, setting down the bike, and she suppressed her giggle, placing her hands on his chest. "You're funny."

He kissed her nose. "You're cute." He held on to her hips, a hopeful gleam in his eyes. "Can't I sleep over?"

"No." He dropped his forehead to her shoulder petulantly, and she stumbled under his weight. "Why not?"

"Because," she said, forcing his head up. It weighed fifty pounds. All that ego. "You need to go to work tomorrow. You left all the lights on in your house. You have to—"

Jason stifled her words with his mouth, his fingers weaving into her hair, holding her in place. Little by little, her body gave in to him, first with her arms around his middle, then her tongue tangling with his, then arching against him as he stepped her backward to the couch. The flames that rose in Gem's veins had become so much a part of her when Jason touched her that she almost didn't feel it anymore.

Almost.

In one quick motion, she was out of his arms, her hands moving up in defense.

"Fine." He lowered his voice, grouchy.

She gave him a chaste peck on the cheek, careful to avoid getting too close. One more kiss like that, and it'd be all over. "Another time."

20

The next day, Jason sat down at his desk after lunch and opened his email. There was one from Gem. He scoffed dubiously, figuring it must have been quite a sacrifice for her to even turn on a computer. He opened it up.

Just a little reminder to let you know I'm thinking about you.

He clicked open the attachment, and his jaw dropped.

Gem's naked body covered his screen. Her long hair was the only form of modesty besides a sheet that hung limply from her left hand. He picked up his phone, taking his eyes off the monitor long enough to dial her number.

"Hey, you," she answered in a smoky voice.

"You can't send me stuff like this on my *work* email, Gemma. I'll get in trouble."

"With whom? Aren't you basically second-in-command?"

"Yeah, but—"

"You don't like it?" she pouted, all breathy and suggestive. He made a sort of guttural sound from somewhere deep inside his body, and she laughed. "Can I come over tonight?"

"Of course. Pack a bag so you can slee—shit." Jason smacked

his hand to his forehead. "I forgot. I'm meeting my friends after work to watch the game."

"Oh." She deflated, Marilyn Monroe voice gone. "Okay."

"You can meet us," he said, scrambling to make it up to her, but there was a slight pause before she spoke.

"No, that's okay."

"I want you to come. Please?"

"But I'll be all sweaty from yoga."

Jason sat back in his chair, the terribly inappropriate but incredibly sexy picture still up on his computer screen. He smiled at it. "Perfect. I like you like that."

She snorted. "How about I meet you at your place later?"

"No. Come to The Grill when you're done with class."

"I don't know."

He pretended not to hear her. "Great. I'll see you later," he said and hung up before she could argue. He downloaded the picture to his phone and erased it from his computer. Two could play her game. He texted Gem.

I can't wait to get your beautiful, naked ass in my bed. Smack it for sending such a naughty picture.

He put his phone down, staring at it, waiting for a reply. After a few minutes recounting all the sex positions he had yet to try with her, he readjusted his pants and got back to work.

That evening, Jason and his friends sat at a high-top covered in beer and wings, a play-off baseball game showing on every TV screen. A player slid home, and the place went crazy. Jason and his friends hooted and clapped; some random guy from the table over even high-fived them. That was when he spotted her.

Gem sheepishly waved at him from the entrance, and his smile instantly grew bigger at the sight of her bundled up in a plush cardigan and scarf, her cheeks flushed red from the cold air. He motioned her over, introducing her to the guys at the table. "Gem, this is Kevin and Luke." His friends shook hands with her, and Jason kissed her temple before sitting down. "How was your day?"

"Good. How was yours?" She arched her eyebrow, a hint of a smile on her lips.

Her hair was knotted on top of her head, but he wound a loose strand of it around his index finger. "Picked up this afternoon."

"Oh yeah? Why?" she asked all innocent-like, and he responded with a tug on her hair before pulling her chair closer to his.

"Gem," Kevin began, swallowing a bite of his chicken wing, red sauce on his fingers, "you hungry?" She cringed at the sight of the bone in his hand, and he furrowed his bushy eyebrows at her. "What?"

Jason answered for her. "She's a vegan."

Luke, a veritable garbage can, shook his head. "That sucks, man. I couldn't live without cheeseburgers."

She shrugged. "You get used to it. Jason's tried some of my food."

He nodded in agreement, glad his friends didn't feel the need to point out how a girl—*his girl*—had invaded their guy night. "Yeah, it's not bad."

"Are you totally disgusted being here?" Kevin asked after polishing off another chicken wing.

Gem smiled indulgently with a laugh. "No, it's fine. To each their own."

"Out!" Luke banged his fist on the table at a play on screen. "I gotta piss."

Kevin also stood up, wiping his hands. "Another pitcher?" he asked no one in particular, before heading to the bar.

"They seem sweet," Gem quipped, and Jason moved his fingers to her thighs, turning her body to face him.

"I like them," he said, leaning in close.

"Then I do too. Besides, this is a much easier test than you'll get from my girls."

"Oh yeah? Should I be scared?"

"Scared, no, but prepared, yes. It's a lot of different...energy when we're together."

"I can't wait to meet them," he said sincerely then wrapped her thick sweater around her tighter. "You look cute all bundled up."

Under the table, she snaked her hand up between his legs, cupping him like she owned him—but who the fuck was he kidding? He'd been hers since that hot August day—and she whispered, "I thought you wanted my naked ass in bed."

He bent to kiss her, but she turned her head, and his lips landed on her cheekbone. She gave him a little squeeze and stood up. "Can you order me a garden salad with vinaigrette? I'm going to freshen up."

He muttered a sulky response as she patted his head and sashayed off. It wasn't until a few minutes after Luke and Kevin returned, and her salad was ordered, that Jason noticed Gem still hadn't returned, and he stalked to the bathroom to find her. The door opened right as his hand reached it.

Gem hopped back in surprise. "What are you doing going into the ladies' room?"

"Looking for you. Thought maybe you fell in."

"Not quite."

The bathrooms were set back in a little hallway, and with no one around, he hauled her to him. His brain had been working in overdrive ever since he'd laid eyes on that picture, and he had to have her. Immediately.

His lips devoured hers, his tongue licking into her mouth in a way that mirrored what he would like to be doing. He backed her up against the wall, the cotton of her cardigan soft against his chest, but he could feel the heat radiating from her body, and he yanked it off. She curled her tongue around his, digging her fingers into his hair as he urged her legs apart with his thigh. When he teased the juncture of her hip and thigh with his fingertips, a soft curse escaped her lips, her shoulders sinking down.

She shifted on her feet, and he backed away, searching her eyes. "What?"

"Your plan to get me naked…"

"Yeah," he breathed, his lips on her neck.

"It's dashed."

He continued nibbling at her throat for a few seconds before her words sank in. Standing up to his full height, he stared down at her. "Huh?"

"I got my period."

Jason's own shoulders sank. "Well, that's inconvenient." He fixed Gem's sweater back around her shoulders and readjusted himself for what felt like the hundredth time that day. "You feeling all right?"

She nodded, scratching the bridge of her nose with her index finger. "You want TMI?"

"Yes." He caught her finger and kissed it. "Always, when it comes to you."

"I'm a little crampy, but my second day is always worse than the first. Like a murder scene."

He had nothing to say and assumed it was better to stay silent in this kind of situation. He kissed her temple then laced his fingers with hers on the way back to the table. Gem's salad was waiting for her, and Kevin and Luke exchanged knowing glances.

Kevin grinned. "That was quick."

Jason mushed his palm against his friend's face. "Shut up."

Gem poured herself a beer from the pitcher, and Kevin raised his glass to her, openly surprised at how she helped herself. "You drink?"

She answered by taking a few gulps then covered her mouth when she let out a tiny, adorable burp.

All three of the guys laughed, and Luke pointed at her. "Didn't expect that to come from a vegan yoga teacher."

She picked at her salad, fumbling over a cherry tomato, probably figuring out that Jason had been talking about her. "I told you," he said, the corner of his mouth curling up into a half smile when she glanced at him, speaking to his friend even though his eyes were on her. "She's full of surprises. In the best ways possible."

THE NEXT MORNING, Gem woke up with the sunrise, the beginnings of a cramp low in her belly. A soft snore rumbled in Jason's chest. She didn't want to leave the warm crook of his arm, but she needed a couple Motrin and some water.

Scooting out of bed, she crept to the bathroom, washed up using Jason's toiletries—a reminder to bring her own—then tossed on one of his hoodies before tiptoeing downstairs to make hot tea. Jason's alarm was set for 6:55 and he almost always pressed snooze twice, so she still had a while before he actually got up.

Tiptoeing back into the bedroom, Gem settled into the big gray chair in the corner with a pencil and a few pieces of blank paper. She smiled at the man sleeping on the bed, his long body sprawled diagonally across the mattress. One arm curled above his head, the other resting on his bare stomach. She began to draw, sketching his powerful form. Her tongue sat at the corner of her mouth in concentration as she outlined his body, contouring the lines and shadows created by his muscles.

BEEP... BEEP... BEEP...

Gem's head shot up from her work, startled by the alarm,

and Jason's arm reached over to hit it, blindly. With his eyes still closed, he rolled onto his side, his hand searching for something. His face nuzzled into the pillow, and he took a deep breath. His face scrunched up, and, finally, his eyes fluttered open.

He squinted, focusing his sight around the room until he found her. "Hey, you," he said, all groggy and rough. "You're up early."

She nodded and went back to work with her pencil.

He yawned. "What are you doing?"

"Drawing."

"What are you drawing?"

"You."

He sat up on an elbow and wiped sleep from his eyes. "Me? Can I see?"

Gem held the pencil between her teeth while she crawled up onto the bed next to him and turned the paper over in her lead-covered fingers. She surveyed his reaction to the sketch, his face lighting up, his normally cool eyes bright blue.

"You have a picture of me. I wanted one of you."

He took the paper to study it, and when he didn't say anything, her nerves got the best of her. She nudged his shoulder with her own. "Do you like it?"

"Yes, of course, yes. You're so talented." He shook his head ever so slightly. "I guess I... It's nice to see me through your eyes. You see me as beautiful."

She tugged the sleeves of his sweatshirt over her hands, trying to gather her thoughts. When she didn't respond, he cupped her knee, offering his own. "When I'm with you, I feel like I'm in a different world. Like my whole life, I've been living in black-and-white, and then you came along and gave everything color. You know what I mean?"

Gem bit her lip, apparently taking a tad too long to respond because he recoiled. "If you're not ready to—"

"No. Jason, no." She grabbed his hands, launching herself

onto his lap. "You make me so happy it hurts. At the end of the night, my cheeks get sore from smiling so much. You kiss me, and my chest feels like it's going to explode. I miss you when we're not together, and when we are, I wish I never had to leave." She rested her forehead against his, her voice wavering with emotion. "It scares me that in just a couple of weeks, I feel so attached to you."

"And me to you," he said, holding her hands against his chest.

She could feel his heartbeat, strong and steady, and with the way hers thumped erratically, she feared she wouldn't be able to keep up with his even pace. "I..." She tried to pull away, but he held on tighter. "I don't want to drown in this."

"I won't let you. I'm not letting you go, Gemma."

21

A week later, Jason brought lunch to Gem at Bare Necessities. With October in full force now, it was way too chilly to eat outside, so they sat down next to each other in an aisle between the all-natural pet supplies and gluten-free cereals.

"Where are we going tonight?" Gem asked, leaning against a big bag of dog food with Jason's long legs crossed at the ankles next to her.

He shoved a piece of sushi into his mouth. "Some steak place."

She picked at her avocado roll. "I'll be eating a cup of soup, I guess."

"It's Frank's birthday, his choice. For your birthday, you can take us to some tofu place if that's what you want." He poked her with chopsticks. "You could always order a New York strip and call it a day."

She snorted. "I'll stick with the breadsticks."

Dipping a piece of his roll in soy sauce, he raised his brow. "So, what did your mom say about us?"

Gem stared at her food like she was dissecting it for a biology assignment.

"Oh, come on, Gemma. I thought you were going to tell her yesterday."

"I was. I didn't."

"Chicken."

Her mouth snapped open to argue, but she shut it just as fast. She *was* chicken.

Jason clacked his chopsticks at her. "She'll eventually figure it out since we'll continue to go places together, and I'll be...I don't know, holding your hand, kissing you."

She pouted. "She's going to make a big deal out of it."

"I am a pretty big deal." He shrugged, and Gem grumbled.

"Doesn't your neck get tired from holding up that big head?"

He leaned toward her as if to kiss her cheek but instead grabbed the last piece of her roll. "Sometimes."

She swatted at him, their usual game. Him stealing her food, her pretending she was actually going to eat it. "Pick me up at six?"

He nodded, swallowing the roll in one bite. "Make sure you bring some slippers or something. I have no socks left since you keep taking all of mine."

Gem thought she hid her sigh, but he caught it. "What?"

"I'm always staying over at your house," she said, and Jason shook his head, evidently not understanding her comment. She went on. "It's a little one-sided, don't you think? Me always having to pack a bag. Why don't you like staying at my apartment?"

"It's not that I don't like staying there. It's that—" he engulfed her in his arms, pulling her close "—I need a big old bed to sleep in. Your bed is too small, Goldilocks, but my bed is just right."

"I'm serious, Jason." She pushed away from him. "I'm always staying at your place. I want you to stay with me tonight."

A pained expression crossed his face, and she pinched him in the arm. "Ouch!" He grabbed his bicep. "I'm kidding. I don't have a problem packing a bag. No need to come to blows."

"You deserve it. My bed is well worn-in and comfortable."

He threw his arm around her neck. "You're right. Who needs leg room when you've got lumps in the mattress?" Gem lifted her fingers to pinch him again, but he caught her hand. "As long as you're next to me, I'd sleep on a rock."

His sincere tone and penetrating gaze left Gem swimming in a puddle of affection, and she rested her head on his shoulder. "It's hard to be mad at you when you're so charming."

He kissed the top of her head. "That's the point."

That night, at ten minutes to six, Gem opened the door for Jason, who might as well have walked out of a catalogue in a dark V-neck sweater, brown leather jacket, and fitted jeans. He shook off George Clooney, who rubbed his head against his leg. "You're not ready."

"And you're early," she said, spinning on her heel, not minding that he followed her back to the bedroom. He let his duffel bag drop to the floor as she let her sweats do the same. After she wiggled into a pair of skinny jeans, he stopped her as she lifted her arms to slip on her top.

"What are you doing?" She batted his hands away.

"I'm early," he crooned, sidling up next to her to nuzzle her neck. His hands roamed over her rib cage and waist. "We do have some time."

She angled her neck to give him better access even as she said, "You start that now, we'll be late."

He slipped his fingers under her bra strap. "So what?"

"So what?" Gem let out a loud guffaw. "*You're* never late." She threw the thin shirt over her head before he could argue. "Here, button me up."

Jason grumbled but gently moved her hair over one shoulder to close the hook and eye. A circle of skin was left open between her shoulder blades, and he bent down to kiss it. When his lips traveled back up to her neck, she narrowly escaped them, bending down to step into her boots.

"Five minutes?" he begged almost comically, and she shook her head. She didn't want to give her mother any more ammunition tonight. It was their big coming out as Gemma and Jason, and that was anxiety-inducing enough.

"Come on. We have all night once we get home. I'll need to de-stress."

At the restaurant, Jason held Gem's hand to walk inside. She tried to escape, but he didn't let go as he opened the door to the expensive steak house. A hostess dressed in all black led them to a table, where Frank and Caroline were seated.

"Hey, Frank, Caroline," Jason said as Gem waved.

Her mother's eyes rounded, pieces clicking into place. "Am I imagining this?" she asked, bobbing her head excitedly. "Are you two...?"

Jason answered by holding up their linked hands and nodded.

"That is wonderful!" Caroline hugged them. "I knew it. I knew you two would make a good match. Didn't I say that, Frank?" She whipped her head back and forth from her husband to her daughter. "I did say that. Oh, this is amazing." She settled back into her seat, dragging Gem to the chair next to her. "Why didn't you tell me? I'm so happy." She clasped her hands together in front of her heart, beaming. "One big happy family."

Jason, appearing much more relaxed than Gem felt, handed Frank an envelope as he sat down. "Happy birthday."

"Thanks, Jay."

"It was Gem's idea. I wanted to get you Depends, but she said that would be rude."

Frank opened the birthday card, and a gift certificate fell out. "Hot Sauce of the Month Club!" He grabbed Gem's hand. "Excellent. Thank you."

A young waitress, probably barely eighteen, in a vest and tie, approached the table. She introduced herself and offered a drink menu along with the specials. Frank ordered a round of appetizers, all of which had some sort of animal in them, and Jason held up his hand to order something else. Assuming he was doing it for her, Gem tapped on his foot under the table. He furrowed his brow, but she only shook her head, not wanting to make a whole thing about it, and reached for the bread basket.

Dinner went relatively smoothly as Frank stayed quiet, sawing his way through the biggest piece of meat in the place, and Caroline stuck to basic questions about Gem and Jason's relationship, no real prying, which Gem was thankful for. For dessert, the waitress brought out a round chocolate cake topped with a few tall candles that Frank repeatedly failed to blow out. After his fifth attempt, he wiped his forehead. "Guess you hit sixty, and the lungs are the first thing to go."

"They're trick candles." Caroline giggled behind a napkin.

Frank's gaze transformed to pure adoration as he reached over the table to kiss Caroline, and Gem wondered what her life would be like at her mother's age. If there would be romance and laughter and...

Jason took hold of her hand under the table, his eyes puddles of some emotion she couldn't read, though from the thoughtful quirk to his lips, maybe it was the same thing she'd been imagining. "Gem, I—"

Before he could finish his sentence, the waitress tripped next to the table, sending a glass pitcher full of water flying high into the air. Its descent to the floor ended with a spectacular smash into a million pieces, but not before most of the liquid made a pit stop all over Gem.

Every head in the restaurant spun to find the clatter, and Gem's breath caught in her throat. Her once-loose cream top was soaked through and almost entirely sheer.

"I'm sorry. I'm so sorry." The young girl apologized from her position on the floor, shock and misery crossing her face. A middle-aged man, who Gem assumed was the manager, sped toward their table. When the waitress spotted him, she wiped her face with the back of her hand. "I'm sorry. I'll get this cleaned up as soon as—"

"It's okay." Gem slipped off her chair to the floor and began to pick up some bigger pieces of glass as the man reached the table. "It was an accident."

"Morgan, in the back, please."

The girl nodded but was slow to get up.

"Now!" he barked.

She ventured another glance at Gem, tears trickling down her cheeks before hurrying off toward the kitchen, head down, broken pitcher in hand. The man offered his hand to Gem. "I am very sorry about this unfortunate incident."

"Don't worry about it." Gem ignored his help, getting up on her own, detecting at the same time the manager did that the outlines of her nipples were distinct through the thin material of her bra and shirt now stuck to her skin.

He cleared his throat and smoothed down his tie. "I would, uh, like to offer a discount on tonight's meal."

Jason stood up, a few inches taller than the manager, to offer his jacket to Gem, and she wrapped herself up in the warmth of it.

"It's no big deal," Gem said.

"I insist," the manager said to her, and then to Frank and Caroline, "I apologize again for this inconvenience on your birthday. You can be assured I will be taking care of the problem."

Most of the patrons in the place were watching the scene unfold, and Gem had a pretty good idea of how this guy would be dealing with his "problem." Morgan was a young girl who tripped; it wasn't the end of the world. She made sure her voice was loud, devoid of any trace of humiliation when she said, "Morgan was very helpful tonight. She was polite and knowledgeable, and if you fire her over a few drops of spilled water, you can be assured you will lose my business here."

Jason snickered beside her, and she surreptitiously nudged him. There was no need for the manager to know her vegan ass wouldn't be stepping foot back in the place.

"Morgan was a great server," Caroline stated with a smile, slipping on her coat.

Frank ushered his wife toward the exit with a, "Food was great!"

Then Jason signed for the check without a word and guided Gem to a quick getaway. Inside the car, she shivered beneath the wet material of her top, and he blasted the heat all the way up. "Better?" She nodded, zipping up his jacket, and he breathed out a quiet laugh. "Man, you've got no fear whatsoever, huh?"

"What?"

"You told off some guy while wearing a see-through shirt and with everyone staring at you. Incredible."

She held her fingers up to the heater. "I couldn't let her get fired."

"No, I know. I know. It's just that not everybody would have done the same thing."

She shrugged, yanking his hand to her thigh, hoping for some body heat to transfer from his palm to her cold legs. "It was no real tragedy, just some water. If somebody has to get ice water thrown on them, I suppose why not me?"

"And that's exactly why you're so incredible because you ask why not you."

She felt her face flush with color at his sentiment, and he cupped her cheeks between his hands.

"You're thoughtful and smart, and I'm so lucky you picked me." He kissed her gently, once, twice, three times before she pulled him close. She kissed him with enough fervor to hopefully show him that she would pick him every time, always.

Back at her apartment, they discarded articles of clothing on the floor as they made their way to her room, expressing words not yet spoken well into the early morning hours until passing out from exhaustion, tangled up in each other's arms.

THE FOLLOWING MORNING, Jason's alarm beeped near his ear, his cell phone stuffed under his pillow. He'd barely gotten a few hours of sleep and dreaded going to work, and with Gem's body sleepily draped over him, he considered taking a sick day.

Last night, being with Caroline and Frank, witnessing their devotion to each other, he couldn't help but visualize his future. He had imagined being sixty and struggling to blow out trick candles while Gem laughed in amused satisfaction next to him. It was Gem he wanted next to him in twenty, forty, sixty years. A lifetime with her would never be enough.

Because he loved her.

The truth had struck him like a slap across the face, and he had been close, so close, to telling her at the restaurant until the water fiasco.

Words somehow seemed insignificant and not nearly enough to describe the world he now inhabited with Gem. It was big and wide, and every day was something new to learn and explore. He couldn't possibly explain all that to her, so when they'd gotten home, he tried again with his mouth and hands.

Smiling in contentment, he carefully lifted Gem's limbs off him and shimmied out of bed to get ready for work. Walking into the living room, he retrieved his forgotten clothes from the previous night and spied his jacket clumped on the floor underneath Mr. Clooney. He shooed the cat away, his eyes almost popping out of his head when he saw the ruined material. Scratches and holes dotted the new brown leather. He gritted his teeth and stomped back to Gem's bedroom to wake her up. "I'm going to kill that goddamn cat."

"What?" Gem picked up her head from her pillow, squinting awake. "What's wrong?"

"My jacket." He held it up. "Look at it. It's brand-new."

She got up, still rubbing sleep from her eyes, and assessed the evidence. "It has character now."

"Character," he repeated in a huff.

"What?" Her eyebrows knit together, and the fact that she didn't seem to care that his stuff had been destroyed pissed him off. She bought almost all her clothes at thrift stores, and he totally respected whatever she wanted to do. The favor was not returned.

"This is real leather," he told her. "It cost me a couple hundred dollars."

"I'm sorry," she said, getting up from the bed to take it from him for a few moments before handing it back. "But maybe you shouldn't spend your money on such expensive things. It's only a jacket."

When she brushed past him to go to the kitchen, he trailed her. "What's wrong with spending money on nice stuff? I earned it. I shouldn't have to come here and watch it get ruined."

"It's not ruined." Gem flicked on the coffeepot then held her hands up like he was a rabid animal, and that pissed him off too. "Calm down."

He marched down the hall, cursing, and came back with his bag, stepping into his shoes.

"Where are you going?"

"Home." He put on the butchered jacket. He was tired and going to be late for work.

"Why?"

"Why?" He threw his arms out at her flippant attitude. "Because I don't want to be here anymore. Because you're acting as if I'm the jackass for being angry, when it was your cat that ripped holes in my jacket."

"I'm sorry, but I just don't understand—" she said, and he cut her off with a huff. Ten minutes ago, he was thinking about staying in bed with the woman he loved, and now they were arguing. Of course.

Fearing he'd lose his temper, more than he already had, he clenched his jaw, measuring his words. "Gemma, I get that you hate capitalism, animal products, or anything nice—" he threw in that last bit for at least one jab "—but just because you don't like it doesn't mean I can't or-or-or..." He stuttered over his words, his anger blocking out rational thought. "If it goes against what you believe, then you don't care about it." He went on in a higher voice, imitating her. "It's only a jacket."

She forced out a laugh that bordered on condescension. "You're being ridiculous."

"It's my jacket, Gem. If we were at my house and something of yours got trashed, I'd at least apologize."

"I'm sorry," she said, although the damage had already been done.

"You want to know why I always want to go to my place? Because your cat claws up everything, you never throw anything out, and you have a turtle, a fish, and a fucking compost heap in your kitchen. Jesus, you might as well live in a tent."

Gem flinched at his words and took a beat in which Jason wished he could pick his words out from the air and shove them back into his mouth.

She lifted her fingers to her chest and lowered her voice. "I would rather live in a tent with nothing and be happy than spend money on expensive shit just to fill up a closet. So, go ahead. Leave." She stalked toward him. "If that's what you care about, then go. Go home in your fancy car to your big, empty house, with your big televisions and state-of-the-art everything.

I don't need you yelling at me about it." Then she put her hands on her hips for the pièce de résistance, delivered with quiet condemnation. "I hope you're proud of your jacket and all your *stuff* because it'll need to keep you company since I won't."

He deserved her anger. He was angry too, but her words hit their intended target. Air whistled from his lungs, and without anything else to say, he picked his bag and heart up off the floor and left.

22

In the twenty-four hours since their knock-down, drag-out fight, Gem hadn't felt much better. Sure, they had argued before, but what had happened between them yesterday was completely different. Maybe because they knew each other so well now, they could take each other out at the knees.

Jason certainly had done that with Gem. He'd insulted her and her lifestyle choices, and then he'd left. With the slam of her door, the reality of the situation had hit her like a ton of bricks, and she'd sunk to the floor, where she hugged her legs to her chest and cried.

She hadn't meant what she said to him, but like a child, she had wanted to hurt him as badly as he had hurt her. She could practically see him deflate, the fight leaving every part of his body, even his spirit, and guilt lodged in her gut.

The day had crawled by as pain settled in between Gem's ribs, and the urge to call Jason had crossed her mind more than once. But with each passing hour, nothing she sought to say felt like enough. A lackluster yoga class had been followed up by a Tylenol PM and an early bedtime.

Gem had battled her doubts and fears about Jason, but this

fight which ended with him walking out brought them all back to the surface. And the light of a new day didn't make her feel any better. Jason had a soft and genuine heart, but he guarded it with a façade built of bravado and styled perfection, and she both loved and hated that about him. She admired how hard he worked and how he was so open about what he wanted, but there was no material good in the world that could provide him the stability and security he wanted.

But she could.

Gem didn't know how to do a lot of things. She was crap at remembering birthdays and anniversaries, almost never paid a bill on time, and had lost her driver's license so many times she'd made friends with Bomani, who worked the DMV desk. But Gem was really good at loving people.

She loved that even though Jason had thrown a fit about George Clooney, he secretly gave him treats and pats when he thought she wasn't looking. She loved the way he protected her, from giving her his jacket at the restaurant to making sure she always felt in control of the decisions about their relationship. She loved him, and she wanted to make him feel as stable and secure as he made her feel.

Normally, she'd FaceTime the girls if she was this upset or needed advice, but she wanted to figure this out on her own. She needed to work through their first real fight, be an adult about this. Hopefully, there was still something to work through. Deciding on a plan of action, she dressed and headed out the door.

A few hours later, Gem wound her way through the offices of Santos & Mitchell, speaking briefly to Joann, who pointed her in the direction of Jason's office.

His door was open, his head down in his hands. He looked miserable. Like Gem felt.

"Hey, you." Her voice was hoarse, and she cleared her throat. "Can I come in?"

His body jerked like he'd been hit with an electric shock, and he stood up behind his desk. With his bloodshot eyes, she guessed he hadn't slept much.

"I just called you," he said.

She took a few unsure steps inside. "I forgot my phone at home."

They stared at each other in silence as the seconds ticked on into what felt like years.

"I'm sorry," they said at the same time, then laughed at the awkwardness of it all.

"I'm surprised to see you." Jason stepped around his desk, muttering a rushed explanation, "Not that I'm not glad you are here. I am. I'm really glad you're here."

Gem's heart fluttered at his unmistakable tension, a sign that maybe things weren't as bad as she anticipated. "You're rambling."

"I know." He shook his head, a sad sort of smile threatening his lips. "I don't know what to say besides I'm sorry." He sat on the front of his desk, his shoulders hanging in defeat.

She positioned herself between his knees. "I shouldn't have said that your materialistic or I would leave you. It's no excuse, but I was—"

"Angry. I know." He placed his hands on her hips. "I was angry too. You're right. It's ridiculous to get so upset about a jacket. I never want you to think that I care more about material things than I do about you."

Gem opened her bag. "I am sorry George ruined your jacket, and you're right, if it were something of mine, I would have been upset. We may not hold the same value for certain things, but I want you to know I won't ever judge you for it. It's still strange sometimes," she said, a repentant pout on her lips, and Jason traced her bottom lip with his thumb, inviting her to finish the thought she struggled with. "It's strange sometimes to remember it's not only me anymore. I'm stubborn and stuck in my ways, and being with you is forcing me to challenge my views and..."

"Me too, Gem. As soon as I said what I did, I wanted to take it all back. I didn't mean it. I love your place and your habits. They're weird and wonderful, and I wouldn't want you to be anything else than exactly what you are." He dropped his forehead to hers, breathing his words into her mouth. "A little vegan socialist who has a devil cat and sucks at loading the dishwasher."

Gem tossed her head back and laughed, feeling lighter than she had in years. Stepping backward, she held up a dark jacket from her bag. "I got this for you. It's not real leather, and I bought it from a thrift store."

He swiftly looped his arms inside it.

"I won't be offended if you hate it," she said, tugging on the well-worn, spotted collar.

"It's perfect. Like you. Thank you." He pulled her into a tight hug, his nose buried deep in her hair. "I'm so sorry, Gem."

"Me too."

Jason straightened up, taking her with him, kissing away her reservations about them not fitting into each other's lives. True, they were opposites—from their music choices and diets to their bank accounts—but that wasn't what mattered. As long as they stayed true to each other and what they were together, they would be okay.

"You'll still come to the auction with me tomorrow?" she asked as he tucked a wayward strand of hair behind her ear, his fingers lingering on her neck.

"Of course."

Their lips met, consuming each other with fierce licks and nips. It had only been a day, yet a heavy longing rose in her as if they had been apart for months. She yanked at his tie, loosening it from around his neck, but he cursed and held her at arm's length. "We can't. Not here."

Gem blinked around the room; she'd almost forgotten they were in his office. Although, it wasn't like they were out in public. They were alone and would remain undisturbed. She locked his door then turned to him, smiling at his frightened rabbit look.

"Gemma, I'm working."

"Well..." She slowly made her way back to him. "It seems like you need a break."

He checked his watch. "I have a meeting in ten minutes."

"Perfect." She stood on her toes, sucking and nibbling at his throat as she dragged her hands down his chest, lightly scratching her nails down his sides until she reached his pants.

"You're a troublemaker," he said, his voice hoarse as she unbuckled his belt and knelt down to the floor.

"Maybe you need a little more trouble in your life." She dropped his pants and underwear to his knees, and he let out a deep, throaty groan when she kissed his hip bone.

"That's why I keep you around."

She agreed with a hum as she took his cock between her lips, and above her, he leaned his hands on his desk.

"If this is your way of apologizing, I think I might pick a fight more often."

Gem swirled her tongue in circles around the tip before taking over with her hand so she could stare up at him. When he traced his thumb over her bottom lip, she nipped at it. "This is my way of saying I know how hard it is for you to move out of your rigid comfort zone. Thank you for bending for me."

He let out a mix of a choked laugh and a moan when she licked back up his length before sliding him back into her mouth.

"You look so pretty on your knees like this," he murmured, and she preened at the praise.

Gem didn't like to give up power, obviously, and Jason knew that, which was why he probably stared down at her with such respect and emotion. She wanted show him in whatever way she could that he meant the world to her.

As if he could read her mind, he said, "I'd bend over backward if it made you happy." Then she wrapped her hands around the backs of his legs, and he let his head drop back to his shoulders. "Christ...Gem..." With a few long pulls and just a little scrape of teeth, she soon felt his thighs bunching under her fingers. He breathed harshly, biting out, "I'm gonna come."

And when she didn't stop, he gathered all of her hair in one of his hands to watch her swallow. She blinked up at him to find him gazing adoringly down at her. "Gemma, I..." He yanked her up from the carpet by her elbow and held her against his chest so she could hear his heartbeat in his chest. "Gem, I lo—"

She cut off his words with a kiss. The first time either one of them said those words to the other, it wasn't going to be in his office with rug burn on her knees. "I like you too."

He snorted a chuckle and stepped away from her to put himself to rights. "How am I supposed to work after that?"

She lifted one innocent shoulder and backed up to the door, unlocking it. "I'm sure you'll pull it together for your meeting."

"Shit. My meeting! I'm gonna be late." He scrambled to grab his laptop and folders and stuck a pen behind his ear before ushering Gem out of his office with a smack on her ass. He ran out ahead of her, down the hall. "Stop laughing, Gemma. It's your fault!"

She only laughed louder.

FRIDAY NIGHT, Jason opened Gem's apartment door with an annoyed shake of his head. He called her name over Joni Mitchell blaring through an iPod in the kitchen, and when she didn't answer, he found her in the bedroom, dancing while she braided a few strands of her hair like a crown around the top of her head.

He propped himself against the doorframe, appreciating the entertainment her lithe body provided. When the song changed, he gave her a round of applause, and she spotted him in the mirror, not at all startled by his sudden presence. "Creep, hanging out like that, lurking in corners."

"You're lucky it's me and not some ax murderer. Your front door is unlocked."

Gem sashayed up to him, dragging a finger down his pectoral muscle, her fingernail scraping along his checkered blue dress shirt. "I am lucky." Then she flicked up his navy tie, purposely skewing the clip. "This color really brings out your eyes."

He fixed the clip back in place then smoothed down his tie. "Thank you, but you should lock the door." He held on to her arms, forcing her to look at him. "Seriously. Anybody could have barged in here."

She leaned up to kiss him. "I left it open for you. There's only you."

The balloon in his chest inflated with her words, *only you*. If it weren't for her holding his hand to playfully spin underneath his arm, he might have floated away.

There was only Gem.

Whirling away from him so her dress floated around her, she held up her arms. "What do you think?"

The dress was somehow both loose and sexy, with long sleeves and a skirt with a slit up the side. Although the pattern reminded him of something that belonged on a kitchen table-cloth with polka dots and flowers, she could've been wearing a burlap sack and he'd still think she was the most beautiful person on earth. "I think you look like a rich woman who went to the mountains for a weekend nature retreat. She did it for the 'gram."

She cracked up and nudged his shoulder. "That's exactly what I was going for."

"I figured."

At the art museum, Gem led the way, rattling off the name of almost every painting housed there. The party was on the second floor, in a large reception hall where the pieces to be auctioned off were exhibited. There must have been well over two hundred people in attendance, and Gem snagged a glass of champagne from a passing server as a tall man—even taller than Jason—greeted her with a kiss on the cheek. With his receding hairline and wrinkled forehead, Jason pegged the man at about the same age as Frank.

Gem introduced him to Jason as the curator of the museum. "Simon has been my mentor for many years."

He waved his hands in disagreement. "I have done nothing for Gemma besides give her a job. The talent this young woman possesses is far beyond anything I could have taught her." He switched his attention to Jason and offered him a stiff hand-shake. A warning. "She is very special, as I'm sure you are aware."

"Yes. Very special." Jason nodded, and Simon smiled, seem-ingly pacified, before holding his elbow out to Gem. "The mayor is here. She brought Congressman Carey with her this time."

She glanced back at Jason, gesturing with her head to follow, and they ended up next to a small group of attendees. Witnessing Gem hold court with the two government officials and fellow artists, he felt a little intimidated but mostly over-whelmingly proud. She spoke passionately about her work with the children, the importance of creative outlets available to them, and the need to keep art in schools. Simon invited the congressmen to meet the few art students who were present and volunteered Gem to give him a tour of the museum.

She squeezed Jason's fingers. "I'm sorry. I didn't think

I'd be—"

"Do your thing. I'll be fine."

She kissed his cheek before escorting the congressman and mayor to the other end of the room, eventually lost in a sea of people. Grabbing a glass of water, Jason strolled around the exhibit, studying a clay bust, a few abstract paintings, and one very unusual piece of metal work. It was titled "A Mother's Gift," but to Jason, it only looked like misshapen pieces of bronze metal. He rotated his head almost upside down. Maybe he was at the wrong angle. "Nope, still don't get it."

"What are you doing?"

Jason swirled upright at the sound of Cole's voice. The kid stood next to him in a suit and tie, and they fist-bumped. "Hey, buddy. Nice to see you here."

"Yeah. I came over so people don't think you're weird, talking to yourself."

"Good looking out, man."

"Do you want to see my picture?" Cole asked, the excitement streaming out of him.

"Of course. That's why I'm here." The little boy showed him to a wall with student work and pointed to a picture of a tree-lined street. It was no van Gogh, yet still pretty impressive for a ten-year-old. "Amazing. Did you do that with Miss Gem?"

"Yeah. It's watercolor." Cole proceeded to explain the process of painting it, and Jason found himself shadowing him as he talked about art class and Miss Gem. Jason saw himself in Cole, in the way he didn't bother to breathe when going off on a tangent about a subject he loved, and how he bounced on his toes to reach for a high five. Just like Jason used to do with his dad.

Cole's mother eventually collected her son, leaving Jason to continue through the exhibit alone, searching for Gem's piece. Since she'd refused to show it to him, he had to rely on the plaques to find it, having no idea what she'd created. He located her name printed below a large charcoal drawing. He stood back, marveling at it.

Gem had depicted a portrait of young love. A man, looking suspiciously familiar, sat in profile, sprawled beneath a tree with a book in hand and his long legs crossed at the ankle. His head, covered with a mop of hair, was tilted up against the trunk, his eyes above him, focused on a young woman, lying on a branch jutting out from the side of the tree. Her hair cascaded down her back in long waves, and one hand rested under her cheek, while the other dangled a feather above her lover's head. Their faces expressed total adoration and contentment.

Jason pressed his hand to his heart, awestruck by the beauty of it. He had, of course, seen many of Gem's scrawling designs around her apartment, and he had sat patiently while she sketched his eyes or hands, but the scene in front of him was truly magnificent in its simplicity of romance in black-and-white.

"You like it?"

Wrenched from his thoughts, Jason angled himself to the man next to him who looked vaguely familiar. He wore a dark suit, and Jason was suddenly very aware that he'd forgone the suit jacket tonight. The man held his drink aloft in greeting.

"I do," Jason replied.

"Me too. I've gotten to know the artist a little, and I think this is one of her best pieces. Gemma Turney has a very interesting perspective. Are you familiar with her?"

Jason eyed him. "I am. How do you know her?"

"I was introduced to Gemma last year. We went out on a few dates, but she ghosted me. Broke my heart." He muffled a laugh, his eyes shining in a way that told Jason he wasn't exactly telling the truth and maybe he was still interested. That idea had Jason curling his hands into fists, especially when the guy said, "She's quite a woman."

It was then Jason remembered who this man was. "You're the

news guy. Colin Mann."

"Yes." Colin Mann, the local news anchor, had a head full of brown hair, perfectly straight, white teeth, a Hollywood tan, and a deep voice meant for broadcasting. "Nice to meet you."

"Jason Mitchell," he said, accepting Colin's hand. "Gem's boyfriend."

The two men shook, sizing each other up, both standing a little taller, puffing out their chests. Colin was the first to break free. "You are familiar with her then, huh?" He smirked and pointed to Gem's art. "Are you planning on bidding?"

"Of course." Jason wanted nothing more than to smack Colin's smarmy grin off his face. What a douchebag this guy was.

"Well, I hope you brought your wallet because you got yourself some competition for this one."

The double meaning was not lost on Jason, and he excused himself to find Gem. When he caught up with her, he held on to her waist, kissing the skin behind her ear. The whole Bridget situation made itself perfectly clear. He'd been sympathetic to Gem's jealousy before, but he'd never fully understood it until now.

She leaned into his touch. "What have you been up to?"

"Exploring," he said, though he couldn't hide the irritation in his voice. "Are you really going to auction off your drawing?" He scrunched up his face when she nodded. "You can't."

"Why not?"

"You can't, Gem. I don't want some asshole buying it."

She arched a questioning eyebrow, and he ground his teeth. "I met Colin Mann."

"Oh." The word contained volumes, but she only shrugged. "It's just a picture. I could always draw more."

Jason shook his head in disagreement. "But that's us—"

With her index finger on his lips, she kissed the corner of his mouth, effectively ending the argument, and Simon took his place behind a small podium, announcing he would begin the auction, but first, he brought a woman to the stage. She introduced herself as Elizabeth, the president of Artist Point, and gave a short speech on the history of the charity, thanking a few important people, Gem being one of them. Jason held her a little tighter.

The first piece of art auctioned off was a small oil painting, followed by a lot of uninteresting landscapes. Gem explained the nuances of color and different mediums used in each work before, finally, her picture was put on the block. The bidding quickly escalated to a few hundred, but it was Colin who upped the ante to one thousand dollars.

"Fifteen hundred," Jason pronounced loudly. Gem tugged on his hand, but he ignored her. The crowd watched with rapt attention as the two men warred, the tension growing higher with each rising number. A collective gasp resounded over the room when the newscaster bid three thousand dollars.

Jason was about to raise his hand, but Gem grabbed it. "Enough, Jason. Stop."

Simon started counting down, and Jason's eyes darted between her picture, Colin, and back to Gem. "I don't want him to have it."

She held his face between her hands, forcing his eyes to hers. "You have me, Jason. You have nothing to prove to him." He grumbled under his breath, and she kissed him. "You have me."

Simon awarded the prize to Colin, who was asked to come onstage so everyone could acknowledge his generous contribution to the charity. He waved to his audience, an arrogant smile plastered across his face, and Jason let out an angry growl. Gem repeated her statement, pulling his arms around her waist.

Toward the end of the auction, the paintings by the students were offered up. Even though their work was only being auctioned for fun, the kids took it quite seriously, especially Cole, who whooped in delight at the front of the stage.

Jason's animosity to Colin, his pride in Gem, and his friendship with Cole had him raising his hand to point at Cole's landscape. "Five hundred dollars."

"Wow!" Cole shouted out. "I'm rich."

The room broke out in laughter. His parents quickly tried to correct him, explaining he didn't receive the five hundred dollars; it went to the charity.

"Sorry, buddy," Jason said, patting the boy's back. "But your painting is going to look great on my wall." Cole ran up to the podium to snatch his artwork from Simon's hands and happily handed it over to his friend. "I will take good care of it," he promised as Gem eased her hand around his elbow, towing him to a quiet corner.

"You didn't have to do that," she said, her hands winding into his hair telling a different story.

"Yes, I did. Cole's your student, and if I can't have your work because—" he stopped short, wanting to put Colin Mann out of his head. "You are in this too," he said, pointing to Cole's painting. "You're in all those kids' works. They love you and—"

"I love you."

Jason froze at her blurted words. "What did you say?"

She dragged her fingers down his jaw, over his shoulder, to rest in the middle of his chest. "I love you."

He enclosed Gem's cheeks in his hands, his thumbs stroking her cheekbones, nose, and lips. He touched every part of her face, memorizing it with his fingertips. If he could, he'd sculpt her out of clay, show her how beautiful she was. Show her what she looked like through his eyes. "I love you too, Gemma." His words left his lungs with a rush of air, breathing life into them. "I love you."

Then they kissed. A sweet yet timid first kiss of two people who loved each other, and when they broke apart, smiling like two idiots in love, he laughed. And then she laughed. And then they kissed again.

After a moment, Gem backed away from him. She had that twinkle in her eyes. The twinkle that told him she had an idea.

"Come on." She towed him down a flight of steps to the first floor and turned to a deserted hall with offices. She pulled him into a small conference room with a square table and chairs, then locked the door behind them. Jason immediately took her in his arms, hoisting her onto the table, devouring her pleas with his mouth. His teeth bit at her neck, fingers dug into her waist. She hooked her fingers under his waistband, but he stopped her hand from moving. "I don't have a condom."

"I don't care. I love you. I need you. Now."

And that was it. He undid his pants, lifted her dress, and crashed into her again. She wrapped her legs around his hips as his hands clutched the table for stability, and she guided him into her, sighing with relief. There was no barrier between them. Nothing but her warm sweetness filling his senses.

She was everywhere. Her hands at his back, her breath on his skin, and he looked, smelled, tasted his fill. He wanted to remember everything about this moment and about the woman he loved.

They were both close to coming, and he bent over her, his lips grazing her collarbone as he whispered over and over how much he loved her, touching the spot between her legs until she panted against his ear, drowning out the echo of his heartbeat.

I love you, it drummed. *I love you. I love you.*

With one last thrust, Jason came, releasing hot liquid that overflowed between Gem's thighs as he rested his forehead on her shoulder. Their ragged breathing resonated in the quiet space, and she kissed his neck over and over again until he picked up his head.

His eyes were heavy, a lazy smile spread from cheek to cheek. "Well, Gemma, you have every piece of me now. Don't hurt me."

"Never."

23

By the time the November chill rolled in, Gem and Jason had fallen into an easy routine. They spent almost every night together, cooking dinners and laughing before tumbling into bed. Every once in a while, Gem could convince him to do something he considered reckless, like skinny-dipping in the freezing lake or having sex on the local high school's baseball field. He always put up a fight about it, but she knew he loved it.

Their relationship was easy and natural and fun, when they weren't arguing. But that could be fun too, sometimes.

Gem dropped her key to Jason's house on the kitchen table and untied her scarf, calling for him. He answered from upstairs. "I'm doing laundry."

She found him in the bedroom, in gray sweatpants, bare-chested, and a pile of clothes on the bed.

"Hey, you," she drawled, watching him gently fold one of her tops.

"How was yoga?" he asked without taking his eyes off his chore.

She sat on the edge of the bed, admiring his body. "Tiring."

"Tired? Really?" He egged her on with a teasing lilt of his

lips. "I ran five miles and then did a whole bunch of pull-ups at the gym today." He used her underwear as a slingshot, the black thong bouncing off her cheek. "You did breathing exercises."

She scowled. "You think you're so tough. You can't even touch your toes."

He raised an eyebrow at her before opening a drawer to put his clothes away and, without notice, took a running leap onto the bed, bowling Gem over. He held one of her legs up by his shoulder and nestled in the wide opening. "You're right. You are the flexible one." He pulled a tube sock off her foot. "Stealing my socks again, I see."

"They're so comfortable, I can't help—" She shrieked when he took a bite at her calf. "Hey! Play nice."

"I am." His words were barely audible as he sucked at the skin beneath her ear.

Gem let out a hum, relishing in the pressure of Jason's body weight on top of hers. "I have to shower," she breathed, angling her neck so he could kiss along the other side of her throat.

"But you smell so good." He nipped her earlobe. "Vanilla and sweat. Sweet and salty."

Fighting was pointless. She melted underneath him, and he slowly peeled off her clothes. His lips moved over hers as his hand brushed the inside of her thighs before finally settling on the soft skin between her legs. He teased her open, his fingers long since familiar with the touch and tempo she needed.

"I love you," he whispered against her breastbone before covering her nipple with a luscious kiss. Gem was slick with want and delirious from two orgasms by the time Jason rolled off the bed to put on a condom. He swiftly returned, raising her leg over his shoulder again. He placed a trail of kisses up her calf, ending at her knee, then sank into her with a low grunt, gently rocking his hips against her.

She tangled her fingers in his golden hair, licking the skin of his chest, damp from effort. His breathing quickly became uneven, the muscles in his arms and legs tightening with each movement, straining in his race to make sure she came one more time. True to his promise, he worked hard, perfecting the ways he could bring her to orgasm with a lot of practice—it was one of his best qualities—and she moaned her release with Jason following soon after, arching his neck.

His long torso was covered in a sheen of sweat as he lay down next to Gem. "Shower?" he asked, wiping at his upper lip, and she answered by skipping off toward the bathroom. She was mid-shampoo when Jason took over. He rinsed her hair and finger-combed conditioner through her long tresses.

"I was thinking..."

She turned around underneath the stream of water to face him.

"All right, so..."

She reached for a bar of soap, waiting patiently for him to continue. "Yeah?" When he still struggled to find his words, she washed Jason's shoulders, chest, and stomach. "You going to tell me?"

"I was thinking. Remember the night at the museum?"

She bit her bottom lip. How could she forget? "Yes. I remember." She guided him by the shoulders, turning him away from her so she could soap up his back. "Is that all you were thinking?"

He dropped his head as she kneaded away the tight knots in his neck. "That feels great."

A few minutes passed before Gem finished her all-over body massage. She was working on his hair when he circled back around to face her, drops of shampoo falling from his forehead, his face still plagued by something.

"You know, Jason, we're in this nice warm shower, naked, soaping each other up, and somehow you look like you're not enjoying it at all. I think I might be offended."

"I was remembering how I wasn't wearing a condom." He

closed his eyes to rinse his hair and face, dousing his body with handfuls of water. "I was thinking you should go on the pill. We wouldn't have to use condoms anymore."

Gem didn't answer. Instead, she crossed her arms over her chest, suddenly very uninterested in this conversation. After a minute, he wiped at his face, squinting through the bubbles still on him. "What?"

"How can you ask me that?" She left the shower in a huff. "It's like you don't know me at all." She grabbed a towel, and he hurried to shut off the water, following her into the bedroom. He held out his hands, dripping wet, while she ignored him, dressing quickly.

He held on to her arms, halting her steps. "I'm sorry."

"For what?"

"I don't know."

She rolled her eyes. "You can't apologize for something you don't know you did."

"So tell me what I did, and I'll apologize for that."

"Gah!" She ripped out of his grip. "You're such a caveman. I'm not taking a birth control pill," she said and marched down the hall.

Jason, still clad in a towel, traipsed right after her as she threw laundry into the washing machine. He shut the door, keeping Gem from escaping him again. "If I ask you another question, are you going to yell at me?" When she cocked her head at him to continue, he asked, "Why don't you like the pill?"

She narrowed her eyes. "Seriously? You want me to put hormones in my body?"

"You already have hormones," he told her, running his hands over his wet hair.

"Thank you for letting me know. And, yes, my hormones are working just fine. I'm not going to alter them. If nature wanted me to have different levels of them, I would. I'm not going on the pill.." She gestured to his crotch. "But feel free to get a vasectomy if you want to go bareback so badly."

This time, Jason folded his arms. "Don't be so dramatic. It was only a suggestion."

"Suggestion overruled." She turned back to the laundry and jammed the start button on the washer when Jason snapped his towel on her butt. She let out a squeal, holding on to her behind.

"Forgot one," he taunted, holding the towel out to her, completely naked.

She couldn't hide her smile.

"Come here," he said, wrapping the cotton towel around her like a robe, immobilizing her arms.

As he tossed her over his shoulder to bring her back to bed, she smacked his butt. "Wait, wait, wait."

He set her feet down on the floor and pushed her onto the mattress with one finger. "What?"

"I don't have class next week because of the holiday, and Laney's going to be in Chicago for some kind of conference. Her boyfriend is tagging along, and we thought we could all meet up for drinks."

"Yeah, I'd love to meet these best friends of yours." Then he opened the towel, unwinding her like a top.

THE FOLLOWING WEEK, Gem and Jason met Laney and Bobby for drinks in Rockford, about midway between Galena and Chicago.

"Remind me again which one Laney is." Jason draped his arm over the back of her chair.

"She's originally from outside of Philadelphia but lives in San Francisco now. She's the prettiest one out of all of us," she said, bobbing her head along to the three-piece band playing Celtic folk music.

"I highly doubt that." He placed a kiss behind her ear. "She's the one getting her doctorate?"

"No, that's Sam. She's in Michigan right now for school."

"I think I need a diagram or something." He drew an imaginary square on the table. "Okay," he said, trying again. "Sam is the one in school with the purple hair?"

"I think it's mermaid-colored now, actually."

"You know what?" He waved his hand. "I'll figure it out eventually." Though, he didn't have to wait long. Laney and her boyfriend showed up, and the two girls squawked in excitement while Jason introduced himself to Bobby Magnate.

"Hey, mate," he said with an Australian accent, which had Gem leaning back out of Laney's embrace.

"Hey, mate. I'm Gemma."

"Laney's told me a lot about you. Shall we?" Bobby asked, holding his hands out so they would all take their seats.

Over their few hours together, the girls mostly chatted, while Bobby sometimes added in some colorful sayings of Aussie slang Jason had never heard. Laney, with blond hair, blue eyes, and a tiny mole by her nose, did have a kind of old-school Hollywood vibe about her, although she munched on peanuts, drank beer, and laughed louder than anyone in the place. She told great stories about her travels and job with the baseball team, but the only thing he cared about was how happy Gem was to be with her friend.

"So, Jason," Laney said, putting her elbows on the table and her chin in her hands, "you've managed to capture our pixie friend. You got Gem trapped in a drawer like *Peter Pan* or what?"

"Captured? I don't know about that. I think it's the other way around."

Laney smiled wide. "I'm happy to finally be able to do this. We never get to see each other." She looked to Gem. "When's the next time?"

"I don't know. Sam mentioned she was going home for New

Year's for a few days, but Bronte will probably be with Hunter."
Gem rolled her eyes, and Jason briefly wondered what that was
about before she continued. "Maybe your birthday?"

"Oi, babe, January, right?" Bobby said, toying with a few ends
of Laney's hair. "I've got the restaurant opening then."

Gem snapped her fingers. "Oh yeah. I want to hear all about
that."

Bobby leaned back in his chair and gave them a short
summary about how he'd made a name for himself in Sydney as
a restaurateur, then moved to America to open up a place in
New York City. He was apparently really popular in the food
world, even had some guest judge gigs on Food Network shows.
He had plans to open another restaurant in the Bay Area, which
was where he met Laney. "I'm trying to convince the missus
here to become the communications director for the Magnate
Group, but I've yet to win her over."

Laney lifted a shoulder. "I drive a hard bargain."

"So, not January for the girls' weekend, then?" Gem said.
"Might be a while till we're all back together again."

Laney agreed with a frown, and Jason took that as his cue to
get up. He invited Bobby to head to the bar with him, giving the
girls a chance to talk alone for a bit. Bobby was a nice guy,
although he had a wandering eye when it came to the female
bartender and the woman sitting opposite them at the other end
of the bar.

At the end of the night, Gem and Laney hugged, kissed each
other's cheeks, then hugged again. Jason shook Bobby's hand,
and they parted ways.

Back at Gem's apartment, Jason plopped on the sofa. George
Clooney curled up in a ball next to him. "I think he's starting to
like me."

"He should, you've been around long enough." Gem took a
seat on his other side and took hold of his hand to wrap his arm
around her neck. "Did you have fun tonight?"

"Of course. I always have fun with you. It was nice to see you with Laney. You guys are obviously really close, so I'm happy you got to spend time with her."

"The four of us are all really different, but they're like my sisters. I don't have anyone else in my life like them." She craned her neck back, her eyes a little droopy with sleep. "It was important for me that you meet Laney. I wish it could've been all of them, but thanks for coming tonight."

He kissed her forehead. "You don't need to thank me for that. I had fun, and I really like her. Jury's still out on Bobby, though."

"Really?" She gasped. "Why? He's so hot and with that accent..." When she bit her lower lip theatrically, he jostled her.

"I guess he's hot," he said with a surly shrug, and she laughed. "He just didn't seem real interested in Laney or, like, in anything you two were saying. It was all about him—at least, that's the impression I got."

"Interesting." Gem's eyes went unfocused, probably thinking through that, and he rested his cheek on her head, telling her the one thing he'd been contemplating for a while now. "We should move in together."

She jerked back, forcing his head up. "What?"

"Do you want to move in with me?"

She pulled her feet up onto the couch, curling in on herself, pointedly not answering, and he sat up straight, releasing his arm from around her shoulders to take her chin between his thumb and index finger. "Move in with me."

"Why?"

He huffed out a laugh. He thought it rather plain. "I'm tired of spending half the week here and half the week at my house. We should live together and stop all this back-and-forth."

Her eyes shifted to somewhere beyond him, and Jason didn't realize she'd have such a hard time with this suggestion. They were in love with each other, spent so much time together, this seemed like the logical next step, but Gem practically vibrated with nerves.

He could physically feel her hesitation.

"What about Mr. Clooney?"

He moved his hands to her neck, his thumbs gliding along the slope of her jaw and collarbone, and he let out an exaggerated groan in play disgust. "I guess he can come too. And Leonardo and Spot, which, by the way, is a really weird name for a fish."

"It's ironic."

He smiled, glad she could joke around instead of how she was acting a moment ago. "So?"

"I don't know," she said after an eternity.

"What don't you know?"

She pulled out of his grasp, taking his hands in hers. "It's just—"

"I love you, Gem." His tone was no longer playful.

"I love you too."

"Then what is it? I don't get it."

She shrugged, and he held back a grumble of irritation. He didn't want to push her into anything and suspected this had something to do with how self-conscious she was about her supposed failures. She didn't bring it up often, but she'd remarked about the differences in their careers and the amount of money they each made a few times.

"If this is about the mortgage or bills or whatever—"

"Jason." Her gaze fell to the couch, where she played with a fray of the material. "I love you, and I want to be with you, but this is all still very new."

"I know," he agreed, wanting to give her the space and time she needed, while also keeping her all to himself.

"It's all just…a lot." She slowly picked up her eyes to meet his. "Can we put a pin in this and talk about it after the new year?"

He breathed deeply. He could give her that; the new year was only a few weeks away. "Yeah, okay," he said, trying to mask his disappointment.

"I'm not saying no." She stood up, tugging on his hand to follow, and he unfolded from the couch, letting her wrap her arms around his waist. "Don't be mad at me."

"I'm not mad."

"Don't be upset."

"I'm not upset." When she eyed him skeptically, the corners of his mouth turned up. "I am not upset. I'll wait. As long as you want me to, I'll wait."

"Then let's not make you wait any longer to take those pants off, huh?"

24

Gem woke up with a knot in her throat. Stomach twisting, she threw her hand over her mouth, sprinting to the bathroom. She fell to the floor, barely making it to the toilet before throwing up.

"Gemma? Are you okay?"

Still retching, she couldn't answer Jason.

"Gemma?" He dropped down on his knees next to her, holding her hair back. When her stomach finally settled, she rested her arms on the seat, and he stroked her head. "How do you feel?"

She breathed deeply, in her nose and out her mouth, eyes closed. "Terrible."

He handed her a cold washcloth, and she swiped it over her face and neck. "Maybe it was the beer?"

After brushing her teeth and taking a few sips of water from the faucet, she looked at herself in the mirror. "I only had one glass."

He shrugged, rubbing her back in soothing circles. "Do you feel better?"

"I guess. What time is it?"

"A little after four."

Gem slunk back to bed, and Jason tucked her into his side, kissing her temple, and she quickly fell back to sleep. A few hours later, Jason shook her awake. He sat on the edge of the bed, fully dressed for work. "I'm leaving. Are you planning on getting up anytime soon?"

She only closed her eyes.

"Are you still feeling sick?" he asked, pressing his palm to her forehead.

"I'm so tired."

"Guess we can't go out on weeknights anymore, old lady."

She garbled a curse and tucked the covers around her head.

"I'll check in with you later," he said and kissed her head through the covers. "Love you."

A few minutes later, she forced herself out of bed and into the shower. Feeling much better after getting dressed and eating a little cereal, she fired off a text to Laney on her way to work. **Do you feel okay today? I puked this morning, maybe from the food?**

I'm fine. Hope you feel better! Laney replied moments later.

Being the day before Thanksgiving, customers were few and far between at Bare Necessities, but Andrew kept Gem busy by forcing her to cut out advertisements for Black Friday in exchange for buying lunch. She was in the middle of a vegetable burrito when Jason called.

"Hey, you." Gem dabbed her mouth with a napkin as she greeted him.

"Hey. What are you up to?"

"I'm being forced to go through every sale paper in the state. Andrew wants a new toaster for his kitchen and a vacuum for his mother-in-law."

"Sounds awful. Want to trade jobs?"

She snorted. "If I had your job, I'd be making houses out of mud and tires."

Jason's deep laughter on the other end of the phone coaxed a smile out of her. "Did you eat lunch?"

She picked up a few beans that had fallen out of the burrito and popped them in her mouth. "In the middle of it. Andrew bought Mexican."

"I'm starving. I've been in meetings all day. But I'm glad you're better."

Pushing the rest of her lunch away, Gem rested on her elbow. "I never got to say thank you for helping me this morning. You're a good nurse."

"Next time we play nurse and patient, I don't want you to be actually sick. You've got—" He stopped mid-sentence, and Gem heard muffled voices on the other end of the phone. "Gem, I've got to go. Let me know if you need anything, okay?"

"Okay. I love you."

"You too."

Gem clicked her phone off to find Andrew bent over the counter, hands on either side of his face, staring at her with princess eyes. "What?"

He uncurled himself. "You and your..." He folded his hands next to his ear, lifting a leg up behind him, belting out a silly little tune.

"What about it?" Gem asked, throwing away her leftovers, not hungry anymore.

"You're extra swoony today. Although if I were sleeping with that Adonis, I'd be swooning too."

"He wants me to move in with him," Gem said, her stomach feeling a little queasy.

"What?" Andrew jumped up like a jungle cat to sit on the counter. "Tell me everything. What did he say? What did you say?"

She skimmed her fingers over her throat, struggling with

her decision and this apparent food poisoning. "He said it was stupid that we are always going from his place to my place, we should just make it one place."

"And?" Andrew circled his fingers.

"And..." Gem bit her lip. "And I said that it was a big deal, and we should talk about it after the new year."

He laced his fingers together, placing them on his leg, one crossed over the other—lecture mode—and Gem groaned inwardly. "From one girl to another," he said with a stiff shake of his head, "you are such a pussy when it comes to love."

"I hate that word used in that context." She tied up her hair, suddenly hot.

"Yes, I know," Andrew said, waving his hand by his head. "The vagina is the strongest organ, able to survive childbirth, blah, blah. I've sat through your TED Talk, so now you need to sit through mine."

Gem clunked her head on the counter, letting it cool her cheek.

"He loves you, you love him, you have to stop pretending you don't know it. That boy has shown up for you over and over, right? I know it was all hate you, fuck you in the beginning, but he's shown you how he can and will support you."

Too drained to argue, Gem let him continue, even as her throat grew thick. She took another deep breath.

"If you want to be with him, be with him. You can't let your past dictate your future. Not every man will walk out on you. Or, if you can't work through your fear, you'll always be stuck where you are, without that beautiful man." He sighed exaggeratedly. "And that would be the real travesty."

Andrew made sense, Gem knew that, but still. It was hard to take that big of a leap. She required baby steps, and saying I love you to Jason already felt like walking before she'd learned to crawl.

Andrew hopped to the floor, fixing his hair. "Besides, it's

bound to happen anyway, right? First comes love, then comes marriage, then comes the baby in the baby carriage."

Gem shook her head, her thoughts and stomach churning, and opened a bottle of green tea. As she tried to take a sip, her insides lurched. The nausea came back full force, and she covered her mouth. "I'm going to be sick."

In a flash, Andrew had the garbage can in front of her. In between gagging fits, Gem explained she was sick from last night.

"Sweetie, I don't think it's from beer or bad food."

Gem hung her head between her knees. "I think you're right."

"It's probably a stomach bug. Go home and rest."

"No, I'm okay," she said, shoving aside her bangs stuck to her damp forehead.

"Go home." Andrew held up Gem's bag and pressed a small bottle of ginger into her palm. "Take this. It'll help settle your stomach."

A FEW HOURS LATER, Jason opened Gem's apartment door with his arms full of shopping bags. She smiled, glancing up from the television, and yawned an inaudible greeting. She didn't look bad, color in her cheeks, but maybe a little tired.

He unpacked the bags in the kitchen before handing her a Gatorade and settling down on the couch. Gathering the blanket around her toes, he placed them gently in his lap. "You think you need to call the doctor?"

"It's probably a twenty-four-hour thing. I'm feeling better anyway."

"Are you sure?" When she nodded, he pointed to the blue liquid. "Drink," he ordered.

She slowly sipped from the bottle. "You should sleep at home tonight, quarantine me."

"Nope." He rubbed her legs. "You said it yourself, I'm a good nurse."

"Go home," she argued rather unconvincingly.

"You say the word, and my home becomes your home."

She ignored him, snuggling deeper into the blanket.

"Or we can stay up late watching cheesy pre-Christmas Christmas movies on this broken-down sofa in your apartment, and then tomorrow, we can take a ride to my place so I can change before dinner."

"Yeah, that sounds good." Gem covered her cheeky smile with the blanket.

"You're lucky I like you." He pinched her little toe and hunkered down for the night, surrounded by Gem, a comforter, and a barrage of bad holiday movies.

Early the next morning, Jason stirred from sleep, his left side tingling with pins and needles. They'd fallen asleep on the couch, and he rolled his sore neck from side to side then untangled his legs from around Gem, falling off the edge.

Startled, Gem picked her head up off a pillow. "You all right?"

"That thing is not made for two people." He stood up, massaging his shoulder. "The one at my place is a lot nicer."

Gem struggled to get up, throwing the blanket off her, saying sharply, "I get it. Your house is better than mine. I should move in with you, I get it."

"Whoa, whoa, whoa." He held up his hands, waiting until she lost that pinched look of hers then picked up the blanket from the floor. "I'm kidding. I wasn't trying to start a fight."

"I'm tired and sore." She took a few deep breaths, wiping the sleep from her eyes. "I'm sorry. I didn't mean to snap at you."

"Still sick?"

She shrugged.

"Want breakfast?" When she shrugged again, he wrapped his arms around her, and she burrowed her head into the spot he knew was her favorite, her temple under his collarbone, her nose tucked into the center of his chest. "How about you lie back down, I make us some coffee, then we watch the parade?"

"You watch the Thanksgiving Day parade?"

"Of course I do. It's an American tradition. As are the legs of the Rockettes," he said, and Gem bit his pec. He laughed, smacking her thigh. "But your legs are much nicer."

Walking her backward, he guided her down to the cushions with an arm around her middle and the other on the back of the couch. She arched toward him, wrapping her arms around his neck. He kissed her. "Feeling better?"

She answered against his lips. "Mm-hmm."

"Are you sure?"

She nodded, widening her legs so he could settle between them, and he rested his weight on top of her. Letting his hands roam from her hip to knee and back, he kissed her neck, but after only a few seconds, her breath caught. "Wait. Wait."

Jason backed off, sitting on the couch next to her. "All right?"

Her hands went to her chest. "I feel...off. Like, everything is making me feel..." She grimaced, her hands motioning vaguely at her chest.

"Well, I have been known to take a woman's breath away a time or two," he said, and Gem punched weakly at his shoulder. "Here." He patted his lap. "Lie down."

She rested her head on his thighs, and he combed his fingers through her hair. Maybe it was her pale complexion from being sick, but he did notice she looked *off*.

He turned on the television, finding the parade right as the commentators announced the Radio City Rockettes.

A FEW HOURS LATER, Gem and Jason sat at a festive table straight from Martha Stewart. A gold leaf tablecloth was topped with two white candles, a centerpiece of acorns and colorful miniature pumpkins, and overflowing bowls of every kind of steaming hot vegetable. Caroline carried in a huge dish of mashed potatoes between two oven mitts.

"You do realize there are only four of us, right?" Gem asked her, moving dishes to make room.

"Yes, I realize that, Gemma, but it's Thanksgiving." She whacked at her daughter with the oversized gloves.

Jason sat up taller, snatching a stalk of asparagus. "Everything looks wonderful, Caroline."

"Thank you. At least someone appreciates it. Wait until you see the—"

"Turkey's here!" Frank carried in a giant, deep-fried turkey on a platter painted with miniature turkeys along the rim. He placed it in the middle of the table.

Gem ignored how the smell of the meat turned her stomach and pointed to the platter. "Where did you find that?"

"The turkey? I went—" Frank started but was interrupted by his wife.

"I was cleaning out a few things when I came across that art project." Caroline looked to Jason. "Gemmie painted that plate when she was twelve."

Jason ruffled Gem's hair. "My little Picasso."

Frank pointed his finger at his guests. "Drinks? Wine? Some pitorro, Gem?"

"No, no, no." She waved her hands in defeat. "I'm a little—" She gestured to her stomach.

"She's got a bug or something," Jason said, tracing circles on the nape of her neck.

She'd felt like such crap, she hadn't bothered to wash her hair and had thrown it up in a bun. While Jason dressed in *real* clothes, Gem couldn't bear to put on anything other than a sweatshirt and leggings.

Caroline stood up from the table. "Do you want me to make you soup? I can make you the kind you like with the stars."

"I'm fine. I'm fine." She was not fine. "Sit down, let's eat."

Frank clapped. "Yes, dig in!"

After everyone's bellies were full, except for Gem, who mostly ate a few forkfuls of sweet potatoes, they all got up to clear the table. Caroline opened a Tupperware to place the leftovers in. "I hear Jason's birthday is in a few weeks."

Gem nodded. "Twenty-eight." She spooned the corn into a smaller bowl, raising her voice so Jason would hear in the other room. "I'm dating an old man!"

He appeared next to her, sliding a gravy boat onto the counter, a lecherous grin on his pretty face. "Yeah, I'm a whole two and a half years older than you. Practically robbing the cradle."

"What are you going to do for your big day?" Caroline asked, placing glasses in the dishwasher.

"I don't know. It's just another day."

Caroline waved a fork in the air. "You two should do something special, maybe take a trip. A weekend getaway."

"Who's taking a trip?" Frank stepped into the kitchen, opening the refrigerator.

"Gem and Jason," Caroline answered before pivoting around to see her husband with his head buried in the freezer. "And what are you doing? We just ate."

"Looking for dessert. I need vanilla ice cream with my apple pie."

As Frank and her mother bickered about when to bring out the pies, Gem moved to the counter to finish cleaning up. She forked the turkey into a plastic container, but the smell of it churned her insides. She dropped the greasy meat into the sink before yanking open the cabinet under the sink and vomiting all her guts into the garbage bin.

"Gemma! Oh my gosh, are you okay?" her mom asked.

After a few moments, Gem steadied herself and stood up, reaching for the faucet to rinse her mouth out with cold water.

"You should make an appointment with the doctor," her mother said.

Jason threw his hands out at his sides. "That's what I told her."

"Maybe she's pregnant," Frank joked, munching on the forgotten turkey.

25

"You're pregnant. Congratulations!" Dr. Garcia happily gave the results of Gem's test.

Her heart skipped. Her stomach dropped. "I'm what?"

The doctor pushed his glasses farther up his nose. "About six or seven weeks along, I'd say, but you'll need to make an appointment with your OB/GYN to know for sure. Get an ultrasound."

Having convinced herself it was the flu, Gem had suffered through one week of the daily vomiting, sometimes multiple times a day, before she'd called to make an appointment with her doctor. It wasn't until the nurse asked her when her last period was that she officially started to freak out.

And now that she'd received the news, the walls had begun to close in. Everything got a little hazy, a little gray, and the paper cover of the cold table stuck to her sweaty palms when she tried to stand. Dr. Garcia was saying something about morning sickness and vitamins when she threw up all over the linoleum floor.

The next few minutes blurred as a nurse rushed in to help. Her body responded to the directions given, but her mind had totally shut down. A far-off voice told her to "Sit down. Put your head between your legs. Breathe deep. Sip this water." But it all sounded like the teacher from *Charlie Brown*.

It was the jolt of a cold, wet cloth that brought those synapses back to proper function.

"Your blood pressure is coming down."

Gem glanced to her left, at a middle-aged nurse wearing scrubs covered with spotted puppies. She patted Gem's shoulder. "Feeling any better?"

Better? Better than what?

Gem's throat felt thick and rough. She attempted to speak. Nothing but a croak released. She angled her head to the nurse, whose understanding smile broke through the fog in her brain.

"I'm pregnant?" she questioned, although it came out flat and lifeless.

The nurse nodded. "Yes, I know."

Gem's blank expression must have tipped off the older woman. "Do you want to be pregnant?"

Searching the room for an escape, Gem remained silent as the question echoed off the stark white walls. A little too white. Her eyes burned from the brightness of it all, and she pressed her fingers into her eye sockets. "I don't know."

She hoped this was all a bad dream, yet when she opened her eyes back up, the nurse was crouched in front of her chair, her hands patting Gem's knees. "It's a surprise, huh? I was stunned when I found out I was having my first baby. It was a few days after the honeymoon, and we had barely moved in to our house. We weren't ready. I wasn't ready to be a mom at all, but you eventually figure it out, you know?" The older woman tilted her head. "Why don't you go home, digest this new information, have a good sleep tonight, and call us back tomorrow. We will put you in touch with some excellent obstetricians, if you need it. Sound good?"

Gem nodded. What sounded good? The information? The sleep? The obstetrician?

Somehow, she found her way home and into bed without consciously walking or driving anywhere. In fact, it seemed as if her brain had completely disappeared. There was nothing, just a black hole up there. She stared at the ceiling of her bedroom, her body completely immobilized with shock.

It wasn't until Jason's voice rang out for her that the shock turned to sheer terror. She scrambled underneath the covers and turned her back toward the door, feigning sleep. Her body trembled, and she prayed he couldn't see her shaking when he poked his head in the door.

He crept to the bed, so heartbreakingly careful not to wake her, and placed a soft, sweet kiss against her hair before shutting the door behind him on his way out. Her eyes stung as tears formed and fell down her cheeks. She was so young and still had so much life ahead of her. For all the plans she'd avoided making in her life, not getting pregnant was one plan she'd intended on keeping. She didn't want to end up like Caroline, getting knocked up and spending her life following men around.

She pressed a quaking hand to her stomach. It didn't feel any different. Her eyes scanned her body. It didn't look any different. But then why was her life being turned upside down by this alien thing inside her?

Anger boiled up. She clenched her fingers together, wishing today had never happened. Wishing that night at the museum had never happened. Wishing none of this had ever happened.

And then as quickly as the anger came, it was eroded by a wave of guilt. A fresh well of tears sprang from the corners of her eyes. She was a terrible person.

She messaged the girls. **SOS SOS SOS SOS SOS SOS**

Sinking down to the floor, she held her phone to her face, squeezing her eyes closed, trying and failing to regulate her breathing. Soon, her palm vibrated with a group FaceTime call. She opened it up, and Sam's face filled the screen. "What's wrong?"

"I think we should wait for the other girls."

"Why are you whispering?"

"Because..." Gem hung her head. "Let's wait, okay?"

Next, Bronte came on, silent in her assessment of Gem, then finally Laney, whose big grin instantly dropped. "Oh Jesus. What is it?"

Gem pressed the volume button to lower it then crawled to the corner of her room so Jason wouldn't hear from his spot in the kitchen. He was banging pots and pans around in there, probably making her dinner like the wonderful person he was, and she let herself cry in front of her friends.

"I'm pregnant."

Bronte covered her gasp with her hand.

"It's okay, it's okay, you don't need to cry. We're here," Sam said. "Are you all right?"

"No, I'm freaking the fuck out."

The girls gave her time to dry her eyes, and Gem stared into the screen of her phone, her best friends staring right back at her.

"When did you find out?" Bronte asked.

"A few hours ago."

Laney plopped her head in her hand. "Did you tell Jason?" When Gem shook her head, she moved closer to her screen. "You don't seem happy."

"Because I don't know how I feel about it."

"Do you want to keep it?" Sam asked, and Gem shrugged. At this point, she honestly didn't know. "You know I had an abortion," Sam reminded her.

Gem nodded. The girls had been with her as she took the pill, watched a *Twilight* movie marathon, and held her hand when she was in pain.

"We'll support whatever you want to do," Laney said, and Gem's eyes flooded with tears again.

Bronte's mouth turned down in a frown, her eyes big and blue and glassy. Whenever anyone cried, so did she. Grabbing a tissue, she said, "It's your decision, but I think you have to tell Jason."

"I don't know," Sam said quietly. "It's not his decision. It's yours. I don't know if you have to tell him."

Bronte blew her nose. "If she wants to be with him, I think she should."

With the two sides presented, Gem was even more confused.

Laney smiled. It was fake but appreciated anyway. "Jason loves you. No matter what you decide to do—keep it or not—I'm sure if you talked to him, explained to him how you're feeling, you'd feel better about it all."

Yeah, but the problem was she couldn't explain it to him because she didn't know. Their relationship was so new, only three months old. She couldn't see how this—being pregnant—could make such a young relationship work when there was still so much unknown.

She didn't know the first thing about being in a long-term relationship, and she sure as hell didn't know anything about being a mother. How could she bring a new life into this world when she was still stumbling around in her own life?

IN THE KITCHEN, Jason made supper. Tomato soup from a can and vegan grilled cheese sandwiches. It was no four-star meal, but he figured it would be easy on Gem's stomach. He hoped that her doctor had finally given her some answers today. This was too many days to be so sick. He'd automatically feared for the worst and spent hours WebMDing her symptoms, which said it could be a multitude of things from kidney failure to gallstones, even lead poisoning.

It was the latter that made him double down on wanting Gem to move in with him. She needed out of this pit of an apartment and into his house. His bed.

Hearing the shower turn on in the bathroom, he hurried to finish the dinner, and in the middle of setting down the plates, her shuffling footsteps came down the hall.

"You look like hell," he murmured. Her hair was wet and flat against her head, her face red and puffy like she'd been crying, and her limp body was covered in oversized flannel pajamas. He smoothed his hands over her face and hair. "What's wrong? What did the doctor say?"

"Bad case of the flu," she said after a few moments of burrowing into his palms.

"The flu? Really?"

She nodded, her eyes downcast.

"Did they give you anything?"

"Uh, no." She pulled away from his grasp and sat in a chair at the table, staring into her bowl of soup. "I guess there's really nothing you can do for it. Just have to stay hydrated and...whatever."

Jason sank into his chair across from her, watching her swallow a few spoonfuls of the red broth before he started eating. "I'm glad it's only the flu and not something worse."

"Mm-hmm."

"Are you feeling any better? Even a little bit? I wanted to go pick out a Christmas tree this weekend, but if you're not feeling up to it, we can do it later."

Gem's eyes slowly drifted up to him, and he encouraged her with a smile. "I think you should go home. I don't want to get you sick." He shook his head, but she continued. "The doctor said I am contagious, so I think it would be better if you stayed away from me for a while."

He popped a piece of grilled cheese into his mouth. "I get the flu shot every year. I'll be fine."

She shook her head. "It's a new strain. That's why I'm so sick."

"It's okay, Gem, really—"

"No!" She stood up from the table with a flourish, her chair grating against the floor.

His eyes widened at her outburst. She was sick, but she didn't have to take it out on him. "What's wrong? I'm sorry that you aren't feeling well, but Christ, you're moody lately."

She closed her eyes and seemed to calm down, measuring her words when she said, "I would really appreciate it if you left me alone for a little while." She pressed both hands to her stomach, and he worried for a second that she might throw up. He moved to help her, but she stopped him, holding out her hand.

Logically, Jason knew she wasn't deliberately trying to hurt him. She was sick and wanted some space until she felt better, but he still resented her stubborn tendencies. Rather than arguing, he cleared their plates without saying another word.

If she wanted him to let her be for a while, he would. He didn't understand it or like it, but what else could he do? He brushed past her, threw on his shoes and coat, and grabbed his keys before opening the door.

"Jason."

He pivoted in the doorway, facing her. She looked drained, her shoulders hunched over and her skin colorless, nothing like his vivacious Gem. She couldn't help that she was sick and feeling out of sorts, and Jason scolded himself for his frustration at her.

"I'm sorry," she apologized, hugging her arms around her chest, her eyes studying the floor.

He traced the line of her chin with his fingertip, pushing it up so she'd meet his gaze. "Me too." He tapped her nose. "I only want you to get better, okay?"

Her brown eyes bounced between his, and he could tell she was thinking about something. Whatever it was, it formed a pit in the bottom of his stomach.

"I love you," she said.

He didn't push her to tell him what was really on her mind, instead saying, "I love you too."

Out of the corner of his eye, Mr. Clooney emerged from the kitchen, red smeared around his whiskers. "It looks like your cat just mauled a mouse," Jason said, pointing at the furball. Gem groaned, stepping toward George to pick him up, but he scurried away. "Can cats eat tomato soup?"

He wondered if maybe he should google it, but Gem only shrugged, her eyes suspiciously bloodshot as if she might cry. "If he's lucky enough to make it out of a dog fight with only one eye missing, he'll probably survive eating tomato soup. Right?"

"Are you sure you're okay?" he asked, and she nodded, leaning her cheek into his for a kiss. He pressed his palm against it—she didn't feel like she had a temperature—then kissed her cheek and temple, pretending he didn't care about why she'd lied to him. He jammed his hands into his coat pockets. "I'll talk to you later," he told her, before turning around to leave.

She didn't answer, only shut the door behind him.

26

Gem's phone buzzed with a text message alert. She knew it was Jason before she picked it up. **Morning, gorgeous.**

She had been avoiding him, resorting to a relationship of texting. It buzzed again. **Feeling better today?**

She slumped in her bed, the back of her head banging against the top of the headboard, and she winced in pain before typing back a message. **Headache.**

It had been five days since she had unceremoniously kicked him out of her apartment on the pretext of an extreme contagion. She had gotten her physical space, but she somehow felt more claustrophobic, strangled with the knowledge of what she was hiding. She'd thought she would have a clear head, be able to make some decisions, but in the past few days, she had made no progress. She didn't even know how or where to start.

She survived on a few hours of sleep each night, plagued with nightmares that involved being run over by strollers and dropping babies on their heads. Though, the days were much worse. Between the morning sickness—which was really around-the-clock sickness—and the lack of sleep, she was a walking zombie. She couldn't concentrate at work, had to call off teaching yoga because she had no energy, and begged for a substitute for her art classes. She looked so haggard, no one had trouble believing she was sick, but she knew at some point she would have to come clean.

Another buzz from her phone. **I miss your face.**

She could hear Jason's playful tone in her head and imagined the crooked smile on his lips as he typed away. She wanted to hide from the text, from the world, from everything, and was about to bury her head under the covers when the doorbell rang. With a blanket wrapped around her shoulders, she opened the door to her mother. Dressed in a long red coat and scarf, Caroline held shopping bags at her sides.

"Gemma Rose, I didn't know if you were dead or alive. You're not answering any of my calls."

Gem fell to the sofa, leaving her mother to invite herself in. "I'm alive."

Her mother pursed her lips. "You need to go back to the doctor. Whatever he put you on is not working, and we need you back to full strength for the party."

"Party?" Gem yawned.

"You would know if you ever picked up your phone."

Gem mocked her mother by showing she could physically pick up her cell phone.

"Honestly, Gemma," Caroline chided as she put the plastic bags on the coffee table to rummage through them. "We're planning a surprise birthday party for Jason." She held up a glittering line of letters that she'd undoubtedly bought from a party supply store.

H-A-P-P-Y-B-I-R-T-H-D- A-Y-!

Gem groaned. Great, to top off her week in self-exile, she needed to find a way to shut down this party. "Mom, I don't think that's a good idea."

Her mother scrutinized her with narrow eyes, her hands on her hips. "Why not? It's your boyfriend's birthday. This is the first time we can celebrate something together, all four of us, and I thought it would be nice to give him this gift."

"It is." Gem squirmed under her mother's gaze. "It's just that..." She lowered her eyes to her blanket, picking at an imaginary pull in the fabric.

Caroline sat down at Gem's feet. "Honey, what's wrong?" When Gem shrugged, she curved her hands around Gem's calves. "I've never seen you like this. I don't think this is the flu. Maybe I should take you to the hospital."

"No."

"Maybe it's mono. Let me see your glands."

Gem cracked when Caroline reached for her throat, blurting out, "I'm pregnant!"

Her mother sat back, her hands frozen halfway between herself and Gem.

"I don't have the flu. I don't have mono. I don't have meningitis or any other type of virus. I'm pregnant."

Their eyes met. Both deep brown and brimming with tears, but Caroline's face lit up in ecstasy. "Gemmie, you're having a baby. That is so wonderful!" She hugged Gem tight to her. "How do you feel?"

Gem heaved out a breath, closing her eyes while trying to discern the exact emotions she was feeling. Fear and regret, then shame for feeling the first two. But mostly, panic.

None to be admitted out loud. "Fine, I guess."

"Does Jason know?"

"No."

Caroline glared at her daughter. "It is Jason's, isn't it, Gemma?"

"Yes, of course, Mom. I love Jason. Of course it's his."

Back to smiling, Caroline rested her hand over her heart. "Well, what's the problem? You should be so excited. You're going to be a mommy!"

"I know. I should be excited," Gem replied. "I should be, and I'm not."

"All new moms feel overwhelmed. Don't worry," her mom said, in possibly the kindest voice she'd ever used with Gem. "It will pass. You'll figure it out. I did."

"Yeah, after twenty-five years."

That came out harsher than Gem wanted it to, and Caroline lost the glint in her eyes. "Being pregnant is difficult, but you are not going to take it out on me."

She moved to stand, and Gem grabbed her wrist. "I'm sorry, Mom. I didn't..." She let out a shaky breath. "I didn't mean it. I'm just... I'm scared."

And then she cried.

Her mother sat back down, pulling Gem almost into her lap as she wrapped her arms around her shoulders and head, letting her get every last tear out until Gem was positive she was dried up.

"I don't know what to do," Gem said, backing away to wipe at her cheeks.

"Do?"

Gem nodded, dragging the back of her sleeve under her nose.

"Do with a baby? You feed it and—"

"No. I mean, if I want it."

"Oh." Her mother nodded and folded her hands in her lap. Whatever lecture Gem expected, it was certainly not, "Your grandparents wanted me to get an abortion."

Gem lurched back in surprise. "What?"

With a deep breath, Caroline smiled sweetly, combing her hand through Gem's hair, saying, "You need to take a shower. You smell. Worse than usual."

"Mom!"

She laughed and sat back against the cushions to get comfortable. "Okay. When I told your grandparents I was pregnant, they told me to get an abortion. They said I was ruining my life, that I wouldn't finish college, that your father was a good-for-nothing."

Gem snorted.

"*Most* of what they said wasn't true," her mother acquiesced. Her mom did eventually finish college and went on to open up a very successful boutique. Although, her father...he absolutely was a "good-for-nothing."

"Why didn't you get an abortion?"

Lifting her gaze to the wall, her mother didn't answer for a while. "Growing up, I didn't always feel loved all the time. Sometimes it seemed as if whether I was born or not, my parents' lives wouldn't have changed. And I don't think I realized how big of a hole I had inside me until I found out I was pregnant." She turned her eyes to Gem as she reached for her hand. "I was scared, and I was worried about your father. It wasn't like I didn't know the type of guy he was. I may be a perpetual romantic, but I'm not stupid. I had hoped he would be the man and father he had promised he was going to be, but I made the decision to have a baby, have you, because it was what I wanted. I wanted someone to love."

Gem swallowed past the lump in her throat, feeling slightly nauseated. "But I don't know how to be someone's mom."

"I don't either."

Mom and daughter both laughed. A short moment of levity after days of what felt like a dark cave Gem couldn't find her way out of. Finally, her mom was there, shining some light.

"No one ever knows how to be a parent. Those books they tell you to read are totally useless. But once the baby comes, you figure it out. It's kind of instinctive."

Gem pointed to the now-empty fishbowl in her kitchen, where Spot used to reside. She'd found the fish floating belly up in the murky water this morning. "How am I supposed to take care of a baby? I can barely take care of my pets. I can barely take care of myself."

A few part-time jobs, a crappy apartment, a dead fish, that was what she had in this world. She didn't know how to be a mother when she was still figuring out how to be an adult, and no matter what Jason said, how often he told her he'd support her, it didn't matter.

All those men who'd dated and married her mother promised the same thing, which was why Gem had always focused on being fiercely independent. She might not have always made the best or smartest decisions, but she'd made them on her own. She'd learned not to rely on anyone else, so when they would inevitably leave, it wouldn't matter. Jason had walked out on her once after an argument; who was to say he wouldn't do it again?

She couldn't control the flashbacks flittering through her memory. The faces of the men who had waltzed in and out of her mother's life, out of Gem's life. Some were kind and treated Gem well, some weren't, though all of them vowed forever, and none of them kept their promise. None of them stayed. Married or not, they left Caroline. They left Gem.

As if her mother could read her mind, she said, "Jason is not like your father. He is not like any of the men who have come and gone in our lives, and there were a lot. I'm sorry about that, Gemma. If there is one thing I would change, it would be that. You didn't deserve to live like that, and I know how it's affected you."

Gem felt her eyes sting with tears again. Honestly, if this was what she had in store for the next seven months, she didn't know how she'd handle it. Then again, if she was thinking about the next seven months, maybe she really did want it.

"I've never known you to be afraid, Gemma."

Gem huffed. That sounded suspiciously like a dare.

"Jason's a good man," her mother continued, tugging Gem

closer to her. "He will be a great father, and you will be a wonderful mother. Much better than I ever was." Taking Gem's face in her hands, her mom said, "Don't make your decision about your pregnancy because you're afraid you can't do it. You can. Make your decision on what you *want*. I will be here to help you no matter what you decide. Whether you want to be a mom now or in the future or never. With or without Jason."

Gem bit her lip to keep her tears at bay and nodded. She was scared, her nightmares were proof of that, but if she thought about her future, she knew she wanted Jason in it. And when she imagined Jason in this future, she imagined him singing to a baby, tossing a toddler in the air, watching some middle school math contest because whatever child they had would, without a doubt, be a nerd.

"You wrote an essay in the seventh grade."

Gem let out a watery laugh at whatever her mother was about to say because she'd stored up every single one of her school projects and assignments.

"It was about how you wanted to change the world." Her mother sniffled and reached for a tissue from the box on the coffee table to dab at her eyes. Then she kissed Gem's forehead. "You have changed the world, Gemma, because you're in it. You changed the world for the better."

It was no use; the tears started up again, and Gem fell into her mother's arms. Because she loved her mother more than words could express. And she was going to have a baby.

27

It was Saturday, the day of the big surprise birthday bash, and Gem was the cover story. Jason was supposed to pick her up to go Christmas shopping, then bring her back to his place, where everyone would be waiting. In the blur of the last few days, Gem had forgotten to get him a birthday present, but she assumed the *big news* would be present enough.

In a turn of events, she was dressed and ready long before he was set to arrive, and she wore down the floorboards pacing the living room, wringing her hands. She hadn't come up with exactly what she was going to say, but she hoped it would come to her in the moment.

Mr. Clooney lay on the floor, meowing loudly, and stopped Gem in her tracks. She had neglected to feed him today, and he wasn't happy about it. She mumbled an apology to him as she walked to the kitchen, where she fed him before moving on to Leonardo. Spot's empty bowl still sat on the counter, untouched. She wasn't sure what to do with it. Much like she wasn't sure what the future held, but as her mother and friends had repeatedly assured her, she would figure it out with Jason.

Busy with cleaning up, she didn't hear Jason enter until he

was next to her, touching her shoulder. She swung around her, pressing her hand to her heart.

"Sorry, I didn't mean to scare you," he said, easing his hands around her waist. He wore a blue sweater that matched his eyes, and when he kissed her neck, she almost swooned in his arms.

"Hi."

"You look better," he said, his gaze roaming over her from top to bottom.

"I feel better."

"Good." He brushed his knuckle down her cheek, his eyes shining brightly, staring down at her affectionately. Now was the time. She only had to be brave.

"Jason, I've been lying to you."

His eyebrows furrowed.

"I don't have the flu."

"But what about the doctor and—"

"I never had the flu."

He searched her face for understanding. "I don't get it."

"I'm sorry I made you worry, but I needed some time."

His eyebrows crimped, his voice taking a harder edge. "Some time?"

"To think." Gem raised a trembling hand to tuck her hair behind her ears, but he got to it first. His fingers barely grazed the sensitive skin of her earlobe, enough to send electricity through her bones.

"You're shaking. Did you eat today?" he asked, and she nodded. She'd kept down some crackers and an orange popsicle. With his hands on her, she was having trouble finding her words, so she stepped out of his grasp.

"Are you going to tell me why you've been avoiding me?" The way his words came out like a joke should have eased her, but the rigid set of his shoulders told her he was pissed, and she was quickly losing her nerve.

"I'm sorry, Jason. I...I've been having a hard time and didn't know how to tell you."

"What, Gem? You're freaking me out."

She reflexively pressed her hands to her stomach. "I haven't been feeling well. I've been sick every day, that part was true. But it isn't the flu that's making me sick. I'm..." She lifted her gaze to his, hoping her growing smile would quell his anger at her. "I'm pregnant."

He blinked.

Took two steps back.

Then blinked again.

"You're what?"

"I'm pregnant."

He shook his head like he had water in his ears. "I don't— why–why didn't you tell me? How long have you known?"

This wasn't exactly the reaction she was expecting, but she could understand. She was shocked too. "I really did go to the doctor. That day you made me soup and grilled cheese. I found out then."

"And you didn't tell me." He lifted a finger first at her then at himself, his voice growing not in warmth but in a painful fury that had Gem's smile dropping. "Why didn't you tell me?"

"I was afraid. I—"

"Afraid of me? So, you lied to me instead. Jesus." He dragged his hands through his hair and down his face. "Gem, I don't get it."

She rushed out an explanation. "I felt like I was being suffocated. Like I was being forced to do things I wasn't ready for."

"I'm forcing you?" His voice rose another octave. "I'm forcing you? To do what? Because as it stands now, I'm not forcing you to do anything. You're the one forcing me."

Gem blanched, her arms dropping to her sides, and for a split second, something that looked like regret crossed Jason's features. But it was gone before she could be sure.

They stared at each other for a moment, and when Gem didn't say anything else, he spun away from her, his fists clenching and unclenching at his sides. His shoulders rose and fell with deep breaths that she could see even through his coat. "You lied to me. You knew for two weeks and didn't tell me. How could you not tell me?"

Gem shook her head, even though he couldn't see with his back to her. "I'm sorry. I didn't know how and—"

"I'm sorry too," he said, cutting her off. "I need to go."

"What? No. Jason." He shook off her hand when she grabbed his arm as he headed to the door. "Please, listen to me. I had stuff to deal with. It had nothing to do with you."

He huffed, whipping his face around to look down at her. "It's not you, it's me... That's what you're going with? I didn't think you were such a cliché."

She gasped, pressing one hand to her chest, where her heart broke underneath her ribs, and one to her stomach, where her baby—their baby—was growing. And then he walked out the door.

She stared at it for a few minutes, too stunned to move, too dazed to cry.

Jason had changed, bent so far from his straight and narrow, and maybe this was too much, too far. Gem had asked him to bend so much, he finally snapped.

And all her worst fears were about to come true. She was pregnant, unprepared and ill-equipped to become a parent, and the perfect world that Gem and Jason had built together ended with the slam of the door.

Like mother, like daughter, history was repeating itself.

OUTSIDE, Jason punched his fist into the brick wall of the apartment building. His knuckles split, but the physical pain was nothing compared to the way his chest felt as if it had been split in two.

He jumped into his car, peeling out of the parking lot, much like the first night he and Gem met. Although, unlike that day, he didn't have to wonder what it was like to be with her. He knew. A goddamn roller coaster, that's what it was.

And it was all getting to be too much. The ups and downs, the push and pull. The secrets and lies.

"Asshole!" he yelled at himself, laughing incredulously. He had lived his life thinking if he could do everything right, be perfect, the people around him would never wound him. He was an idiot because, of course, that wasn't true. The one person he loved most in the world had hidden this huge, life-changing thing from him. The one person he loved most in the world had cut him in two.

And then to give him that line about it being her and not him. Of course it was him. Otherwise, she wouldn't have avoided him; she wouldn't have been lying all these days. She didn't trust him, didn't respect him enough to give him the truth. And... "Fuck!"

He opened all the windows in the car and blared some screaming emo music, trying desperately to drown out the millions of thoughts racing through his mind as he drove onto the highway, hitting one hundred miles per hour. He didn't know how to process any of this, his anger, his hurt, his surprise, his utter confusion. Just a few weeks ago, she had told him she didn't want to move in with him, and suddenly, they were going to have a baby.

A baby.

What the actual fuck.

After a few hours of aimless driving, he pulled into his garage, thoroughly windswept and heartbroken. He jostled his keys into the back door, and he was immediately blown away.

"Surprise!"

A crowd of friends and coworkers huddled in the kitchen, smiling and laughing. Jason stood stock-still, eyes closed, hoping he'd imagined this whole disaster of a day.

Maybe it was a dream.

What happened with Gem was a nightmare.

He opened one eye at a time—fuck, they were still there—to find the group had descended on him. They handed him off, down the line, well-wishes from all. They thrust cards and presents into his hands. When he made his way to the edge of the crowd, Frank encircled him in a bear hug.

"Happy birthday, kid."

"Thanks."

"Gotcha good, huh?"

"You got me," he deadpanned.

Frank chuckled, smacking Jason's shoulder before moving on to entertain a few of his guests, and Caroline bounded up to him, hugging and kissing his cheeks. "Happy birthday, sweetheart!" She took his coat. "Where's Gem?"

"Not here."

"Yes, I can see that." She playfully pinched his arm. "Where is she?" When he shrugged, she narrowed her eyes, smile long gone. "Jason, where is my daughter?"

He met her gaze, unsure of what to say or do. "At her apartment."

"Why?"

He didn't know how much Caroline knew about their *situation*, and he sure as shit didn't know how much he was supposed to say. If anything at all. He shrugged.

"Jason."

Luke and Kevin appeared at Jason's side, luring his attention away. They spoke animatedly about the great tickets they had scored for an NBA game, but Caroline clenched his arm, holding him in place, her eyes concerned. "What about the baby?"

Jason could only meet her gaze with a hardened jaw. He couldn't answer her question because he didn't have an answer.

Caroline rushed away, her hand pressed to her temple, muttering curse words that he'd never thought he'd hear come out of her mouth. He didn't know what a heart attack felt like, but he had a pretty good guess of it from the shooting pain in his chest. He felt his skin go cold, and his knees literally shook underneath him.

"You okay, man?" Kevin asked.

Jason staggered into the living room, and his two friends followed him to a couch, where he plopped down, his body numb.

"You look like you're going to puke," Luke said. Kevin nodded in agreement.

Jason's mouth went dry, words becoming harder and harder to form as his tongue stuck to the roof of his mouth. He couldn't seem to focus, his eyes blurry, his brain like a train charging down a track without brakes.

"What's going on?" Kevin urged.

"Gem's pregnant."

The heads of his friends whipped around to each other and then back at Jason. "Pregnant?" they repeated together.

He nodded, silent.

"It's okay, man. It'll be fine," Luke said, patting his shoulder, although he didn't sound very assured.

Kevin blew out a breath. "I need a drink for this."

Jason licked his parched lips and held up his hand. "Shit, me too."

"Hold on," Luke said, standing up. "I saw somebody brought you whiskey. You really want a drink?"

Jason rubbed his fingers over his forehead then nodded. Like the good friend he was, Luke retrieved the bottle. He unscrewed the top and swallowed a gulp straight from the bottle before passing it to Jason, who twisted it over in his hands. With a sigh, he put the bottle to his lips and took a long pull. The last time he had tasted alcohol was over ten years ago, but tonight seemed like the night to break the dry spell. He winced at the burn in his throat and gave it to Kevin.

The three sat together, passing the bottle back and forth, slowly getting drunk.

28

Thump.

Thump.

Thump.

Gem tried to ignore the low, constant sound. She assumed it was the person in the apartment next to hers stomping around, but eventually, it grew too loud to ignore. Getting up to investigate, she realized it was coming from outside her apartment. She opened her front door to find Jason sprawled on the floor, his leg bent up as if he'd been hitting the wall with his foot, and he toppled inside the apartment like a sack of potatoes.

"Jason?"

He looked up at her, glassy-eyed. "You rang?"

"What are you doing?" When he eventually scrambled to his feet, she got a whiff of him, reeking of alcohol. "You've been drinking."

He stood up to his full height, hanging on to the doorframe for balance as he leaned inside, pronouncing each word slowly and distinctly. "Very astute observation, Gemmie."

"How did you get here?"

"I rode my bike."

"Don't be a jerk."

He smirked, wobbly and derisively. "Can I come in? This jerk wants to talk to you."

She stood in the door, blocking him. "I don't think we should have this conversation right now. Especially when you're like this."

"We have to have this conversation." He loomed over her, his hands above her head on the doorframe. "Now."

Their bodies were so close that her chest met his torso with the rise and fall of each breath, and he stared down at her with red eyes. His mouth slanted down in something that looked an awful lot like loathing, and she slumped against the doorframe. "Jason, please…"

She wanted a life with Jason, one full of laughter and kids and vegan pizza, and had cried about him walking out on her with her mom, who had arrived earlier to talk. She'd told Gem about how he'd walked into the party, looking wrecked. Not that Gem could blame him.

She'd looked and felt that way for a while. And when she finally had her ducks in a row, her life figured out, she had turned his inside out. By hiding away from him, she was able to do some soul-searching, but she'd obviously shattered his heart in the process. She did need to talk to him, but she feared this time she had really fucked it up.

"I'm mad as hell," he said. "Of all the things you are, I never thought you to be a liar."

Her attention snapped back to him, her eyes narrowing on his lips, wanting to be sure of every syllable he spoke.

"But you're full of surprises, aren't you?" he said. He was drunk and angry, and she tried not to take any of his words to heart, but it was almost impossible with the way he looked at her. As if he hated her.

Really hated her.

"I'm driving you home," she said, leaving the door open to

265

walk back inside.

"Not until you tell me why you lied."

"I didn't lie." She grabbed her keys from the coffee table.

"Lie of omission."

She ignored him and stalked to the kitchen, where her coat hung on a chair. He closed the door and trailed her, halting her from putting her arms inside. "Why didn't you tell me you're pregnant?"

The answer was too long to tell him now, and she shook her head.

"If you were hiding this, what else have you been hiding?"

She held up her hand, attempting to stop this. Jason wasn't in the right frame of mind for this particular chat, nor did she want to have it at three in the morning.

He plunked down on a chair and slammed his fist on the table. "Tell me!"

Her eyebrows shot up at his outburst, but her alarm only served her own temper. "I am not going to talk about this with you when you're drunk and it's the middle of the night. Stop screaming." She wound her hair up on the top of her head as sweat beaded on her neck. "You're acting like a dickhead."

He let out an irritated breath through his nose, leaning back in his chair so its front legs hovered above the floor. "These raging hormones have certainly brought out your mean side, haven't they?"

"No. You did."

The chair plopped back down. "You don't get to be angry right now, Gemma. I got that market cornered. I was totally blindsided by you today—for not one, but two reasons. You tell me you're pregnant and that you've been afraid to tell me for two weeks. Two weeks!" He pulled at his hair as he hung his head, his elbows propped up on his knees. "I don't understand," he began, but he stopped when his voice quaked.

"I'm sorry."

"You've been sick, and I was so worried, and you didn't care that I thought..." He sniffled and wiped at his face. "The internet told me it could have been anything. Lead poisoning, cancer, a tapeworm."

She dared to brush her hand over his hair, linking her fingers with his until he looked at her. "You're an engineer. How could you believe everything WebMD says?"

"Because I'm an engineer, Gemma!" He shook off her hand. "That's what I do. I research and read and make Excel spreadsheets. How could you not think I wouldn't worry? I love you! I fucking love you with everything inside of me, Gem, and you..." He dropped his eyes toward the floor, not bothering to wipe his tears anymore. "You have this thing inside you now, and you kept it from me. How can you love me like I love you, with everything inside of you, if you keep it from me?"

She had trouble following all of his thoughts, but she got the gist of it. He felt betrayed. She had broken him, broken him so much he had resorted to drinking, which he had a personal aversion to. Yet, here he was, drunk as a skunk, confessing his heartbreak in fits and starts.

"After everything I've been through with my parents...after everything we've been through, how could you not tell me? We don't keep secrets from each other. We argue and fight, but we don't keep secrets," he said, his words slow and quiet, his head in his hands.

Gem took the same pose, her elbows on the table, guilty sobs racking her body, and yet there was still a small part of her that knew she'd had to do what she'd done to get to this point of self-assurance. This was what he needed to do.

After many silent minutes, Gem dried her eyes and ventured an uneasy touch to Jason's shoulder. He was still. "I'm sorry, Jason."

Nothing.

She slipped off her chair and knelt in front of him, her brow furrowing when she took in his calm face. She poked him. "Jason?"

He breathed slow and even, asleep.

She huffed, half annoyed and half relieved he had passed out with his head in his hands. He may have walked out on her before, but he was here now. And that was a good thing, no matter what happened next.

She went back to bed, replaying the last few weeks in her mind until the early morning hours when her brain finally gave up fighting her body. Her eyes drooped closed as the sun rose, streaking through her window shade.

29

Jason cracked one eye open, his body sputtering to life, and he immediately clapped his lid shut, a headache building behind his temples. He gradually picked his head up off the table, disoriented for a moment as the room spun around him. He grunted, blinking, trying to remember how he ended up asleep in Gem's kitchen.

Bits and pieces of last night broke through the fog, his chest heavy with the memories. He smacked his lips, his dry mouth stale with whiskey and desperate for water. He stood up, his joints cracking in response, and swayed on shaky legs to the sink, where he dipped his lips to the stream.

"He lives."

Jason whirled around a little too fast, and he grimaced, clinging to the counter to get his bearings. After rolling his neck to get the kink out and waiting until his brain had a chance to catch up, he studied Gem—wet-haired and fresh-faced—before bending over the countertop, heartbroken and hungover.

Quietly making her way around the cabinets, Gem put two pieces of bread in the toaster and brewed a pot of coffee. When the toast was ready, she put it on a plate then dropped it and two ibuprofen next to him with a tall glass of water. He gulped down the red capsules and sagged back to the counter.

"What was your drink of choice last night?"

"Jack Daniel's," he said around a bit of toast that was like sand in his mouth.

Gem's lips tipped up in a slight smile as she handed him a cup of black coffee. "Lightweight," she joked. "Did it make you feel any better?"

Ignoring the coffee, he picked at the counter with his index finger. "I didn't want to feel anything. I wanted to forget." He let out a frustrated laugh. "But that's stupid, right? How do you forget that the love of your life is hiding the fact that she's pregnant?"

He cupped the back of his neck with both hands, staring down at the floor, the crack running alongside the bottom cabinets. "Why, Gem? What did I do?"

She stepped toward him. "You didn't do anything. It was me."

He dragged his eyes to hers, raising one eyebrow.

"It's true. That's why I couldn't tell you."

He dropped his hands, confusion and anger clouding his reason so he could only say, "I didn't know I could be so mad at you."

She nodded, as if it was a forgone conclusion. As if they were a forgone conclusion, and he got that heart attack pain again.

"My head is so..." Gem circled her hands on either side of her head. "I didn't know what I wanted to do."

"To do?" he repeated, his confusion clearing up a bit. "Like, if you wanted to keep it or not?"

She nodded.

"Okay," he said, moving toward her. "Why couldn't you talk to me about it? You hiding it makes me feel like you don't trust me." He swiped his hand across his forehead, his head pounding. But he needed an answer. "Do you trust me?"

"How could I tell you? You're always so wonderful and good

at everything, and I'm a screw-up. I'm barely making it through my daily life as it is." She threw her hands up at a sudden thought. "And I killed my goldfish! How can I raise a baby when I can't even keep a goldfish alive?"

He couldn't help it; a pitiful chuckle escaped from the back of his throat, and Gem threw her hands over her face.

"Let me get this straight," he said, moving away from the counter to tug at her wrists, lowering her arms. "I'm awesome at life, and you suck at it?"

She nodded.

"And you were afraid to tell me you're pregnant because you killed a goldfish?"

"In essence, yeah." She nodded again.

"You are out of your mind." He didn't know whether to laugh or leave, he was so pissed. "No one can keep a goldfish alive."

"But I'm just figuring out how to be an adult—and your girl-friend, for that matter. I have no idea how to be a mother." Her eyes misted over. "I'm scared I'm going to mess this up. I'm scared I'll mess it up, and you'll leave me. Like you did yesterday."

The puzzle pieces fit together in his head, despite his brain still functioning below capacity. It all made sense. He didn't like it. In fact, he hated it. But he got it.

"First of all, Gemma, I swear, I will *never* leave you," he said, the pain of not being with Gemma worse than any hangover or heart attack. "I know I haven't had a lot of time to earn your trust, but please hear me when I say, there is nothing I would love more than to be with you for the rest of my life. Okay? I'm sorry I walked out on you yesterday. I needed time to think and process it."

When she nodded, he continued, "You think, because of your experiences, that you have to do everything on your own, but you don't. I want you to do what you want, live your dreams, and I will be here to support you. I don't want you to be afraid that I'll sneak out one night after a fight or something. I am not going anywhere."

Giving in a little, she slanted closer to him as one tear fell over her cheek. Jason wiped it away.

"Second of all, you are not a screw-up or a mess or any other asinine idea of what you think you are." He held her face between his hands, forcing her to look him in the eye. "You are brilliant, creative, kind, and so fucking stubborn. When you put your mind to something, you do it. You jump in headfirst, you're brave and wild, and you think I'm this, like, robot who never makes mistakes, but I only ever do things I know I can be good at. I don't like to color outside the lines, and you, Gemma, you are an artist. You showed me how life is better when you take chances."

When Gem chewed on her bottom lip, he tugged it free of her teeth, and she nestled into his touch. "I...I never expected to fall in love with you so fast. I never expected—" Her hands cupped her flat belly. "I never expected us to have a baby so soon."

"So..." His heart fluttered in a funny way, his stomach flopping around, slightly nauseous. "That means you actually want to have this baby?"

Her gaze skirted around behind him for a few moments before landing back on him. She nodded. "But do you?"

Frantic now, desperate for her to understand his feelings, he couldn't stop his words from tumbling out. "I know this isn't what you expected. It's not what I expected either, but we can do this. I want to do this with you. I will make mistakes. You will make mistakes. Let's make mistakes together."

A corner of her lips rose, her brown eyes finding life again. And that gave him life.

"With your good heart and my good looks, this baby is going to turn out amazing, no matter how bad we screw up."

"Get out of here." Gem laughed, a balm to his weary soul, and he hugged her tight to his body. He leaned down to kiss her, but she suddenly broke away from him. "With everything going on, I didn't get you a birthday present."

He scooped her back up in his arms. "You really think I care about a birthday present? I don't. I only want you."

His hands tangled in her hair as he lowered his lips to hers. It was their first real kiss in over two weeks. Jason dipped his tongue into her mouth, a man tasting his first drink of water after a long drought, and she wrapped her arms around his neck, allowing him better access to her.

One of his hands slipped over her spine to her backside, and a startled squeak leaped from her throat when he gave her ass a good squeeze. She smiled against his lips, her hands roaming over the planes of his chest before her fingers clawed at his shirt, yanking him closer. She trailed kisses down his jaw, before settling next to his Adam's apple, where her teeth nipped at the tender flesh.

"God, I missed you," he bit out, wrapping his arms around her waist, taking much of her weight against him in a snug embrace. He crushed his lips to hers, his patience wearing thin with the need to get her underneath him, and walked them toward the bedroom. The toe of his shoe caught on a broken piece of linoleum, and he stumbled, clunking their heads together.

"Ow."

"Shit. Sorry."

They separated a few inches, laughing. Jason kissed the reddening circle on Gem's forehead, changing his mind. "You want to go for a drive?"

She traced the purple bags under his eyes. "You don't want to take a nap first?"

He shook his head and grabbed her coat. "No, I have to show you something. Come on."

A light snow covered the hard ground as Gem and Jason stepped out of her car, their breaths leaving their mouths in puffs of smoke. He led her by the hand to the middle of an open field, and she took in the sights around them, the sparse, flat land dotted with evergreen trees and a low-lying mountain range in the distance. "This is what you had to show me?"

He nodded. "We're breaking ground in the spring."

She pointed to the ground. "Oh? This is it? This is going to be your famous environmentally green development?"

He held his arms open. "What do you think?"

"I think it's a tremendous waste of resources," she said, her dark eyes twinkling at the line she'd tossed at him a few months ago.

He took both of her hands in his then brought them to his chest. "How much would you hate it if I wasted some of those resources on a house for us?"

"Huh?"

"I want to make you the house of your dreams. Mud, tires, Coke bottles, whatever."

Gem stuttered, and he placed his hands on her waist, bending his knees so they were eye to eye. "I want to take care of you, and I think having a house you love is a good start."

"But you already have one," she pointed out as if he'd forgotten.

"Yes, I do. But *we* need a house. You, me, and this—" he placed a hand on her belly "—thing we made need a house."

"Why don't—"

"There is no way you are talking me out of this. Your sarcasm and name-calling will not change my mind."

"You can't—"

Jason silenced her with a finger on her lips. "You said you're afraid, but so am I. As long as we take care of each other, we can do anything. So, let's agree to take care of each other and worry about the details later."

He ran his hands over her hair, his eyes memorizing every line of her face, her freckles, her lips. He could stare at her and never tire of it.

Finally, she smiled. "I can't believe you dragged me out to the middle of nowhere in this freezing weather when I'm pregnant. You want this baby of yours to catch a cold?"

"So, say yes already."

She rolled her eyes. "Yes. Yes, I want a house with solar panels and overhead lighting and ceiling fans and a vegetable garden. Yes, of course, that's what I want."

He kissed her. "So, we're doing this? We're having a baby?"

She lifted one shoulder. "I guess we are."

He hooted and spun her in a circle before putting her down with a kiss on the tip of her frozen nose. "Let's get you back into the heat." He guided her to the car, where he opened the passenger side door and helped her in.

"I'm only, like, two months along and completely capable of getting in and out of cars myself."

Jason shut the door and got behind the wheel. "Hey, I said I'd take care of you, and I will. Now, are you hungry? Is the baby hungry? Is it craving anything? You want ice cream?" He shook his head. "No, it's too cold for ice cream." He tossed her a look. "Unless you want some. Do you want some? How about break-fast? You want waffles or something?"

Gem leaned over the console, sealing her lips over his, heightening the pressure of the kiss by forcing his head back against the headrest. She paid extra attention to his bottom lip, drawing it between her teeth.

Jason unhurriedly opened his eyes to her, dazed by the sudden, passionate kiss. "What was that for?"

"You were rambling." She strapped on her seat belt. "Now take me home and take me to bed."

He started the car, gunning the engine. "Yes, ma'am."

EPILOGUE

"You're doing so good."

"Shut up."

"No, really, you're the strongest person I know."

"Shut. Up."

"Just keep breathing, like we practiced. Focus on—"

"Jason. I swear to everything unholy, I will rip off your balls and shove them down your throat. I don't want to hear your platitudes. Shut up and get me the epidural!"

Jason reared back as Gem fumed in the hospital bed, her hands in a stranglehold on the rails. Sweat beaded on her upper lip and brow, her hair wrapped up in a messy bun that hung limply on the side of her head.

"You said you wanted to do it natural."

"I know what I fucking said, Jason, and I changed my mind. Stop trying to convince me otherwise. Get a nurse in here. Now!" Her shout cut off with a hiss of pain, and her face turned beet red once again as another contraction blipped on the monitor next to the bed. She exhaled and shifted onto her side toward him, her face racked with pain. "Jason."

"I'm here, I'm here," he said, not knowing what to do first, completely helpless.

After nine rough months of Gem struggling with severe morning sickness for the first half and then being so exhausted and swollen at the end, it was apparent this baby did not want to leave its home. The OB/GYN waited a week and a half at Gem's insistence to see if he or she would make their way into the world on their own, but eventually, the doctor said Gemma needed to be induced.

Gem wasn't happy about it but agreed, and she'd spent the first few hours of the day stoically taking each contraction in stride as the nurse pumped up the Pitocin little by little. She had taken a walk, tried to bounce on a ball, and even spent some time on all fours—anything to ease her discomfort. But once the shaking set in, Jason's anxiety skyrocketed. The nurse assured him it was totally normal, simply Gemma's body's reaction to the adrenaline, but he couldn't stand it anymore. Between her increasing temper and pain, he wanted to avoid being murdered so he could actually meet his baby.

"Uh, excuse me," Jason said, jogging out to the nurses station. "My girlfriend's in a lot of pain, and she'd like the epidural now. Please. As quickly as you could get it to her."

The nurse—a pleasant-enough woman who surely had a name, though he'd long forgotten it—smiled congenially and said, "I'll let the doctor know."

"Okay, great. Thanks."

"Gem, they're coming," he said, back at her side. "Pretty soon, you won't feel anything."

"Great, because right now, it feels—" She gritted her teeth, holding back half a scream as another contraction hit, and Jason yanked at his hair.

After witnessing this, he had no idea why people had babies at all. He didn't know whether to get down on his knees in appreciation for Gemma or to apologize for putting her through this.

"Fuck!" she yelled at the end of the contraction, breathing slightly easier. "It feels like a watermelon is trying to come out of my ass. Stop laughing, you asshole, and get over here."

Jason dropped to the bed. "What do you need?"

"I'm so hot. Take my socks off."

He did. "What else?"

She frowned, looking wholly spent. "Have this baby for me."

He took her hand in his, finding it warm and clammy, and kissed the back of it. "I wish I could. I really, really, really wish I could."

"Is my mom here?"

Jason nodded, but another contraction took hold—they were coming so fast now—and this time, she let out a primal yell to get through it.

"Do you want me to go get her?" he asked when it was over, but she could only shake her head. He ran back out to the nurses station. "Is the doctor coming soon?"

The nurse pointed to the female doctor coming around the corner. "Right now."

"Great. Good. Perfect." He led the way for the doctor like a flower girl at a wedding. "She wants an epidural now, please."

The doctor smiled. "How are you feeling, Dad?"

"Terrible."

She laughed. "Not uncommon."

Gem moaned, so did Jason, and the doctor slid on gloves. "Let's see if you've progressed any further, and then we'll assess if you're able to get the epidural or not."

"*If?*" Jason repeated, and the doctor nodded, positioning herself at the foot of the bed, her face changing almost immediately when her hand disappeared under the hospital gown, between Gem's legs. "What? What is it?"

"That's ten centimeters. Plus one station."

"What does—" Jason's question was cut short by Gem's guttural moan, and the doctor said something to the nurse, setting a flurry of activity into motion. More nurses and medical students entered the room, introducing themselves, but Gem didn't pay attention and Jason plumb didn't give a shit.

"Gemma, there is no time for an epidural anymore. Your baby is ready, so we're going to start pushing, okay?"

"No." Gem shook her head. "No."

"Right now?" Jason asked, his stomach in knots. "She has to do it without anything for the pain?"

The doctor nodded. "Yes. The baby is ready now."

Jason sank down next to Gem, trying to sound more confident than he felt. "Okay. You can do this."

"No, I can't. It hurts." She squeezed her eyes shut, and he couldn't tell if it was sweat or tears that formed in the corners.

"I know it does, but you can get through it." He smoothed her hair back from her face. "You're almost done."

The nurse instructed Gem to lean forward and hold the backs of her legs. Jason took hold of one for support as the doctor suited up with a mask and gown, a light shining down on her when she sat at the foot of the bed.

"Gemma, when you feel your next contraction, take a deep breath and bear down," the doctor said. "Nice, deep breaths, you can do this."

Mere seconds later, a contraction hit, and Gem bore down, whatever that meant.

"Nice, Gemma. Great job," the doctor said. "The head is right there. Give this next one a big push."

"I can't. I can't. It hurts," Gem said, inhaling deeply with a wince, and then her breath caught. "I—ah!" She screamed and pushed and cried. "It's burning!"

"Push, push, push, push, push," the doctor chanted.

Gem screamed again, and Jason thought he might pass out.

"The head is out. You feel that?"

Gem shook her head, her whole body trembling. "I don't feel anything but burning. I'm being ripped in two," she whimpered, slanting her bloodshot eyes up to Jason, and he had never been so in love with her. "I can't do it anymore."

"Yes, you can," he told her then leaned over, getting a glimpse of the wrinkly, circular thing poking out from between her legs. That was *their baby*. "You *are* doing this. I can see him."

"How do you know it's a him?" she said, her mouth curling up in momentary jest before twisting in pain.

"Push, Gemma," the doctor ordered. "One more push."

She breathed out a garbled cry, her face covered in a mixture of sweat and tears, and she had never been as beautiful than in that moment.

The doctor chanted again, this time, "Good, good, good, good. Here it comes."

"Holy shit," Jason said, watching as the good doctor pulled out the rest of his baby's body while Gem sagged into the pillow. "That's our baby."

The doctor held up the bloody, mucus-covered, little alien. "Congratulations on your baby girl."

Jason wheezed out a breath, overwhelmed with so much love he thought he might burst. A nurse took the baby to clean her off, and he cut the umbilical cord, a little dizzy, a lot in love.

His eyes glazed over with tears, and he knelt down next to Gem, who smiled and cried, her hands still shaking as she held their baby in her arms. With the help of the nurse, they positioned her on Gem's chest, swaddled in a blanket and cap, still a little goopy and gross and utterly perfect.

The doctor started talking about placentas and stitches and other horrible things, but Jason could only focus on the two women in his life now.

"It's a girl," Gemma whispered, a content smile curving her lips, her hands gently patting the baby's back. How she could have ever thought she'd mess this up was beyond him. "What do we call her?"

He propped his head next to Gem's shoulder, exactly in line with his daughter's scrunched-up face, her tiny mouth wriggling up and down a bit. "You don't like the name we had picked out?"

Gem flinched, and Jason glanced down to where the doctor worked on her, a medical student by her side. He saw a needle and thread and flinched too.

"I don't know," Gem whispered. "Seems a little plain now that I've seen her."

Jason nodded. "Okay, whatever you think. I'd call her Wednesday if you wanted," he said, referring to the day of the week, but when Gem shot him an interested look, he shook his head, backtracking. "I'm joking."

"I'm not. Like Wednesday Addams. I kind of love it."

He lightly drew his fingertip along his baby's cheek and then Gem's. "I'll make you a deal. You agree to marry me, and you can name the baby whatever you want."

She huffed out an exhausted laugh. "That's a terrible deal." She grinned sleepily at him. "I would have agreed to marry you without any conditions."

Jason kissed her forehead. "I love you so much. I'm not letting you or this little girl go. Ever."

Gem lifted her chin, seeking a kiss, but the baby let out a tiny wail.

"I think it's time we try nursing," one of the nurses said, and Jason backed away, letting them do their thing, ducking out to deliver the news to Frank and Caroline.

Jason didn't believe he could contain any more joy inside his body, but when he walked back into the hospital room to see the love of his life gazing down at the other love of his life while she fed her, his heart proved how flexible it was, expanding by the second. More and more love. More and more joy. He checked his chest, sure he would see the outline of his heart shoving through his skin like a cartoon.

After the room had cleared, and Gem had a chance to clean up, and Frank and Caroline met their first grandchild, Jason crawled into bed next to his fiancée. She glowed. He was sure if he could somehow engineer a way to capture her smile, he'd be able to power their house with it. "When I texted the girls earlier to update them, I told them you'd call. Do you want to do that now or later?"

She lifted a serene shoulder, seemingly unbothered by anything, even after twelve hours of labor. "We can do it now."

Jason opened up a new FaceTime call and held out the phone so the screen could capture all three of them in it. In seconds, Bronte, Sam, and Laney showed up, alternating between peals of delight and sweet coos.

"I'd like to introduce you," Gem started, catching Jason's eye before continuing, "to Willow Jane Mitchell."

"Willow Jane!" Laney crowed.

"She's beautiful," Bronte said, crying. "You did such a good job."

"How do you feel?" Sam asked.

"Terrible." Gem laughed. "But also, really happy."

Jason's eyes teared up for what felt like the thirty-eighth time in the last two hours. "Jane? For my mom?"

"For your mom," she said, a little wobble to her lip. "Is that all right?"

"Yes, of course." He kissed her. "I love the name. I love you. I love Willow. I love everybody," he said with a drunken chuckle and tipped his head to the girls on the screen. "I love you guys."

They all laughed.

Gem gazed down at Willow, who closed her eyes, her eyelashes settled on heavenly pink cheeks. "I think she fell asleep." Gem pushed her lips out in an attempt to shush everyone, then said to the girls in a whisper, "I'd also like to introduce you to my fiancé too."

The girls all screamed, Willow woke up crying, Gem rolled her eyes, and Jason smiled.

True perfection.

THANK you for reading Hating Mr. Perfect! If you enjoyed it, please leave a review, and don't forget to sign up for my newsletter on my website for a bonus Gem and Jason epilogue!

KEEP READING for a sneak peak of Bronte's story, Falling for Mr. Wrong

FALLING FOR MR. WRONG

SNEAK PEEK

After two days together, they should have been used to it, but Willow's wail could wake the dead, and Bronte twitched from her position on the couch, where she'd been sprawled out.

Laney snorted a laugh. "Maybe she'll be a good singer when she's older."

Sam discreetly reached for the remote, raising the volume of the *Golden Girls* episode they were watching as Gem stood up.

But then Jason's voice called down from upstairs. "Don't move, Gemma! I got her!"

Gem plopped back down and offered a sad smile to Bronte. "Happy birthday."

Bronte only waved her fork, which was covered in blue icing from her cake. "There has never been a better one. I'm with my best friends, and I got the flower."

Gem wrinkled her nose at that. Laney had bought the cake, which was not vegan, so Gem wasn't eating it. Although she did have a very large stack of her own homemade cookies that were supposed to help her breastfeed, leaving her not completely without sweets.

With Willow still crying upstairs, Gem pouted. "I'm sorry we aren't out getting drunk or something," she said, all forlorn. "I feel so old."

"You kinda are." Sam pointed the remote at her. "You're a mom now."

Bronte nodded, even though a twinge of jealousy settled into her bones when Jason plodded quickly down the stairs, his daughter wrapped up in a monkey print muslin blanket. He cringed at Gem while Willow cried against his shoulder. "I think she wants her mama."

The girls all laughed, proving Sam's point.

Jason Mitchell, Gemma's fiancé, was dressed casually in sweatpants and a T-shirt. He was a tall, muscular, preppy type and looked totally opposite of the guy Bronte imagined wild child Gem would end up with, if any at all. But here she was, in a brand-new home with a beautiful, screeching baby.

Jason passed Willow off to Gem, asking, "Do you need anything? More water?" When Gem nodded, he grabbed her gigantic aluminum water bottle before pointing to the other girls. "Ladies? Anything? More wine? Cake? Pretzels, chips?"

Laney lifted her glass with a few drops of pink wine left in it. "I wouldn't be opposed if you guys want to open another bottle."

Sam and Bronte both looked to each other and then shrugged. Jason took that as his answer. "'Nother bottle coming up."

"This is great," Sam said, settling her back against the couch.

Laney shifted over to comb her fingers through Sam's rose-gold hair, separating it into three groups to braid. "What is?"

"This," she said with a gesture around the room.

"This?" Gem asked, popping out her boob to feed Willow.

A look of horror crossed Sam's face. "No, not that. I mean..." She circled her arm again. "You built this whole family, and it's really nice to be here."

"I somehow convinced you three to stay in my house with my ten-week-old under the guise of Bronte's birthday weekend, but really, it was so I could remember what the *before* times were like." A ghost of a smile tugged at Gem's lips. "Don't lie and tell me you're enjoying this tiny banshee," she said, nodding to her daughter.

"I'm not lying. Being in this house is like living in a sign from Target, you know?" Sam lifted her hand as if reading it on the wall. "Love lives here."

Gem mumbled out a, "Dork," as she tamped down a smile.

"No, it's true." Bronte put her plate and fork on the table. Unlike Gem, who had been raised by a single mom, and Sam, who struggled with her parents' divorce, Bronte grew up with a great family and wonderful parents, which made her want more of the same. As a kid, Bronte dreamed of finding her person and beginning her own family. She assumed she'd be the first out of her friends to do it, and now that she'd witnessed one of her best friends attain what she wanted, it only made Bronte's desire for marriage and family grow.

Gem tossed Bronte a look. "We should be out celebrating, but instead..." She trailed off, adjusting her hold on Willow.

Bronte waved her off. "We had our spa day and went out to dinner last night. I'm having fun with my girls here."

Willow whimpered as if to say *Me too!* and the four women all laughed.

Jason reappeared from the kitchen, carrying a bottle of wine and Gem's water bottle, which he gave to her first before refilling all their wineglasses.

"We even have our own handsome butler," Laney said, lifting her wine in a salute.

"Pleasure to be of service." Jason grinned then plopped down next to Gem, dropping an arm around her shoulders.

"It's still weird sometimes," she said. "Like, Willow will wake up in the middle of the night, and for a second, I forget where I am and *who* I am. It takes me a minute to remember I have a kid now."

"You forget about me too?" Jason quipped, towing Gem in closer to him.

"I could never," she said sweetly. Then she added with a bit more bite, "You snore too loud to ignore."

Jason jostled Gem playfully, whispering something in her ear that made her cheeks flame as she smiled. She elbowed him away to scoop Willow from her breast and onto her shoulder.

Laney finished Sam's hair with a clap and leaped up. "Bobby snores too, but no matter what, I can never wake him up to stop."

At that, Sam lifted her hands above her head, stretching. "That's why I enjoy sleeping alone."

Laney grabbed her phone, always one to document everything, a social media queen. "Jason, if you please?"

He nodded and stood to take her phone, while Laney, Sam, and Bronte all found seats on either side and in front of Gem and Willow.

"On three," Jason said, positioning the phone up.

"Happy birthday, Bronte," Sam said from her seat on the floor.

"One."

"Hope it's a good year for you," Laney said, tugging on Bronte's ponytail from the other side of Gem.

"Two."

"And all your wishes come true," Gem added.

"Three."

Jason snapped a few pictures then handed Laney her phone back in exchange for Willow from Gem. "I'll leave you ladies to it." He kissed Gem's forehead. "I'll take the midnight feeding, okay? You've got enough milk stored."

It was only eight o'clock, but Bronte suspected he planned

on staying upstairs the rest of the night with the baby so Gem could have the last few hours with her friends.

"It was nice finally meeting you in person, and I'm really glad you guys could come for the weekend," he said to the group. "Our guest rooms are open whenever you want them."

A chorus of gratitude rang out and barely audible sighs of appreciation when he turned around with Willow in his arms, his long, confident strides on display as he walked away. After a few moments of silence, Laney, Sam, and Bronte all looked at Gem, who blushed with a laugh. "I know, right? He's perfect."

"Like a dream!" Laney crowed.

Sam grabbed the remote once again. "A literal real-life Ken doll."

"I'm happy for you," Bronte said, holding Gem's hand. The two had come a long way since meeting on their college campus the first day as roommates. Bronte had been a mess, crying and already homesick, while Gem was excited to be out of her home state and away from her mother's "douchebag boyfriend." A few days later, they'd met Sam and Laney in a humanities class, but it wasn't until two weeks after that they'd solidified their friendship at a party when some awful guy slipped something in Gem's drink. Bronte, Laney, and Sam immediately swooped in to help her, and the rest was history. Best friends for life.

Gem glowed, her eyes watering, as she squeezed Bronte's hand in return, bringing her back to the present. "Life is good."

Bronte's eyes watered too because she was physically incapable of not crying when someone else cried. "I can tell."

"Are you happy?"

Bronte coasted her gaze around Gem and Jason's living room, the walls a bold but soothing orange with pops of gray and green in the furniture and plants everywhere, and her friends scattered about but close enough to touch. Laney with her foot resting against Gem's thigh and her head on the arm of the sofa, next to Sam, both of them laughing about something on Laney's phone. This was the first time they'd been able to be with one another in person in over a year, and it was well worth the wait.

"Yeah," Bronte said. She may have been jealous of Gem and what she had in this house, but these three girls were as close to her as her own family. This weekend was the happiest she'd been in a long time. "I'm happy."

"Well," Laney started, lifting the wine toward Gem. "Since Jason's called dibs on the midnight feeding, that means you can have a drink, right?"

"You're damn right." Gem wiggled her fingers, and Laney passed her the wine, which she drank right from the bottle—like the lady she was—and they all giggled, telling stories until after two when Gem finally had to go upstairs to pump. Instead of separating into different bedrooms, Laney, Sam, and Bronte all piled into one bed, where they slept all crammed together until exactly six o'clock in the morning.

That was when Willow's howl woke them up. Time for breakfast. Like clockwork, that tiny one was. A girl after Bronte's own heart.

It was exactly fourteen minutes until takeoff, and Chris was cutting it close. He couldn't recall the last time he'd had a layover, let alone traveled on a commercial airline.

Still catching his breath, he walked down the jetway toward the plane, fixing his well-worn baseball cap lower over his brow. At the entrance of the plane, he inhaled a calming breath as he passed those really tempting first-class seats on the way to the cramped and overcrowded ones behind. He scanned the rows laid out in front of him. Almost everyone was already in place with heads bowed over a book or cell phone. Some inspected their cramped surroundings, but no one took any extra notice of him.

No one stared. No one made a fuss, pointed, asked for a picture. Nothing.

Between the gate agent not recognizing him and this, he was sure his star status had not only fallen, but imploded into a black hole.

Was he so egotistical he expected to stand out, be treated differently?

He shook the thought from his head. This was what he wanted, what he needed. To avoid attention.

He made his way to the back of the plane and turned toward his seat, blocked by someone already in the aisle seat. "Excuse me, can I..."

A startling pair of blue eyes blinked up at him expectantly. "Do you need to get in?"

"Yeah."

The young woman stood, allowing him to slide into the row. He settled in his seat with a sigh and, out of the corner of his eye, caught her movements as she sat back down. Opening a magazine, she leaned back into her seat, getting comfortable.

As if that was possible. Chris buckled the seat belt nice and tight. Not that it mattered. If the plane went down, a thin strip of cloth across his lap wasn't going to save him. The thought made him squirm, and he pushed his neck against the headrest, a low groan escaping his throat when one of the flight attendants began the safety speech over the loudspeaker.

"Hey, um, sir, are you okay?"

Chris slanted his gaze to his neighbor. "I'm a little..."

"Don't like flying?"

"No. Not really." Not liking flying was an understatement, especially without the assistance of some alcohol. He'd learned from his first flight that they didn't serve drinks until they were up in the air, and those tiny bottles of vodka were crazy expensive. Didn't stop him from ordering the limit, two, but still. Flying coach was for the birds.

"A few more hours, that's it," he whispered to himself.

"What?"

"Nothing, only trying to calm down." This was why he took private planes on the rare occasion he had to fly anywhere, so he could get drunk and no one would care or notice how scared he was. Though, Wes clearly didn't want to give him even that luxury of having a panic attack in private.

"You can talk to me, if you want. I mean, if it'll help," his seatmate said.

"Okay," he agreed after a deep breath, his body rigid and unmoving, save for a bouncing knee.

The engines roared as the plane taxied toward the runway, and his blood pounded in his ears.

"I'm reading this magazine." She held it up for him. "Do you want to take a quiz? It's to find out your workout personality."

He glanced to her hands which held brightly colored pages with ads for sneakers and sports bras before he faced front again where a flight attendant demonstrated how to put on an oxygen mask.

That must have been enough of an answer for her because she cleared her throat. "What are you most likely to be doing on a Saturday night? A, unwinding with a book and bubble bath. B, going for a run to outdo your best time. C, challenging your friends to a game of poker or scrabble."

Obvious choice. "High stakes poker, C."

"Poker," she repeated, checking off the letter with her pen. "At work, you have a reputation for being... A, the independent and sometimes hard-nosed one, who strives for personal best. B, the laid-back one to organize projects on your own. Or C, the social butterfly who energizes everyone."

"Social butterfly, I guess," he said as if that wasn't the exact reason he had been sent on this sojourn.

She checked off the box. "Last one. After a bad day, what would cheer you up most? Indulging in your favorite dessert, the knowledge you can overcome any obstacle, or a pep talk from a friend?"

The pilot called for the flight attendants to have a seat and prepare for takeoff. Chris closed his eyes, grimacing in anticipation. "Can the pep talk be naked?"

Falling for Mr. Wrong is available now!

ABOUT THE AUTHOR

Suzanne's storied history in literature began when she was first published in the 5th Grade Poetry Anthology of 1997 with a poem titled Snowy Day in May. She continued her career with a much lauded Angelfire website featuring multiple novels of *NSYNC fanfiction. School, boys, and eventual full-time jobs got in the way here and there, but she kept on writing, including a screenplay which she directed to bring to the big screen in 2013. These days she writes stories about life, love, and bringing down the patriarchy in between wrangling a few beasts, some human, some not. And she's funny, she swears it.